THE TOWER'S ALCHEMIST

THE GRAY TOWER TRILOGY #1

ALESHA L. ESCOBAR

Edited by
AMANDA LYONS

Creative
Alchemy

Copyright 2014 by Alesha Escobar
Edited by Amanda Lyons
Published by Creative Alchemy, Inc.
Cover Art by Christian Bentulan

This is a work of fiction. Names, characters, organizations, places and incidents either are the product of the author's imagination or are used fictitiously. If you are enjoying this book, please consider leaving a review. It helps others to find this story and to make an informed decision.

Want free and discounted ebooks? Join my readers lounge today!

https://www.aleshaescobar.com/newsletter

To all those who have inspired me. Thank you.

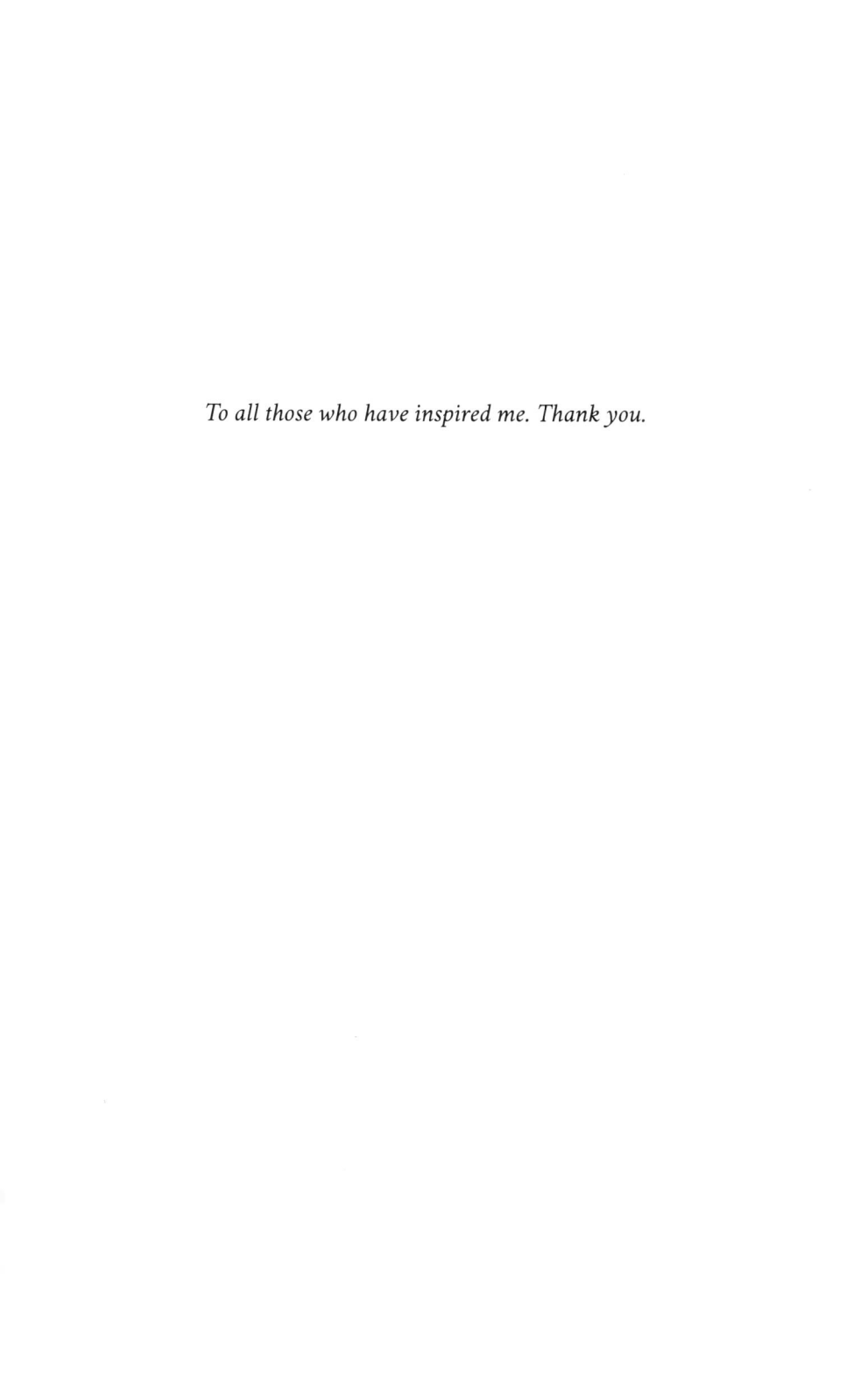

PRAISE FOR THE GRAY TOWER TRILOGY

"Escobar's attention to detail, to bringing an era long past to life in an urban fantasy is wonderful. The secondary characters...are superbly drawn."
—**Open Book Society**

"The story itself is intriguing and unique. It has action, love, suspense, and everything else that makes up a great fantasy story."
—**Goodreads Reader Review**

CONTENTS

Chapter 1	1
Chapter 2	9
Chapter 3	20
Chapter 4	30
Chapter 5	43
Chapter 6	53
Chapter 7	64
Chapter 8	72
Chapter 9	82
Chapter 10	91
Chapter 11	108
Chapter 12	122
Chapter 13	131
Chapter 14	152
Chapter 15	168
Chapter 16	181
Chapter 17	199
Chapter 18	220
Chapter 19	235
Chapter 20	244
Chapter 21	253
About the Author	275
Also by Alesha L. Escobar	277

CHAPTER 1

I never imagined my first trip to Denmark would include crouching in a forest in the dark of night, but at least the beech trees gave Lyder and me much needed cover. I rose to my feet and stood over him, jerking my head to the right to indicate that we needed to pack up and head out. When he waved me off, I shut the transmitter case with my foot and trained my sten gun on him.

He glared at me. "I wasn't done with my radio transmission."

"You went over by five minutes. That means they'll be coming." I had little patience for people who did things that would likely get me killed.

He pulled out a pistol and grabbed the case. "I'm ready."

I flinched when the first gunshot rang. It took the SS little effort to pinpoint our position. Lyder jumped to his feet and ran with me through the forest. I breathed in through my nose and out of my mouth, like I'd do when taking a jog. I felt a cold lump in the pit of my stomach as my shoes haphazardly crushed dry leaves and twigs beneath them. The sound of men's voices and dogs barking followed us, and where the forest cleared, we spotted the bright headlights of a trekker sitting in the middle of the road.

Great, we've just been flanked.

With heavy breaths, we paused and pressed ourselves against the trunk of a tree as if it were all the protection we needed.

"Any bright ideas, Sergeant?" I pulled out my golden knife and began carving repetitions of two alchemical symbols into the soft earth: Fire and Air.

"We make a stand and fight." He dropped the case and pulled out another pistol. "They'll likely force us to surrender once they see my uniform."

"Bad plan." They might take an officer of the Danish army as a prisoner of war, but if they caught a woman in civilian clothing with a gun aimed at them, they'd kill me on the spot—or take me in for interrogation with a nice dose of torture and *then* kill me.

"Drop your weapons," a voice on a loud hailer commanded, first in English and then in German. It came from the trekker. From the other side I heard the dogs' howling grow louder and men's boots trampling crisp leaves.

Lyder raised his guns and fired at one of the SS officers who made his way down from the trekker. It looked like he was hit in the shoulder, but he quickly reciprocated the gunfire. I took the opposite side and aimed my gun, hitting him with a burst of bullets. The officer grunted and fell to the ground. I began feeding my Fire and Air symbols with energy and slowly built up the power I needed in them.

Lyder shivered and stared at me. "What are you doing?"

"Saving our lives." My right hand shook as a warning, but I ignored it and continued. I held off the effects of the spell just long enough so I could blast the other men in range.

We moved to another tree when the SS officers from behind sent gunfire and their vicious dogs our way. When they were close enough, I released the symbols, and sparks began forming in the air. The sparks grew into flames, and joined by Air, became a whirlwind of fire. I directed the firestorm toward everyone behind us, and confusion and panic broke out. Some of the men fell back, while others were caught in the raging flames and burned alive. Still, others ran for cover and waited. I nudged Lyder, who simply stared at the spectacle, and urged him to follow me.

"Emelie," he said, using my current codename. "Why are you going toward the trekker?"

"A trekker only holds two at most. I'd rather go against one soldier than twenty."

I felt something wet trickle down my nose and knew it was blood. I relinquished any remaining hold I had on the firestorm, and with fear, I awaited the inevitable physical exhaustion to creep in.

We headed up the dirt embankment and saw that the trekker still had its lights on, but no one moved there or made any further demands on the loud hailer. Where did the second man go? Lyder suddenly shouted a warning, but it was too late. The man we were looking for had wrapped his arm around Lyder's neck from behind and lifted him up against the embankment with little effort. Lyder dropped his weapons and began kicking his legs in the air and clawing at the man's arm to no avail. His strength was simply inhuman.

"Drop your weapon, or I'll break his neck."

I placed it on the ground in front of me and held my hands up in the air. "Who are you?"

He released Lyder and made a quick blow to the back of his head to knock him unconscious. "A rich man, once I hand you over. They like collecting Tower Slaves."

He jumped from the top of the embankment and landed on his feet. He wore no uniform, only a dark sweater and trousers. I sensed the taint of dark magic on him and I cursed at myself for having wasted so much of my strength earlier.

"I'm not with the Gray Tower." I trembled from fatigue and lowered my arms.

"Doesn't matter." He gave a smug smile, watching me reel from the effects of my previous strong rush of magic.

He pulled out a pair of Czech swivel cuffs. When I sensed the amount of iron present in them, I lifted my wrists and allowed him to cuff me. Obviously this warlock wasn't an alchemist. As soon as the cuffs clicked shut, I threw my arms up high and over his head, pulling him toward me so that the cuffs pressed into the back of his neck. We were locked in an embrace.

I manipulated the iron, letting it do the work for me and turning it into a weapon that would corrode and blacken his flesh. He began struggling and screeching, unable to hit me with a spell because I was right up against him. He *did* put aside the pain long enough to figure out that he could strangle me. He wrapped his hands around my neck and squeezed with the ferocity of desperation.

There we were, in near silence, arms around each other and neither one intending to let go until the other dropped dead. Tonight, however, would not be that night for me. A spray of blood hit me across the face as the corrosion from the iron cuffs ate into part of his neck. I fell down with the weight of his body, coughing and sputtering. After I managed to wriggle free, I tried to find a key on him, but his pockets turned up nothing—except a business card for a Dr. Falk Meier, which made me shudder.

My wrists burned from the spell and my legs felt like rubber. I stumbled over to my sten gun and picked it up before limping over to Lyder. I prodded him and called his name a few times, uttering a silent prayer of thanks when his eyes blinked open. "Lyder, we have to get out of here." I coughed again, but this time it was due to the forest fire smoke billowing toward us.

"Where are my guns?" he groaned.

"There." I nodded over to my right, and he rushed toward the weapons to reclaim them.

The other men who ran off were regrouping and we heard them in the distance. I helped him to his feet and we dashed south alongside the road, trying to make it back into town where my safe house stood. I was already running out of breath and hardly managed to keep up with him.

"You couldn't find a key?" He glanced at my wrists and then his gaze went back to the road.

My eyes narrowed. "Yes, but then I decided that I liked wearing Czechoslovakian handcuffs."

I stumbled and nearly fell, but he caught me and pulled me along with him at a quick pace. I had to give him credit—he wasn't going to stop for anything.

When we reached town, a few resistance fighters who were appointed as lookouts signaled to us and guided us through back alleys until we reached the safe house. Once inside, Lyder immediately shed his uniform jacket and grabbed a bottle of liquor. I, on the other hand, asked my hostess Kanja if she knew how to pick locks.

She grabbed her smallest blade from the kitchen and held it up with a grimace. "I don't know what to do," she said.

"It's okay, I'll walk you through it." I sat at her kitchen table and held out my wrists.

She sat across from me with a frightened expression. "Perhaps Sergeant Lyder—"

"He's busy getting drunk, thank you."

"I'm not drunk yet," Lyder said. "Can't you transmute those cuffs anyway?"

"Maybe one day I'll be able to. Kanja, my wrists are badly hurt. Would you mind?"

She sucked in a deep breath. "Then...tell me what to do."

I guided her through each step, using encouraging words and a soothing voice. When the cuffs clicked open, I winced and gave her a pained smile. "Thank you. You're a very brave young woman."

She couldn't have been older than eighteen, but then losing one's parents and joining the Resistance made one grow up rather quickly. I looked up at Lyder when he set a glass in front of me and poured me a drink. He grew much more subdued.

"To another day of cheating death." He finished off the rest of the bottle.

"Just remember not to go over a thirty-minute broadcast. Ever."

"God, I'm going to have a headache in the morning," he said, turning around and rummaging through Kanja's cabinets.

"I'm going to be aching all over," I complained. I was so exhausted from the fight that I didn't think I had the energy to mend my wrists with magic. I thanked Kanja once more when she went over to the sink and brought a wet towel for me. I had forgotten that my face was bloodstained.

I wiped my forehead and cheeks clean. As soon as I downed my drink, I felt sick. The house suddenly quaked and unnatural screeches filled the air. People from outside began shouting and screaming, and the sound of gunshots popped in long bursts. I didn't even have to look out the window to know that Black Wolves had landed.

"Get into the closet!" I rose from my seat and shoved Kanja toward the bedroom. Lyder was on my heels.

"What's going on out there?" he asked as I pulled them both inside and shut the door.

"Everyone, quiet. Don't move, don't speak, and don't breathe." I sucked in a quick breath when the pain in my wrists flared up, but I managed to get us into the compartment behind the secret panel in the back wall.

I crouched in the compartment and closed my eyes, emptying my mind of any fear or expectations, focusing only on cloaking my abilities. A Circle of Protection would've just served as a beacon for the Wolves—I needed to hide, to be nothing to them.

We heard more gunshots and screams. Somewhere nearby,

glass shattered and a car screeched before colliding into something. When the house shook again with a crash, we thought a grenade had hit the other side of the building. We thought better of it when something heavy with talons came walking down the hallway and scratching up the hardwood floor. I opened my eyes when I heard a grunt. Through a crack in the panel, we saw the Black Wolf's shadow blot out the stream of light coming from beneath the door. Lyder pressed his hand over his mouth, and Kanja pulled out a tiny crucifix and held it close.

Lyder looked like he would sick up at any moment when a set of claws, attached to a human-looking hand, reached beneath the door and spread out. I continued concentrating on cloaking myself and lightly extended it to the others in the closet. My head throbbed and I felt feverish. I knew that if I kept pushing myself, that I'd faint. The only thing that kept me from passing out and hitting the floor was the fact that I wouldn't be able to do it quietly.

The claws ripped the door open with a yank, and I feared the false panel that separated us would not remain secret for long. A garbled voice from outside called to the Wolf and it pulled away, making a long whoosh that resounded throughout the hallway. The kitchen window shattered and the menacing presence that permeated the house dissipated.

None of us moved or spoke for nearly a half hour. Lyder licked his dry lips and finally stuttered. "T-they said if our government surrendered, that they wouldn't send the Black Wolves."

I shook my head. "They're a bunch of liars who can't be trusted. Put that in your next radio broadcast."

Lyder groaned. "I left my radio set out in the forest."

Kanja cleared her throat. "Is it safe to go outside now?"

"It's best we stay here a little longer. Just in case." I placed my hand on her shoulder. My wrists felt slightly numb.

"And you said the Gray Tower trained you?" Lyder threw me a dubious glance.

"Do you want to go fight a half-monster that likes to eat people for lunch? I don't get into tangles with Wolves unless I have to." Besides, I was so drained that I didn't think I could get up and move, even if I had wanted to.

"What time is your pilot coming to pick you up?" Lyder asked.

"Midnight. I'll be ready by then."

"I hope we can see you again," Kanja said with a weak smile.

"I hope so too. Hopefully when we're not under the threat of a painful death."

Lyder chuckled. "Fits the job description, doesn't it?"

"Then maybe I need to find a new job."

I knew I said that every few weeks, but this time I think I meant it. How many more times would I push my limits and run weak and tired with a bloody nose? Or get trapped in a closet with a Black Wolf sniffing at me? Kanja had no business being my host, but she was the only one who volunteered—and probably the only one left alive.

She looked at me with triumph in her eyes, probably unaware of how close we all were to evisceration. I felt guilty at both having her involved and the prospect of never returning to help. In my heart, I knew the truth that I'd have to speak aloud when I made it back to Baker Street—I was tired, and at this stage, I'd be of use to no one.

CHAPTER 2

I really wanted to tell Brande to take his glass of dry Sherry and get the hell out of my office, but you couldn't say that to a wizard without there being trouble. I lowered my gaze and rustled papers on my desk, hoping maybe he'd get the hint, but he obviously felt he had a few last words to say.

"I'll probably be able to see you again in a few months. It's becoming more difficult to enter and leave Prague...I hope you understand."

"Well," I lifted my gaze and met his, "that's what happens when you let a gang of Nazis run into your territory."

"Isabella—"

"When we're over here, I'm Emelie."

He waved his hand and took another sip of Sherry. "Of course, *Emelie*. If we had been ready, perhaps we could've fought them off without any trouble. But now..." he shook his head and it made me feel a pang of guilt for being dismissive.

"We're all trying to do what we can, right?" I placed my hand over his in a conciliatory gesture. I knew how he felt when the Gray Tower did nothing as the SS and German Armed Forces rolled into Czechoslovakia and took over. However, the Order of

Wizards couldn't make a move without being detected by certain enemies of our own.

I knew he would've been first in line to fight off the enemy despite that fact, and that's what I was already doing in my own way. I had to admit that I couldn't escape the nagging feeling that we were so wrapped up in living for a cause, that sometimes it felt like life passed us by. He and I could have easily enjoyed our drinks over a dinner table in a dimly lit nightclub with our bodies swaying to the beat of music. It would have been a nice change of scene from the solitude and monotony of my cramped office.

Knowing Brande though, he probably thought this was just fine—which was a shame, because what girl *wouldn't* want to be seen in public with him? I didn't realize my hand was still touching his as I thought about all this, and he gave me a quizzical look though he didn't withdraw his hand, either.

I pulled my hand away, a little flushed, and just then Ian walked in carrying a file. Brande acknowledged him with a nod and Ian did the same. When Brande faced me again, I saw Ian pointing toward the left wall, at an informational poster that you could find posted in nearly every pub in London nowadays. It portrayed men wearing military uniforms, frozen in laughter with a group of women hanging onto them. A caption at the bottom of the poster read: *What you say to your friends...could be heard by the enemy!*

I always laughed at that poster hanging in here, but I've seen some inexperienced operatives unwittingly betray themselves and their cohorts by not taking that motto to heart.

"Emelie." Ian cleared his throat. "The file is ready." He furtively glanced at Brande.

"I swear I tried to make him leave," I said as I shrugged my shoulders. Ian was even less patient with Brande's presence than I was.

Brande pulled a package from a hidden pocket inside his

trench coat. "Your emerald spectacles, jade powder, and red garnet lipstick."

"Thank you."

I didn't always have time to make or procure enchanted items, and I appreciated whenever he delivered them. Emerald granted the ability to see in the dark; jade's healing powers had saved me from grievous wounds and poison on several occasions, and I used red garnet sparingly as it inspired romantic desires and aggression. I learned a long time ago to manipulate the magical qualities in these stones and work them into everyday items. Whipping out a stone wasn't very subtle, and in my line of work, a lack of subtlety could get you killed.

Brande handed me the coveted items and finished his Sherry. "Perhaps you'll come to the Gray Tower once you're done playing spy with the British." He rose from his seat and shouldered his way past Ian, leaving us alone in the office. I didn't know why, but Brande's comment stung me.

I looked at Ian. "I know what you're going to say—"

"I trust you, not him. Besides, don't you think it's all part of a nefarious plot that the Gray Tower sends *him* over? If Bernadine actually did her job and stopped gushing over him at the reception desk, then maybe I could get a few words out of the bloke."

I let out an irritated sigh. "I swear, sometimes you act as if you don't want a wizard on staff. If that's the case, then you shouldn't have recruited me."

He shook his head as if saying he wasn't going down that road today. "Look, when are you going to let us take this out?" He glanced at the other half of the office, where an empty desk and chair stood collecting dust. Notes and pictures clung to the wall.

"Why do you suddenly care?" My eyes narrowed. I noticed, when I had first joined the Special Operations Executive, that all the men had their own offices, while all the women had to pair up and share, sometimes three to an office.

My officemate and friend was a girl named Stella, whose

husband died in a battle last year. She wanted to help the Resistance in any way she could and successfully ran missions for us, but she hadn't reported back to us since January—now it was the middle of June.

"We've got a new recruit, I think you'll like her."

"Not interested. What do you have for me?" The last thing I needed was a wide-eyed new girl following me around, talking about how swell it was to spy on the Nazis.

He opened the file to reveal a dossier and pointed toward a profile picture of an older gentleman. "I presume you've heard of Dr. Veit Heilwig?"

"The scientist? Yes."

"For the past three months Allied forces have been taking heavy blows from the Nazis on the Western Front. The bastards have been violating the Geneva Protocol and unleashing a new chemical weapon on our soldiers. We have evidence that—"

"There may be more than just chemicals in those weapons?" I fondled the Agate stone set in my ring.

He nodded. "Do you remember that incident with the poisoned food and water?"

"Believe me, I'm not forgetting *that* anytime soon."

The contaminated goods were unwittingly dispersed among Ally soldiers throughout Europe. Over a thousand men died before it could be counteracted and hundreds more were still lying in hospital beds, strangely disfigured and barely alive. All we could do was separate and destroy the contaminated food, and there was still no known cure.

"That was Heilwig's work. Now he's perfected it...they're calling it The Plague. At this rate he'll win the war for Hitler and the Black Wolves, and that's exactly why we need another alchemist to go up against him, neutralize the new chemical weapons he's developed, and take him out."

"You want me to kill him?"

"No, take him out of France. We want to extract him."

"Why do you want him alive?" And how exactly did they want me to kidnap him? You couldn't just walk up to a warlock, cuff him, and tell him to come along. Next time I'd save my plaintive musings about life passing me by in favor of wanting to just live another day. This was going to be a tough mission.

"Just...read the dossier. I've got MI6 breathing down my neck over this one and Morton's just dying for an excuse to discredit us."

"My goodness, we wouldn't want *that*, now would we?" Discredit happened to be the least of my worries, buddy—I could be rotting in Dr. Meier's Nazi experimental program by next week if I failed. Half the things I heard about it I refused to believe, and the other half I resolved to never find out through experience. I swore this would be my last assignment. If I had any sense left, I'd gracefully exit the stage and go quietly live my life elsewhere...preferably with a handsome guy who didn't mind that I created explosions and induced heart attacks.

Ian rolled his eyes. Sometimes I wondered if he wanted to throttle me for my backtalk. "Report to the hangar tomorrow at the appointed time so Richard can take you over to Paris. And don't be late."

"Ian..."

"What is it?"

I felt like squirming in my seat. "You got my resignation letter, right? I put it on your desk this morning."

He pursed his lips. "I wanted to give you some time to think it over. That Denmark job really got to you, didn't it?"

"I'll do this last assignment, but promise me you'll have the final paperwork ready to sign when I return from Paris." My shoulders tensed in anticipation of his objections. I was certain he'd go on about how much SOE needed me.

"All right then," he said in a low voice. "I don't want to see you go, but if that's what you want..."

As he turned and headed toward the door with his gangly

walk, I glanced at the clock on the wall and winced. Ideally my routine would have been to nestle in my reclining chair and eat dinner by 7:00 p.m., but instead 8 o' clock stared back at me without apology. I flipped through the dossier, noting the most important details and memorizing Dr. Heilwig's face. When dropped into Paris tomorrow evening, I won't have the dossier to reference, nor any identification papers or passports on me.

We did this for two reasons: an agent's counterfeit identification could be damaged or lost during transport anyway, and in the case of arrest, the Gestapo often found it difficult to verify or prove she was a spy. I usually obtained papers from trusted sources on an as-needed basis, but if I didn't need them, then I did not carry papers. When I first began this, I found it all exciting because it allowed me to be anyone I wanted. After a few months, I ended up feeling like I was no one.

Sometimes I had to remind myself that *Emelie* was just my code name, and that her preferred mannerisms or activities weren't necessarily the ones Isabella George liked. My officemate Stella went to France often under the name Angela Wyatt, and had chosen it because her mother's first name was Angela and she obsessed over the 16th Century poet Thomas Wyatt.

After my first few missions, I grew apathetic in choosing names. Ian suggested *Emelie* because he said when he was younger, he had always wanted a little sister by that name. Since he never got one and I was the closest thing to it, he had said I should go with the moniker, and I've been using it ever since.

My lips curved into a slight smile at remembering this, but then turned into a frown as I thought about Stella's failure to report back. Wherever she was, I hoped that she had only been delayed and needed to hide with the French Resistance, or was already en route to London. In any case, I wanted Stella's belongings to remain here, untouched. If she happened to return, I didn't want her to think we gave up on her so quickly. In keeping with my weekly routine, I grabbed my dusty handkerchief from my desk drawer and wiped off her belongings.

I wondered, with a twinge of sadness, if anyone would do that for me if I were missing for five months, and I didn't even want to think about what Ian would have to tell my family under those circumstances: *So sorry, your daughter wasn't really working for the U.S. Ambassador to Britain—she was gallivanting about Europe engaging in counter-missions against the Nazis because we couldn't afford Hitler's occult powers to gain an advantage over Allied forces.*

It would kill my mother and brother to find out about me that way, and although pride kept me from saying it, the longer Stella went missing, the more anxious I grew that I could very well be next. Then what? Without a doubt, this would have to be my last mission behind enemy lines.

∾

When I arrived at my flat, I pulled out the few supplies I would take with me to Paris: a wad of francs, the enchanted items Brande brought me, and my golden alchemist's knife. I placed them on my nightstand then headed into the kitchen to fix myself dinner. I went through the cabinets and refrigerator but found nothing that piqued my appetite. My friend Jane Lewis usually came home around this time. She cooked enticing meals like lamb stew and meatloaf. Most importantly, she generously shared them with me.

I still hopelessly tried to make an American dish every now and then, but I would only end up frustrated and yearning for home while my belly rumbled. I decided to see what Jane was cooking and went downstairs to her flat on the first floor. I knocked a couple of times, and she answered the door, wearing a dirty apron and wiping flour from her hands. Her freckled face broke into a smile, and she welcomed me in.

"Please, have a seat, Isabella. I was just finishing the liver sandwiches." She went back into her kitchen and pulled a dish out of the oven.

"Liver sandwiches?" I wanted to grimace, but unless I was cooking for myself, I had no right to object.

"Well, it's more like a meat-filled pastry."

"Filled with liver?" As if I were supposed to overlook *that* fact.

"Not everyone in the world eats loads of fried cows and cheese."

"This is going to be interesting."

"I'm trying to follow the ration recipes from *Woman's Weekly*." She gestured toward the magazine on her coffee table.

"Is it *that* bad?" I went over and grabbed the magazine, flipping through its pages. I took a few moments to scan its housekeeping articles and recipes.

"If you went to buy food more often, you'd know." She arranged the liver sandwiches on two plates and invited me to come sit with her at the dining table.

"You're cooking an awful lot lately." I took a bite and gave silent thanks that she had at least seasoned the meat.

"Well, I'm just honing my housekeeping skills, you know." She bit into her sandwich and turned her left hand to reveal a diamond engagement ring on her finger. She must have slipped it on in the kitchen.

"Congratulations, Jane." With a smile, I got up and threw my arms around her. "I didn't know...have I been away that long?"

"It was all so sudden, even *I'm* still surprised." Her face simply glowed.

"Garret is a lucky man." I frowned when she took it upon herself to plop another sliver of sandwich into my mouth. I wondered if she hid some stew or dumplings in the refrigerator and this was all to torture me.

"And it came at the perfect time. I was wondering last week what I was going to do with myself."

My smile faded. "You were tired, weren't you?"

She nodded and tears formed in her eyes. "I don't want you to get the wrong idea. I still believe in what we're fighting for, but we all have to retire some time, right?"

"Sure we do."

Jane's sister, Anna, had been one of three Special Operations Executive agents arrested by Nazis last October in the Netherlands. She was immediately sentenced to death by firing squad. They had no pity on her because she was a woman; the SS shot her down and threw her body into a heaping pile of other victims.

"Besides," she wiped her face, "I'm getting old and I want babies. All my girlfriends who I grew up with are married off and raising families."

"Well, I'm glad for you, Jane. You deserve a happy life with Garret."

I asked her to recount the whole proposal from beginning to end. I asked to see her ring again and secretly felt a mixture of excitement and envy. Afterward, I offered to clear the table and wash dishes so she wouldn't try to feed me anything else. We made small talk the rest of the time, and she reminded me about some letters she held for me. I thanked her and continued cleaning the kitchen, wiping down the counters and saving scraps of leftover food.

I couldn't help but steal glances of her engagement ring every few minutes and savor the sweet smoothness of the gold it was made of. As an alchemist, I had a natural ability to taste the metallic essence of metals. I eyed the shining round-cut diamond set in the middle and wondered if I would cry or jump with excitement if someone ever proposed to me.

Though my life as a spy did have its share of excitement, I couldn't deny the mental, physical, and even spiritual drain that this line of work had on me. I remembered days when I would refuse to get out of bed because weariness or distress had dragged me down. Even when Ian had sent a car for me, I wouldn't answer. At other times, I'd return from a mission with a stone cold face and impenetrable heart, and then, as soon as I stepped through my doorway, I would start bawling.

I called it being *tired*, and I understood what Jane felt.

I wasn't going to lie to myself. I wanted to be married one day, move somewhere close to my brother and his wife, and watch our kids grow up together. I wanted to be able to stroll through my quiet little neighborhood not having to wonder if the friendly neighbor down the street was an enemy operative with a gun behind his back. I wanted to be in control of how I lived, and I couldn't reconcile this with living and dying by others' orders.

"I should go back up to my flat. I'm going to Paris tomorrow." I came back into the living room and leaned over the sofa to give Jane a peck on the cheek.

"Be careful, do you hear me?"

"You know I will, because I want to make it back for your wedding. When will it be?"

"March, of next year." She got up and walked me over to the door.

"I think I can make it back by then."

She laughed. "You'd better. And I want to come to yours one day."

"I'd have to find a guy to stick with me first."

We said our goodnights and I headed back upstairs, feeling loneliness creep upon me. I quickly changed, got into bed, and began browsing through the letters Jane gave me. Some were bills, others were solicitations for mail order catalogs, and, of course, I received my letter from Jonathan. I tossed the others aside and opened his cryptic letter, written under the pseudonym Sherman Woods.

I told him a long time ago that since I had access to "sensitive information in the ambassador's office," that my employer frowned upon casual and steady communication with family and friends. Johnnie took it upon himself to start writing me once a month using a silly code language we used to communicate in when we were children.

I always found his letters, and the effort he put into them, amusing and gratefully welcomed. In fact, I found the elaborate system we came up with quite impressive. The codes would actually work if I wanted to use them for a real mission. As I read his account of his weekly triumphs and worries, as well as how our mother was faring, I wistfully thought of the look on his face if I were to just show up on his doorstep.

Well, perhaps I could do that once this mission was over. The sooner I extracted Heilwig and got rid of The Plague, the sooner I could be finished and truly go home. I slowly drifted into a restless sleep, hoping for this outcome, and of course, wondering what my final assignment would be like.

CHAPTER 3

The cab driver flinched when he saw the bomb drop. It fell through the sky with a deadly grace, but I didn't bat an eyelash. I pressed my hand against the window and reached out with my senses, making sure that a curse hadn't been laid along with the bomb's contents.

"Are you sure it's safe to go to the air hangar?" He slowed the car.

"It was a leaflet bomber," I told him as we watched a multitude of folded papers eject from the bomb and swirl through the air. The empty container would land without incident, the propaganda leaflets would make their way into people's hands—but hopefully not their hearts.

He wiped his brow. "Thank God. I thought it would explode."

I shook my head at some of the Royal Air Force officers running over and collecting the leaflets. Although the Nazis dropped their leaflet bombs in city centers, where they could reach the civilian population, every now and then a batch would be directed toward a military or industrial site. I didn't know how many Air Force officers gave credence to the propaganda printed on those papers, but it probably wouldn't galvanize them to read about how the impeccable prophet Nostradamus predicted their demise four hundred years ago, or to see pictures of dead Ally soldiers littering the ground. That is, if you believed in their Black Propaganda.

"You can let me out here, thank you." I gave him a squeeze on the shoulder then opened my door.

"SOE isn't paying me enough for this. One day it'll fall out of the sky and hit me right on the head." He let out a nervous laugh.

I smiled back at him and said goodbye. As I exited the car, I saw the sky turn a deep orange, and I knew that at sunset I'd have to board the transport plane to Paris. I heard the engine of a spitfire fighter plane pass over and wondered if it went to hunt down the bomber that dropped the leaflets. As a couple of officers admitted me into the hangar, I spotted one of the pilots running in from the field with a few leaflets in hand.

"Good evening, Emelie."

"Hi, Max." I took one of the leaflets he offered and grunted when I read it. "What are you going to do with these?"

"Burn them...like the others."

That sounded like a good idea, especially since the one I held in my hand made me want to toss it into a fire without looking back. It had a drawing of a dark, crooked tower with a caricature of a wizard perched on top, raining his spells down on frightened people. In bolded letters it said, "The Gray Tower helps now, so it can harm later."

I gave the leaflet back to Max. "Make sure you get rid of all of these."

We halted when Richard approached us with my supply pack and jumpsuit in hand. He gave them to me and pointed toward a changing room. "We're leaving in an hour."

"Lieutenant," Max said, "We got these—"

Richard jerked his thumb in the direction of one of the large storage bins. "We don't need any of that bollocks here. Trash them."

Max immediately headed for the bin to dispose of the leaflets. I was glad Richard refused to even take a look at them. Sometimes I'd get odd stares or snide comments from colleagues at SOE who knew I had trained with the Gray Tower.

At first I had dismissed it as plain ignorance or even a bit of envy on days that I needed my own confidence boosted. However, as the war progressed, I realized that many of them were afraid. In the back of their minds, they probably wondered if I'd turn rogue and blast them all away.

Though the Masters imposed strict rules on members of the Order while at the Gray Tower, they didn't have much to say when it came to being in the outside world. I understood why people, or governments for that matter, would be wary. Still, it didn't hurt to show a little friendliness, especially toward those of us who willingly joined the Ally cause and risked our lives each day.

As Richard turned and started barking orders at the maintenance crew that worked on a bomber, I made my way through the bustle on the hangar floor to the changing room. I felt a little guilty about making this my last assignment, but I promised myself that I'd at least make it my most successful one. The average life expectancy of an SOE agent was just a few months, and I've lasted over a year. So, if one really wanted to get into the mathematics of it, I've basically served a couple of lifetimes.

That had to count for something, right?

∽

When night fell, I rode in a transport plane that could've been shot out of the sky at any second. I poised myself to leap toward the dark terrain of the northern region of France. From there, I'd have to find my way to Paris. Most SOE agents came here by plane or submarine, sneaking their way toward the Maquis resistance fighters or a Nazi target.

We started off doing "small jobs" like operating anti-Nazi radio programs, bringing in food and arms to friends and stranded Ally soldiers, and relaying messages and news back to SOE headquarters. Most of us were women, from all walks of life, from both Europe and America, who wanted to do more for our countries than to stay at home and worry.

The male-dominated intelligence community treated us with disdain, but soon even they couldn't refute our important contributions. "The Ministry of Ungentlemanly Warfare," Winston Churchill once jokingly called us, although the epithet was perfectly apt. We did anything and everything to frustrate the Third Reich and set Europe ablaze, and we weren't afraid to fight dirty.

"Looks like you're the last one in for the week." Richard frowned as he closed the cockpit entrance, made his way over, and knelt next to me. I was already sitting in the area where the drop hole would open and I'd have to jump out with my parachute.

"You say it as if it's a bad thing." I glanced at my hands and clasped them together, unsure of what to say next. He knew my officemate Stella, and he even took a fancy to her. Though he never admitted this, and would vehemently deny it if I ever brought it up, a girl could just tell about these sorts of things.

"How is it faring on your side?" His strong gaze demanded me to face him and answer. He wanted to know if there was any news about Stella, but I had none to offer. I really didn't want to talk about this with him, and I didn't want to plant any nasty seeds of doubt. I wished his co-pilot had come back here to see me off.

I half smiled. "If I'm alive, then I'm faring well. I'll let you know if I hear anything, you know..."

The signal light flashed and the metal panel beneath us slowly opened. A gust of wind encircled us, and I gave a quick nod toward him. Though his facial expression revealed nothing, I felt like I needed to say something to him as a word of encouragement.

"Go, Emelie!" Richard cut me off before I could speak. He didn't do it in a crass or dismissive manner, but perhaps in that moment he realized that he didn't want to dwell on Stella any more than I did.

I took a deep breath and scooted myself forward. The first time I leapt out of a Royal Air Force transport plane, I had barely kept my wits. I kept imagining the Gestapo or SS strolling along a lonely stretch of road and finding me splattered all over. I may have been an alchemist, but I had yet to figure out a potion or elixir to make me airborne.

My parachute released as soon as I jumped out of the plane, and I fell silently through the night air, hoping the white umbrella above me didn't serve as an invitation to enemy gunfire. I thought all was clear as I nearly touched the ground, until I noticed a convertible-top jeep barrel down the road and then slow to a halt.

I knew the patrol officer driving the trekker spotted me, and I cursed under my breath as I skidded across the field. My adrenaline went surging through me as I grabbed my knife from my jumpsuit's outer pocket and cut myself loose. I rolled away and scanned the area, trying to decide whether to lay low or just make a run for it. The only thing I saw was the trekker's headlight beam; blackness enveloped everything else, including me.

I grew up in the city, where we had streetlights and bright theater marquee signs. The one time I actually went on a trip to the forest where there weren't convenient lights stationed to guide my path, I found out just how terrified I was of absolute darkness. I still didn't like the dark, and I dared not move because I wanted to hear where the officer was. All I heard was my heavy breathing, and I was so anxious that the only thing I could do was press the back of my hand to my mouth to stifle the sound.

A shot rang out. I quickly dropped to my knees. I didn't know what direction the bullet came from, and I tried encouraging myself with the morbid thought that there had been plenty of people who survived gunshot wounds. I finally steadied my breathing and gripped my knife, waiting for him to make another move. However, I immediately bucked and dropped my weapon when a pair of arms enclosed me in a fierce grip.

I swung my head back and gave him a good head-butt, making him cry out in pain and release me. I quickly turned around, delivered a left hook, and dodged his fist when he tried to reciprocate. Although we couldn't see each other, we could hear and feel each other's body movements in this deadly dance. I heard him swing at me again. I blocked his strike, but not before losing my balance and landing on my back. Fighting in a jumpsuit could be cumbersome sometimes.

"Who are you?" he asked in German, grabbing hold of me and dragging me by the scruff of my neck. He brought me toward the beaming headlights where he shoved me against the front of the jeep, and I slowly faced him with arms raised in surrender. I had to plan my next move carefully.

"I'm from the Russian Liberation Group," I answered in perfect Russian. "Praskovya sent me." I thought I'd add that part since he cocked his revolver. The Russian Liberation Group had been sending in spies and other reinforcements for their Nazi allies for about a month now. Some of these operatives entered France the same way I had.

"She sent you?" He switched over to speaking Russian. Though his tone sounded doubtful, he lowered his gun slightly.

"You know us...we do everything *backward*, comrade." I prayed the codeword we had intercepted last week still held.

The back of my neck began to burn, and I thought of what I could say next. He saved me the trouble when he slid his gun into his holster and offered me his hand. "Leave it to the Russians to send women to do a man's job. What does Praskovya want?"

I quickly grasped his hand, one of the easiest access points, and honed my magical senses, tracking the rhythm of his heart and the electrical currents in his brain. As his heartbeat slowed and his mind hazed, I spoke to him.

"What's your name?"

"Karl Manfried."

"How many other officers are in the Paris office?"

"Twenty six."

That was a little more than I cared to handle alone. "Why don't you go back to your headquarters and greet your comrades with a Molotov cocktail?"

He slowly nodded and let his hand slip from mine. He headed straight for his trekker and jumped inside. The jeep rumbled and slowly reversed, then made a turn in the direction of the city. By this time, my hands shook from exhaustion, and my head ached from the amount of concentration I mustered to use body magic on him. It also didn't help that I was hungry and irritated. In any case, I needed to make it to my safe house even though it was apparently past curfew. However, I needed as many SS officers off the streets as possible. Hopefully Karl would be the distraction I needed once I reached the city.

I pulled out my foldable bike from the pack attached to the parachute. After spending twenty minutes longer than I usually would setting it up, I unzipped and shed the jumpsuit to reveal a rather tight-fitting milkmaid uniform. I promised myself that I'd make it back to London just to shoot Ian for making me wear this.

I stuffed the jumpsuit into the pack and placed it in the little straw basket attached to the bike's handlebars. I pedaled down the road without looking back. I took note of the Seine River which ran to my right. It looked like I was south of Mantes, just outside of Paris. I kept my eyes open for more trekkers, hoping that I could make it through without any trouble.

When I made it to the city proper, I took some backstreets to avoid a few SS officers on patrol. I pulled my bike up to an alley and slowly walked through. I scowled when I saw an officer in the middle of the alley, against the wall with his woman, blissfully lost in a quick and dirty cuzzy. They either didn't notice or didn't care when I walked by and wrinkled my nose at the scent of garbage and piss.

I wondered if the woman was just another collaborator selling her body for food or gas, or an agent of the Resistance engaged in an act of seduction. Sometimes I wondered what went through women's heads when they did this. I've used my red garnet lipstick twice to kiss men and enthrall them so they would do what I wanted, and those were the least arousing experiences I've ever had. If I were that woman, I'd probably be thinking about how much longer it would be before the deed was done, or why he didn't get a hotel room.

I grew more confident as I turned a corner and headed down another lonely street, but unfortunately fate would not have it be that easy for me. Before I was halfway down the street, two SS officers headed toward me from the opposite end and hailed me. Though I put on a stoic face, my fingers trembled and my heart raced. Our confrontation would be inevitable since they would be complete idiots not to question a milkmaid out riding her bike after curfew.

"Halt right there, *mademoiselle*." The first officer spoke in a syrupy voice.

I saw the glint of a name tag on his uniform and frowned. Supposedly the SS Hitler sent into Paris were the "polite" ones, and I supposed many of them believed themselves an actual legitimate enforcement organization—nevermind the fact that they were occupying someone else's country. The first officer, whose name tag read Adelbert, approached and grabbed hold of my bike.

The second, whose name was Gerhardt, grabbed my arm and spoke to me in French. "A little late to be delivering milk, isn't it?"

"I...I was with my Pierre. I didn't mean to take off so late."

Adelbert leaned my bike against the brick wall of the closed shop we stood in front of. The menacing look in his dark eyes worried me more than the gun in his holster. "Lucky for you that your sweetheart didn't accompany you."

Gerhardt forced me against the wall with my back to him. "Is it the same Pierre who lives by Le Petit bakery?" He asked the question in English.

"I'm sorry," I said back to him in French, "I don't understand much English."

He ran his hands along my body, pretending to frisk me. Hey...one more grope and you'll get a kick to your face!

"Check her bag, Adelbert."

My body tensed and I quickly assessed my options. I could stun Gerhardt with a blow and fight Adelbert, or even beat him to the bag so I could grab my weapons. However, a bullet in the back of my head would end it all. If he opened the pack sitting in the basket, I would be the next one in front of a firing squad. Suddenly an explosion went off a few blocks down. The sky lit up. I prayed the mind-hazed Karl Manfried had carried out my order.

"*Scheisse!* It's the office!" Gerhardt, with a bewildered look on his face as if he couldn't believe someone would dare attack his office, began running in the direction of the fire. Adelbert drew his revolver and followed.

I slid away from the wall and opened and shut my mouth. Thank goodness Gerhardt didn't break my jaw. After rotating my aching shoulders, I hopped on my bike and continued down the street, pedaling as hard as I could until I reached a winding road that led to the dark and quiet neighborhood near Vincennes. I slowed and parked my bike at a small prayer chapel, taking my pack with me and quietly entering.

No one sat or prayed inside, but a beautiful statue of the Madonna oversaw a corner full of flickering candles. I went to the back room, where the caretaker stored his cleaning supplies and extra candles, and I crawled beneath the small table, where a trap-door lay hidden beneath a rug. I lifted it and pulled on the iron handle as I carefully slipped inside. It was tricky getting the rug back over and then closing the door, but I managed to do it, and began trekking through a dark underground passageway.

Though the path led me down a straight line, I wished I had at least swiped a candle. I felt like I was going to be swallowed by the darkness. I didn't feel like going back, so I just went at a steady pace and held my hands out in front of me in case I stumbled. After walking through the underground passage for five minutes, I finally felt the false dirt wall that signaled the end of my journey.

I recalled Ian's instructions for getting to the safe house. I felt for the hidden lever and pulled, and the false wall cracked open. I pried it open further and opened a reinforced wooden door behind it. I quickly slipped through, covering the door the way I found it. I crawled up a ladder and pushed open a trapdoor like the one in the chapel, except this one opened into a tool shed.

I supposed they really wanted to make me work to get here. I was so irritated that I almost broke the trapdoor when I slammed it shut. I paused and listened for any noises—a voice, footsteps, or trekkers. When I was sure no one was nearby, I covered the trapdoor with a rug and crept from the tool shed before I went toward the back of the safe house. I approached and saw an angel ornament hanging in the middle of the back door. I held my pack and stepped forward, giving a slightly urgent knock. I heard slow and hesitant footsteps, and after a few seconds elapsed, someone finally answered from the other side of the door.

"Who is it?" a woman's muffled voice queried in French.

"Emelie." I gave a grateful but tired grin when she opened the door.

"It's late, Emelie."

"Yes, but I have gifts."

"From whom?"

All I wanted at this hour was a hot meal and a soft bed. "From 64 Baker Street."

The woman nodded and smiled. "Then come in, Emelie, and make yourself at home."

CHAPTER 4

At the first rays of dawn, I awoke and went to soak in a hot bath. I tried to expel my bitter feelings from last night's encounter. This was neither the first nor the last time I would run into officers like Adelbert and Gerhardt. Sometimes I wanted to shed my façade and just start hitting them with spells that would make them run back home with their tails between their legs, like the cowardly dogs they were. However, being a vigilante wizard wasn't part of my mission, though sometimes I wished it were.

My limbs still ached from last night's assault, and my shoulders burned with soreness. As I relaxed in the warm water, I noticed a display of waxy soaps on an adjacent shelf, some wrapped, from different regions of France and even other countries.

These were probably small gifts left by guests who've come and gone, some perhaps forever. Looking at the display reminded me of my father, who'd bring my brother and me treats from the different places he had traveled to. For my mother, he'd bring exotic flowers and a heartfelt kiss.

I laughed to myself when I remembered how he would always warn us not to stay up late eating candy. Johnnie and I would hide our treats all over the house in the most unlikely of places so that we could grab them whenever we'd want—and my father found each and every one of them without fail. As a child, I never understood how he had known and anticipated every plan and move we'd make. My favorite part was when he'd tuck us in and read me Emily Dickinson poetry until I fell asleep. I was only eight and didn't completely understand it all, but I always found her poetry fascinating—and I enjoyed the fact that a girl wrote it.

After nearly an hour in my thoughts and memories, I tore myself away from the tub with lethargic movements and got dressed. I hid my supplies beneath a secret panel in the floor before heading to the kitchen. My stomach rumbled when I caught a whiff of the fresh pastries just coming out of the oven.

I greeted Renée, the woman who had admitted me last night, and sat at the table and helped myself to a cup of coffee. She looked rather pleased at my enthusiasm as she placed a couple of pastries on my plate. Though I didn't know her, I knew *of* her, and that she had been with the Resistance since the beginning. I was glad that she had accepted the task of hosting me.

"My husband fought in the Free French Army until a Maquisard betrayed him and murdered him in his sleep." She gestured toward her husband's portrait hanging on the wall. "My son and daughter-in-law were sent off to Dachau, and I've never heard from them since."

I shook my head. "Our enemies knew you were hurting them…you were important." Those Gestapo bastards often kidnapped or killed members of people's families as retribution.

"Have you lost anyone, Emelie?"

"Yes…I mean, I hope not." *Stella, where are you?*

"I once had a guest tell me that he at first thought I was a hard woman because I still fought, despite everything. The truth is, I'm the type of woman who would go into my son's old room and dust off his belongings, fluff his pillow, and sometimes just sit or cry."

"I'm very sorry for your loss." It reminded me of Stella and how I acted as custodian over her items, though I feared the most likely outcome of her fate.

"Thank you."

"May I ask you about Veit Heilwig? Do you know anything about him?" I breathed in the heady and aromatic scent of the coffee before taking another long sip.

"Dr. Heilwig fashions himself a man of great intellect." Renée escaped her somber mood and poured herself some coffee. The fine lines in her face softened. "He is at the university lecturing and poisoning minds."

I broke off a piece of my pastry and ate it before speaking. "Do you know anything else about the chemical weapons being used?"

"I heard that they've transferred more from the south, where Mussolini's men are stationed, but no one really knows where they are coming from. They're probably in a factory in this region, though the Maquis haven't been able to find out which one."

"Perhaps Mathieu could help us with that," I said.

Mathieu Perrine had become the unofficial voice of the Maquis during occupation. His nightly radio broadcasts were a constant thorn in the Gestapo's side. If you ever needed a message to be sent out, or coded instructions to the nearest safe house, or a simple word of encouragement, Mathieu could deliver.

"I'll try to contact him and see, but it won't be easy." She sipped her coffee. "We lost a safe house last week, and I fear the Gestapo is becoming more ruthless."

"I understand. I'll most likely have to get into the university to keep an eye on Heilwig."

"Without credentials?"

"Is Penn in Paris? He can give me the papers I need." I looked askance when she kept staring at me.

"So young." She shook her head. "I don't know if you just seem familiar to me, or if you remind me of myself. Believe it or not, I was like you once. Now I am just old and tired."

"You were one of the first." Though I gazed at her with pride, it was tempered by the sadness in her eyes.

"And perhaps I will be one of the last. Only God knows. Just remember to stay true to yourself, no matter what...that's what I've learned."

"Very sound advice." I drummed my fingers on the table and stared at my Agate stone ring.

"Well, I might as well show you around, Emelie. Would you care to see the garden?"

"Please."

I followed her to the back door that led to the plot of land behind the house. A picket fence enclosed the garden and I could see three small crosses peeking out from beneath the hyacinths. Inscribed on each cross were the words "*Se Souvenir*," which meant "Remember." For most of us, remembering something painful often proved to be difficult, but Renée seemed to embrace it because it was all she had left.

"Do you see the tool shed over there?" She pointed at the wooden structure with its peeling white paint. I cringed a little at having slammed the trapdoor so hard last night.

"I had one of those...at my parents' old house."

"Make sure that you always take the underground passageway beneath the floor that leads to the chapel down the hill. No one must know that you're staying here."

I gazed at her in amazement. "You made that passageway yourself?"

"I can't take credit for it. My husband did it years ago during the Great War, when we thought Paris might be taken."

"Your husband must have been a great man."

"And to think, when he first proposed to me, I turned him down." She chuckled. "He was very intelligent, but not always the best at showing his emotions. Even when he proposed to me, it was more of a logical argument as to why we would be compatible mates. One day, he showed up with flowers and a poem he wrote for me. I knew then that I wanted to marry him."

"And the crosses are for him, and your son and his wife?"

She smoothed her hair, right where a streak of gray stood out. "Three reasons to get out of bed every morning and keep doing my work. I used to hide maps, weapons, and even passports back here. So many people have come through this house, each leaving his own mark."

"What do you hide there now?" The air was quiet—a good quiet, but a sad quiet.

"Nothing. I haven't had a guest in eight months. Soon, SOE will forget about me."

I raised an eyebrow. "This can't be the same woman who I hear inspired so many SOE agents and even saved lives."

She folded her arms. "Is that what they say about me?"

"Well, I don't think the Gestapo has forgotten about you." Even from the garden, I heard trekkers speeding up the hill, and I exchanged glances with her.

"Wait here," she said. "If they come to the door, I'll talk to them." She patted me on my shoulder and headed toward the front, either apathetic to her possible fate or resigned to it.

My heart jumped at the shouting and loud knocks at the door. I listened carefully, just in case Renée needed me. I heard two agents speaking with her, and then a pair of heavy shoes pounding against the floor throughout the house. Doors opened and shut, closets were ransacked, and I thought I even heard the toilet being checked. As the pounding footsteps grew louder, I placed my back against the wall and tiptoed sideways. Just as I turned the corner, the back door opened.

Not waiting to see if the Gestapo agent would explore the backyard further, I made my way toward the front. I froze in place when I heard the second agent with Renée, their voices drifting through an open window right above me.

"Adelbert caught a suspicious woman riding around last night. You wouldn't happen to know anything about that?"

"Mister Karsten—"

"*Agent* Karsten."

"I've only been up a couple of hours."

I flinched and bit my tongue when I heard a thunderous slap. "I asked you about last night, not about this morning."

I was just about to turn the corner and make it to the front of the house when I saw the second agent coming from the other side. I ran back toward the garden, hoping he didn't see me from the corner of his eye. I didn't want to chance running into him, so I stayed in the back, listening for footsteps. When I heard none, I slipped in through the back door. My bare feet padded along the ground once more. I quickly went into Renée's son's old room and stood against the wall, straining to keep track of the conversation and praying I could make it over in time if he decided to pull out a weapon.

"Who had breakfast with you?"

"The old man, Otto, who lives down near the chapel. He's a friend of mine."

"Lorenz, go see Otto."

"Yes, sir." Lorenz left and shut the door.

"How are your Maquis friends, Renée?"

"They cost me my family. I wouldn't quite call them friends."

"I might as well have some refreshments while I'm here. Got anymore coffee?"

"Of course," she responded in a stiff voice, but I heard her go into the kitchen and return.

"Ah, looks delicious. The old man must've left in a hurry." I could hear him scraping a spoon against the bottom of a coffee cup.

"Is there anything else I can get you, Agent Karsten?"

"Sounds like Lorenz is coming back up the road. Are you sure there isn't anything you want to confess?"

"Only the guilty have something to confess, sir."

"Well, let's see if you're the lying whore that I think you are."

The door opened. Lorenz's boots scuffed the floor. "Sir, the old man said he had breakfast this morning with her...and asked if she had any more pastries left."

A torturous silence filled the house, and I stepped closer to the doorway, my heart pounding in my chest and my palms sweating. If anything happened to Renée, I would feel responsible, and I didn't know if I would forgive myself for that.

Karsten grunted. "Then let's not waste any more time. Perhaps we'll stop by again later."

As soon as I heard them depart, and the loud rumble of their trekker fade in the distance, I ran into the living room toward Renée. I gently touched her left cheek and felt a burning sensation where Karsten had struck her. I delivered a cool flow of healing energy through my fingertips and shrank the swollen bruise on her face.

"Are you all right?"

She sighed. "I'll be fine. They know about my husband and son, so every now and then they come and try to scare me."

"Cowards. Thank goodness Otto went along with your story."

"Yes, and it helps that I make only pastries for breakfast anyway."

My hand fell to my side. "I thought I was going to have a heart attack."

"So did I, Emelie." Suddenly she jolted. "Emelie...I knew there was something familiar about you. This may sound strange, but Otto came by a month ago and said he had a letter for you. I didn't know what he was talking about since I hadn't hosted anyone in months, but he was adamant that the letter be given to an Emelie."

"Me? Are you sure?" I didn't receive letters while undercover. This was either extremely important, or terribly dangerous.

"I don't know." She frowned. "But he's very loyal and discreet. You can go see him this afternoon and find out about it."

The letter certainly piqued my curiosity, but it also made me uneasy. I ran through nearly all the people I knew as I tried to guess who would attempt to send me a note under these circumstances. I managed to put aside my worries and offered to clear the table and wash dishes. I didn't forget to thank her for the meal, and especially for her protection. After I got rid of my milkmaid dress and the jumpsuit, I borrowed one of Renée's old shift dresses and a sun hat to cover my head. She packed the remaining pastries and set them in a picnic basket, asking me to thank Otto once more for his aid. I headed out the back door carrying the basket and made my way to the tool shed. Using a candle Renée gave me, I made my way through the dark tunnel.

Wooden beams reinforced the ceiling and walls, and I went a little faster when I thought I felt something scurry across my toes. I exited through the trapdoor in the chapel. Otto wasn't there, and so I walked through the front and headed toward his house, stiffening with each car that passed, and refraining from making eye contact with others.

I wanted to cringe when I spied three SS officers with weapons drawn, and four young men and two women on their knees in a line, hands behind their heads. The situation startled me, and though I had seen death and sent enemies to their deaths, the idea of shooting innocent and defenseless people in the streets like that filled me with a sickening dread. I started running toward them, but when the first gunshot rang, I knew I was too late.

"This will be the punishment for all terrorists!" one of the officers shouted to horrified passersby and witnesses. Once again, the cowards used murder to intimidate their foes.

I slowed my pace as each subsequent shot ripped away the façade of tranquility that the mild summer weather presented. I held back tears of anger as I slowly went up Otto's front steps. I made sure to look at each officer, remembering their name tags and faces, promising that they would one day get what they deserved.

Otto opened the door, ushered me through, and gladly accepted the basket of pastries I brought him. He led me to his sofa and invited me to sit, all the while asking me who had been shot in the street. I shook my head and let the matter go; I was still upset at the sight. I didn't know who those people were, but they certainly weren't terrorists. The real terrorists were wearing swastikas.

"It's a shame." He took a seat next to me. "I fought in the Battle of the Marne over fifteen years ago and thought the Germans wouldn't dare come back after that. Now I must sit here and suffer them shooting people in the streets."

"Do you still work with the Resistance?"

He snorted. "They say I'm too old. They'll let boys who are barely old enough to shave carry messages back and forth, but me? No...Old Otto might break his foot coming down the steps." He muttered a curse word in French, and I reluctantly smirked.

A steaming kettle whistled from the kitchen and he excused himself. I glanced at his coffee table, all covered with newspapers and magazines, and I heard the low humming of the radio. It seemed Otto spent much of his time trying to keep up with current events, though the Nazis filtered or censored most of the information. Mathieu Perrine's radio broadcasts were the only trustworthy source of what really went on with the Allies and the Resistance. I grinned when I saw Otto return with a hot cup of tea for me, and I politely listened as he began telling me about his son Lucien.

"My boy fought alongside the Maquisards and eventually joined the Free French Army." He smacked his lips when I handed him a pastry from the basket. "He's on special assignment in Spain with some Americans. They're trying to bolster public support for the Allied forces—secretly, of course, since General Franco would not openly have any of it. Perhaps you can meet Lucien one day, as he is a fine young man and *unmarried!*"

I smiled again and took a sip of tea as he showed me a picture of Lucien. I didn't want to be rude, but elders were notorious for holding you hostage in a conversation if you let them. I needed to grab my letter and find out who tried to contact me.

"Renée told me you had a letter? May I see it?"

"Yes, yes…I will get it." He nodded his hoary head and shuffled over to a cupboard where he had a secret compartment. At least two pictures of his son, Lucien, hung on every wall. There were also pictures of a beautiful young woman, probably his deceased wife when she was younger.

"Here it is, and it's still sealed." He handed me the letter and then sat across from me, filling his pipe.

"Who gave it to you?" My heart nearly skipped a beat when I recognized the handwriting.

"A courier. I took it and thought maybe he intended it to go to Renée, since she has people stay at her house sometimes. I brought it to her the day I received it, however she insisted that I keep it. I think she was waiting to see if I was fool enough to get caught."

I opened the letter and unfolded the sheet of paper. It had no signature or date:

> *Safe in their alabaster chambers,*
> *untouched by morning and untouched by noon,*
> *sleep the meek members of the resurrection,*
> *rafter of satin, and roof of stone.*
> *I should have shielded you from our friends.*
> *We will meet again.*

I re-read the note until I had committed it to memory. I promptly took it over to the stove and poked it into the fire, watching the paper blacken and curl. The note confused and scared me. My head wagged back and forth in denial, and for a moment I thought someone was playing a cruel joke on me.

"My dear, why did you burn that letter? Was it not important?" Otto came into the kitchen with an anxious expression.

"If you were still active, you'd know to never keep any papers or letters on you. If they were lost or if you were captured...then what?" I didn't want to snap at him, but I had little patience to spare these days.

"I apologize."

"You don't need to...thanks for the letter, and I hope your son returns safely."

I gave him a peck on the cheek and trudged toward the door, once again facing the discomfort of walking back to the chapel. The bodies of the victims had been removed, but their blood still stained the street. I felt like I would go berserk if I saw another SS officer out on the road, but luckily I didn't.

When I returned to the house, Renée saw me trembling, and she pulled me to sit down at the table. I barely heard her questions. I didn't even reach for the glass of water she pushed in front of me. I kept arguing with myself about the note and how my father couldn't have sent it. First, I knew for a fact he wasn't in France, nor would he have been within the last month. Second, he was a very straightforward man, much like Renée's husband. Why would he send me such a cryptic message? Renée kept rubbing my shoulder in a consoling manner and staring into my eyes. She finally fell into silence because she seemed afraid of what I would say.

"I got the letter...from Otto." A letter that was either a lie or pointing toward one.

"Wh-what did it say?"

I took a moment to clear my dry throat. "I think it's from my father."

"Is he in France?"

"He died sixteen years ago in Rome." Both the U.S. Army and the Gray Tower confirmed it.

"My God..." She placed her hand on her chest as she exhaled; her shocked expression mirrored my own. "Are...are you sure he's dead?"

"I don't know anymore." I felt my stomach tighten. If this note had truly been penned by him, then that meant I had been lied to about my father, and so everything I had believed about him...I didn't know what I believed anymore. It was his handwriting, a reference that he knew I would recognize, and it was addressed to my codename—eerily enough, the same name as my favorite poet.

"What did the letter say?"

I repeated the lines to her and realized that the first four lines were an excerpt from an Emily Dickinson poem about time and eternity. Why this poem?

"I have that poetry collection!" Renée shot up and went into her son's old room, leaving me to recall what I *did* know about my father.

He rose through the ranks of the U.S. Army and was also trained by the Gray Tower. Both institutions readily assented to my father being a liaison between the military and the Order of Wizards, and, by all accounts, he served honorably. One November evening, when another Elite Wizard, Serafino Pedraic, came from the Gray Tower to meet with my father in Rome, he found my dad's bloodstained apartment ransacked. No one had seen my father since.

After a lengthy investigation, Serafino arrived at our house along with General Robert Cambria, delivering their final verdict—Major Carson William George was dead. Though I was ten years old, certainly old enough to understand, part of me wanted to deny it and keep believing that my father would come through the front door any day with candy for me and Jonathan, and flowers for my mother. But he never came home.

All other kinds of emotions rose inside me, and I didn't know what to make of them. I believed my father wrote the note, but where was he if he was alive, and why had he been missing all those years? I kept ruminating over his words. What exactly did he mean by shielding me from our friends? He mentioned alabaster chambers and resurrection; could it be about death? Dickinson was a bit preoccupied with it. Maybe it was a warning that someone would die.

"Here it is." Renée nearly bumped into the table. She held the book open and started reading the poem to me, pausing after each stanza to see if I recognized any significance in them.

I shook my head, having only listened to half of her words. "I need to think about all this."

"Sooner or later, it will come to you. You say you haven't seen your father in years...perhaps there were things he said to you or that you've heard while he was still around."

"Maybe."

She closed the book. "Penn is with The Red Lady. Will you be going down to the nightclub later?"

I gestured toward the back, where my guest room stood. "Do you have any extra dresses in that armoire?"

"Do you like purple satin?"

"I'll take it."

CHAPTER 5

Penn Margaux bootlegged liquor, smuggled weapons, and claimed to be a spy from Orleans—but for what it was worth, he wasn't on the Gestapo's side. I had known him for as long as I've been working with SOE, and he always managed to obtain information for me when no one else could, or hand me a passport at the last minute. I even bought ingredients off him that I needed for some spells.

I would usually reach him through *La Dame Rouge*—the Red Lady, Jasmine Léon. She became a wildly popular entertainer at the Éclat nightclub after moving to Paris. While some of the locals believed that the Gestapo didn't shut down the club due to the threat of an utter uprising (the people adored the Red Lady), the truth was that Éclat served as a useful tool for the enemy in the constant game of espionage. The danger lay in the presence of Gestapo agents, both uniformed and plainclothes. They knew half the spies in there, and have blackmailed some into working for them, or betraying employers when it suited their interests.

I once knew a spy from Madrid who had claimed he was sent to gauge how things were going in France. Despite Spain's claim of neutrality, the Gestapo didn't like General Franco sticking his nose where it didn't belong, and so, as the spy left Éclat one night, two agents followed him to a woman's house—his French sweetheart. The problem was that the spy had a wife back in Spain. They used this information against him and forced him to spy on the Spanish government. They even made him turn over information on other spies who came into Éclat. I guess he couldn't take it any longer, because one day his Gestapo handlers found him hanging from his necktie in his hotel room.

This taught me to keep a low profile. I had carefully crafted a persona that blended in easily with the many young women who patronized the club. This also reminded me to remain aware of the fact that people still watched me, just like the others at the club, which meant that I would have to be careful when leaving, and I certainly wouldn't leave with a man. But as foolish and single-minded as many men were, I had seen several leave with women from the club without a thought.

When evening fell, I hailed a taxi to take me down to Éclat. Well, I had to stand near the chapel and flag one down. I kept brushing off my dress and feeling like something was crawling down my back. I swore that I'd find a workable invisibility potion so that I could just go straight to Renée's front door instead of through that creepy underground tunnel. I felt I needed the cab because it would've been awkward to approach the club on foot, and nothing screamed *I'm a Spy Who Doesn't Belong Here* like pulling up on a foldable bike and trying to get into a swanky Parisian nightclub.

I wore a slinky purple gown and a black sequined wrap—and of course, my Agate stone ring, which I never took off. Renée had to beg me to wear full eye makeup, but I had to admit that I liked the rouge on my cheeks and lips, and my hairstyle. I looked damned good, if I did say so myself. I checked my makeup in a compact mirror one last time before tossing it into my purse and instructing the bloated taxi driver to halt.

"If you leave that club alone tonight," he said facing me, "out of compassion I will take you home with me."

"Go to hell." I threw him a few francs and slipped out. Maybe I looked a little too good.

I strutted toward the entrance like I was a Hollywood starlet, making sure to give the doormen a wink and a smile. They readily admitted me. I came in just as Jasmine began singing *Blue Moon* up on stage. People swayed to the music, oblivious to the haziness created by cigarette smoke. The scent of perfume wafted toward me, and I narrowed my eyes as I silently critiqued or approved of some of the ladies' choices in shoes.

I acknowledged a group of handsome guys at one of the tables with a smile, but kept it moving since most of them were spies. I tasted the essences of silverware, gold jewelry, and even guns. There were about twenty tables in there, and those closest to the stage were reserved for Jasmine's most ardent admirers and paramours—or those pretending to be.

I nearly stumbled when I saw *him* sitting at one of those tables. At first I pretended not to see him, but then my gaze met his, and I headed straight toward him like a moth to a flame. I probably shouldn't have made a move to join him, but sitting in that area made it easier to keep an eye on who entered the club; besides, it looked like both of us had business with Jasmine tonight.

"Fancy seeing you here, Emelie." He flashed me a seductive smile.

"It's good to see you again, Drake." His real name was Kenneth Aspen. He knew mine as well. We had obtained illegal copies of one another's files after we first met, which wasn't quite your typical romantic gesture.

"How long are you in Paris?" He pulled out a seat for me next to his and gently brushed his thumb against my cheek. I forced myself not to smile.

"I'm here long enough to enjoy the scenery." I clapped along with the audience and gazed at Jasmine as she finished her ballad. She came down and stopped at a nearby table, where an enthusiastic man with a thick mustache greeted her with flowers.

"The Boss sent me to take a look at some cars." He took his seat and offered me some of his pochouse. I couldn't refuse the stewed fish. It smelled delectable, having been cooked in red wine and flavored with a savory spice.

"Then I'm glad your Boss sent you." I grabbed a knife and fork and dug in.

By "Boss," he meant the Office of Strategic Services (OSS), the American counterpart to SOE, and by "looking at cars" he meant sabotaging factories that produced machinery and weapons for the Nazis. I thought I heard him say that I looked beautiful, but I was already on my feet, welcoming Jasmine into my arms. We planted kisses on one another's cheeks and gave each other a tight hug. As befitting her stage name, she wore a red rose in her hair and a scarlet dress.

"Well, look who's in town!" She accepted a cigarette from a waiter passing by and asked for a lighter. Apparently both Ken and I had messages to slip her (conveniently hidden within our cigarette lighters), because we eagerly asked for her to keep them as gifts. She wiggled her way between us, lighting her cigarette with her own lighter and giving a rich, sultry laugh.

"I've missed you, Emelie...you too, Blondie." She patted Ken's cheek. I glanced toward the front entrance to see who entered and left, before facing them again.

"By the way, Jasmine, there's another gift waiting for you in your dressing room." He gave her a knowing look. It was probably the stipend OSS paid her for her services.

"Is it five thousand, like I asked?" She blew out a thin stream of smoke, her deep-set eyes watching Ken like a hawk.

"Would you mind telling me why you needed an extra two?"

"Things are getting tough around here." She shifted toward me and lazily eyed the band, which started up a tune.

Ken leaned in. "I know about your side operation. For goodness sake, Jasmine, don't get yourself killed."

Not satisfied with just being an informant, she also took it upon herself to hide and smuggle stranded Ally soldiers across the border, Maquis resistance leaders with bounties on their heads and Jews who've fled the slaughter in Czechoslovakia...anyone who needed it. I had been meaning to ask her how she did it and who helped her.

She rolled her eyes and faced me. "How are you, Emelie?"

"I'm doing well, and I love being in Paris. Do you miss New York?" She acknowledged my code phrase referencing Paris, which meant that the city would be ripe with action within the next week or so, and that the Maquisards should be on alert. This time, Ken watched the door.

"I'll tell you what, I don't miss performing in New York." She faced Ken, and I turned to watch the front. "Tell *that* to your Boss. Tell him as long as I can't walk through the front door of a New York club that I'm performing in, then he can kiss my black ass and keep paying me my five grand."

I smirked.

"Jasmine..." Ken began blustering.

"I know, I know—times are changing." She fell back into her earlier jolly mood, welcoming the glasses of cocktails another waiter brought over. "But I just love that Eleanor Roosevelt. Remember that incident a couple of years ago where she left that women's organization and told them off because they were talking about being whites-only? Ha! We need more people like her!"

"Yes, we do." My cocktail glass chimed with hers in a toast.

I always hated when people told me not to aspire to certain things because I was a woman. I couldn't imagine what it would be like to be told this simply because of my skin color. One of the many things I've learned is that when you've been holed up in a safe house with someone who doesn't look like you or speak the same language, but who was ready to break bread with you and even fight by your side—you quickly realized that there were a lot more important things to gripe about. At the end of the day, people were just people—blood, sweat and tears, heart and soul.

"Jasmine," Ken said, gazing at the front entrance, "get your things and go lock yourself in your dressing room. Emelie, I think our covers are blown."

I looked toward the front and saw four Gestapo agents heading through. Ken covertly drew his pistol as Jasmine hid the cigarette lighters beneath her flowers. She rose from her seat and wasted no time in leaving the lounge.

The music died and people shied away or headed toward the exit. For a moment, I hoped that the Gestapo were after someone else, but, sure enough, they came straight toward Ken and me. I felt the presence of other wizards as easily as I detected metals, and, despite the fact that the agents all wore black gabardine jackets with swastika armbands, I knew one or more of them were warlocks in disguise.

I turned back toward the table and immediately retrieved my golden knife from my purse. I began carving the alchemical symbol for the sun on the table's smooth surface. It was a simple circle with a dot in the middle, and since it dominated gold, any spells I performed would be amplified. I carved the zodiac sign for Libra next to it, which would set off my Sublimation spell, which turned solids into gas. I charged the symbols with magical energy until they glowed, and held off the effects until I was ready.

I looked at Ken. "Remember that crime lord in Cairo?"

"You mean the sadistic wacko who wanted to sell a ship-load of grenades up here to the Nazis? Yes, vaguely."

I steadied my shaking hands. "And do you remember when he and his goons confronted us in that bar one night?"

In one smooth move, he jumped away from the table and took a shot at one of the Gestapo agents. All remaining employees and patrons finally broke into an open panic and evacuated the building. Two of the Gestapo officers shot back at him as he dove behind the bar for cover, while the other two agents—the warlocks—came after me. I used more of my energy to create an invisible shield with my Agate stone ring, which helped deflect bullets.

The hairs on the back of my neck stood when I saw the warlocks approaching with searing red daggers. I had seen less fortunate wizards hit with those, and, as soon as it touched a person's flesh, the skin would tear and fold, blood would sizzle and spill forth. My stomach churned, and all I heard was the distant sound of gunfire. I reassured myself with the fact that at least these two warlocks weren't Black Wolves.

With a swift move of his arm, the warlock on the right sent a red-hot dagger flying toward me as he charged forward. I dodged the blazing weapon by dropping to the floor and grabbed hold of him when he came within reach. I flipped him over and made him land on the other side of me with a thud. I quickly rolled in the direction of my table, where I had carved my symbol. The other warlock flung another fiery dagger toward me. I released the Sublimation spell, letting the flames mingle with the gas accumulated in order to create an explosion. The building shook as I dashed away to avoid the blast, and I took cover behind the bar where Ken had been. One of the Gestapo agents that had engaged Ken lay dead by a doorway. It led to an emergency hall exit. I heard a physical fight ensuing in the hallway.

I began coughing from the smoke that filled the room and knew that I had to leave the lounge if I wanted to keep breathing. On hands and knees, I peeked around the corner of the bar and saw only one of the warlocks still standing. The bastard had been waiting for me. He spun a pestilential black mist that flew straight toward my face. I didn't jerk back quickly enough to escape it and grunted in pain when my eyes burned. My vision blurred and darkened to black—I was blinded.

I rushed in a panic toward the doorway, tripping over the dead agent's body and bracing my fall with my hands. I crawled in the direction where I remembered the door standing and heard the warlock's footsteps and heavy breathing. I stiffened and timed the swing of my leg just in time to kick him. I didn't know where my stiletto landed, but the kick stunned him, and I got back onto my feet, rushing through the doorway and staggering down the hallway.

Believe it or not, I began to worry. I wondered why the warlock didn't blast me with another spell since I was vulnerable and running blind. When the obvious answer dawned on me, I started running even faster. I cursed when I stubbed my toe against a utility box against the wall in the hallway and nearly lost my balance. The warlock caught up to me and I swung my knife, driving my blade into him. He cried out in pain and struck me; I hit the wall with a smack and tried to pry his forearm away from my neck.

I froze when I felt the blade of my golden knife sweep across my cheek. I heard his harsh breathing and felt the heat of his breath near my neck. I squirmed when he made a cut across my shoulder with the knife.

"God, no..." My voice grew hoarse and I was sick to my stomach. Repulsed, I felt his mouth on my wound, lapping up the blood flow.

A single gunshot reverberated throughout the hallway, and I jolted. I felt the pull of his body as we both slid down and hit the floor.

"Isabella! What happened?" I heard footsteps and knew that it was Ken who rushed to my side. I heard a rustling of clothes and felt his jacket being wrapped around me as he helped me to my feet.

"Ken..." My darkened sight seemed to spin in gray and red colors all about me. I tried to speak, but my throat burned with every syllable uttered.

"That's a nasty cut you have. We need to get you patched up

quick to stop the bleeding."

"Ken..."

"What is it?" He held me with a firm grip and pulled me along down the hallway.

"Cut his head off."

"What?"

People in the normal world called them vampires. To wizards, they were a nasty bunch of warlocks called Cruenti. Blood Magic was one of the most powerful forms, and Cruenti fed off other wizards. They drank wizards' blood to cast spells, enhance their own powers...and to regenerate from gunshot wounds.

"Hurry up and do it before we both die."

He must've looked at me as if I were crazy, but he didn't bother to argue. I gripped the extra pistol he pressed into my hand and was about to tell him that I couldn't see anything, but decided to say nothing to avoid delaying him. I heard him go over to what sounded like the utility box. He opened it, probably grabbing an axe, and stalked toward the Cruenti.

I heard his nervous breaths and then a pause. "He's dead."

Suddenly I heard Ken shout in disgust and shock, and the Cruenti roared as repeated thuds filled the hallway. I visualized the sickening tearing of flesh and crushing of bone, and forced myself to speak when I heard Ken's attack cease.

"Did you get him?"

He breathed heavily. The axe clattered against the floor at the other end of the hall. "Yeah...I got him."

"Do you see my knife?"

"Erm...do you still want it?"

"Please? I'd get it myself, but he blinded me with a spell."

I heard him make a low grunt and grab my knife. He walked back toward me in quick strides. My legs grew weak, and my head throbbed and grew feverish. I sank to my knees, pressing my hand against the wall for support.

"Let's get out of here and get you healed." Though his voice shook, his hold on me remained firm. Under any other circumstances I would've refused to let him carry me, but my legs felt like rubber, and I could barely stay conscious.

"Got a first aid kit in your car?" I hissed through clenched teeth as the cool evening air stung my exposed wound. I heard sirens blare and the rumble of fire truck engines.

"Yeah, but, baby...you're going to need a lot more than that."

"Renée Apolline...my jade powder."

"I'll get you there."

"Thank you." I shut my eyes and leaned into him as I closed out the spinning gray and red colors. I hoped that the jade powder would completely restore my sight.

CHAPTER 6

I awoke to the sound of birds chirping. I squinted my eyes at the sunlight streaming through the bedroom window and smiled to myself, feeling immense relief for having my eyesight back. I brushed my fingers across the bandage that had been applied to my wound, and although it felt a little sore, I could tell that the jade powder had once again healed me. I didn't know how much remained, but it would take weeks for me to obtain more.

I was in my guest room at Renée's and strangely felt a sense of safety and comfort, despite the danger that lurked outside in the city. This room felt like my little sanctuary, and for this moment at least, I just lay in blissful silence.

Then, the thought of that Cruenti last night crept upon me and made me shudder. I began wondering how my cover was blown in the first place. Now I would have to change my codename and even wear disguises. If I pulled out now and asked the Maquis to get me across the border to Spain, it certainly wouldn't be shameful. However, I didn't want to fail at what I intended to be my last mission, and I certainly didn't want to feel like I've belittled the sacrifices of others.

I also didn't want to return to Ian empty-handed so that

Joshua Morton from MI6 could berate us. Besides, if I took care of Veit Heilwig and his chemical weapons, I could finally retire like I wanted to.

I shifted when I heard a knock at the door. "Come in."

Renée came in with a bowl of soup. "How are you?"

"Better...I guess." I sat up and took the bowl from her.

"You were in and out of consciousness since last night. I was worried."

As soon as she said that, my head throbbed and my body tensed. All I wanted was to fall back asleep again. "Where's Drake?"

"He said he would try to find his Maquisard contacts. He told me he'd be back before dinner."

My vision hazed, and my eyelids grew heavy. "I think I'm going to rest some more. Can you wake me when he comes?"

I felt a delicate hand on my sweaty forehead, and then on my cheek. The door opened and closed, and then I was asleep. It was a deep and quiet rest, but in some eerie way I felt like I was lost in nothingness. I wondered if this was what death felt like. I must've lain half-dreaming and seeing grays until I finally had another nightmarish memory of that Cruenti. I swung and tossed, fighting an enemy that wasn't there, until I ended up accidentally kicking Ken, who was sprawled at the foot of the bed. He shifted and groaned.

"How are you feeling?" I asked. I sat up, quelling my irritation at not being woken earlier. At least he was here and not out in the streets. It was dark again.

"Don't ask." He pulled himself toward me and laid his head on the pillow next to me. His swollen black eye was barely noticeable. It must've really hurt, or else he wouldn't have used the jade powder.

"Did you finish off the powder?" I caressed his swollen eye with my thumb.

"There's a pinch left. I put it away for you."

"Keep it. You've earned it."

"Thanks."

"Did you find your contacts?" I pulled my legs under me and began playing with my ring. I felt trapped, like I couldn't do anything or go anywhere. Now that the enemy had targeted me, I would have agents like Karsten waiting for me on every corner, ready to arrest and torture me before finally handing me over to a firing squad—or worse, to Dr. Meier's experimental program.

"Yes, I found them, but we have to be careful." His serious look made it seem like he was really saying *I* needed to be careful. "I still have to finish my assignment with OSS and can't leave just yet."

I nodded. "I also have to stay. I can't go back to London without finishing what I started."

"You've been out all day."

I frowned. My mind was still a little murky. "What day is it?"

"It's the twenty first...happy birthday."

"Some birthday." My stomach ached with hunger.

"At least we're alive." He propped himself up on his right elbow and began slowly planting a trail of kisses up my arm until he reached my shoulder. I leaned in to kiss him back, but a knock at the door made us pause.

"Giving you a head start, *mes amis*." A high-pitched cackle resonated from behind the door. Ken and I both sighed.

"Come in, Penn." Ken turned on the lamp and went to open the door for him. Renée was on Penn's heels, carrying a tray of bread and fruit with a small carafe of juice and a couple of glasses.

"Good evening!" Penn took the tray from Renée and steadied it on the bed next to me. He slid onto the bed and helped himself to a slice of bread. "We could use an extra glass, and some wine...and cheese, if you have any, Renée."

She glared at him before turning and heading down the hallway. Penn regarded Ken with a smile and offered me a glass of juice.

"Thank you." I gulped it down.

"Jasmine sent you?" Ken grabbed his shirt which was hanging on the bedpost and threw it on.

"Jasmine's upset about what happened down at Éclat. The club won't be able to reopen for another couple of weeks and she doesn't do business at home. So, if you have any further messages, give them to me now." He grabbed a few grapes and plopped them into his mouth. He wiped his hand on his vest and pulled a cigarette lighter from his pocket.

"For me?" Ken asked.

Penn motioned for him to take it. "I believe you'll be able to find what you're looking for once you decode the cipher. The Americans picked up the signal by RADAR."

I felt a dull ache in my side and got up. Renée made a soothing tea in the kitchen which I suspected she bought from a Practitioner. Those types of teas were the best—and sometimes the most dangerous. There were plenty of charlatans masquerading as healers "certified by the Gray Tower" who put God-knew-what into those mixes. Anyhow, I could vouch for the fact that you didn't leave the Gray Tower with a certificate. As I stepped out into the hallway, I heard Ken growl in frustration.

"Dammit, Penn. This isn't necessarily my area of expertise…I can barely decipher this crap."

I laughed to myself when I heard Penn retort, "What do I look like, a spy dictionary? Get your Maquisard friends to help break the code."

I made my way toward the kitchen and faintly heard Ken say, "Great, now I'll have to go out looking for my contacts. If I get shot or obliterated by a warlock, I'm coming back to haunt you."

I met Renée in the kitchen. She had the wine bottle in one hand and slices of cheese on a plate in the other. I thanked her for her foresight when she gestured toward a hot cup of tea sitting on the counter. I grabbed the drink and headed back toward the guest room, quickly running a hand through my hair and imagining what I must've looked like. I came back in and sat on the bed, eyeing the plate of bread that had just a few slices left.

"Did Jasmine leave anything for me?" I swatted Penn's hand when I saw him reach for another slice of bread. I took it for myself.

"Give me three or four days. Ever since your little spat, there have been increased measures to guard against counterfeit papers. This morning, they machine-gunned an entire post office full of people just to send us a message. I'll be lucky if I'm even able to accomplish this."

Renée offered each of us some wine and a single slice of cheese. "I apologize, but...you know, the rationing."

We accepted with thanks, and once Penn had his fill of wine, he bade us goodbye and set out to do his work. I kept coming up with excuses for Ken to stay, but we both knew that he had his assignment to complete and I had mine. As he left to go meet his Maquisard contacts in Mantes, I realized with frustration that this was why a stable romance with him wouldn't work: there was no stability to be had. We would spend days together and then not see each other for weeks; the closest we ever got to having a real date was dinner in an Egyptian bar which devolved into a gunfight with criminals.

If it weren't for our circumstances, and if it weren't for our obligations to SOE and OSS, I could see myself with him, and accepting his proposal. Then, like Jane Lewis, I could wear my diamond ring and catch up on *Woman's Weekly*, all the while glowing with joy. For now, I settled for flirtatious banter, stolen kisses, and exchanging reluctant goodbyes.

However, this time as we parted ways, a nagging question burned in my mind: Why did he tell Penn he was going to find his Maquisard contacts when he had already done so?

∼

Three days had passed, and I received no news of Penn or if he managed to obtain the credentials I needed. This was disheartening to say the least, but I kept myself busy the first couple of days by helping Renée around the house. When I got tired of that, the next day I read nearly every magazine in my room, assuring Renée that I was doing "research" (that is, if you counted fantasizing about luxury vacation homes and the latest fashions). As evening approached, I took a break and went to my room, where I laid across the bed and avidly listened to Mathieu Perrine's underground radio broadcast.

In a fervent tone he reported bits of information he received on Operation Barbarossa. Apparently Hitler had been serious when he said he wanted to help himself to the Soviet's lands and resources. Though the two were tentative allies, it was only a matter of time before betrayal occurred. The so-called Führer probably used the Black Wolves to launch the invasion, just like he used them to take Czechoslovakia. If they knew that the Gray Tower was within their reach…perhaps my father's warning had something to do with just that. I grew anxious at the thought, and hoped that Penn wouldn't take yet another three days to get back to me. It seemed I would have more than the Gestapo to contend with.

The Black Wolves were a coven of powerful warlocks led by a Cruenti named Octavian Eckhard. The Wolves had been around as long as the Order of Wizards, and for centuries engaged in a mostly covert war with us that finally brought itself out into the open within the last twenty years. Hitler was known for his obsession with the occult, and blinded by arrogance and avarice, he eagerly accepted an alliance with the Black Wolves. It didn't surprise me that the warlocks fought alongside the Nazis, but what did baffle me was how they knew to come directly after Ken and me. It was one thing to uncover me as a spy, and something more to uncover me as a spy who was an Apprentice Wizard. I turned my attention toward Renée when she entered my room. I returned her smile, though I didn't feel like smiling.

"Let's get started, Emelie...or should I say, Noelle?" She carried a black sack with her and a set of papers that she handed me. This time I did smile in earnest. Once again, Penn came through for me.

"Tell Penn that he's the killer-diller." I had to admit that I was impressed. I thought I would have to wait at least another day, maybe two.

"Tell him yourself, Noelle."

The door swung open and Penn walked in with a limp and a black eye that was just beginning to heal. "There are a lot of unfriendly people in the world, Noelle. Make sure you take care of this identity. It's the best I could get."

I made room for him on the bed so he could sit. I gently cupped his chin and concentrated on a wave of healing energy that tingled through my fingertips and reached out to flow through his body. I felt his heartbeat, steady and strong, and I even a bit of his fatigue as his lungs slowly expanded with air. His muscles ached. He shuddered at the sensation of the spell, and when I was done, he squeezed my hand in silent thanks.

I acknowledged his gesture. "If you ever need me for anything...*legal*, that is...I'll be there."

He faced Renée. "You hear that? I'm not such a lazy pilferer after all."

Renée swung her hand through the air and laughed. "Well, I didn't quite use those words. Jasmine must have a heart of gold to keep you around."

He nudged me. "Or maybe it's what I can do for Jasmine is why she keeps me around, eh?"

"*Exécrable!* Such talk!"

I shook my head at their banter and scanned the papers. My new name was Noelle Armande, and my cover was that I came from Dijon as a late registrant to the university's summer program. Now that my papers were in order, I could go to the school and present them. I needed to sit in Heilwig's class and find the opportunity to extract him.

"The Nazis must be coming down even harder on everyone." I folded the papers and set them aside. Usually Penn would provide me with much more, but at least this was passable.

"I wasn't exaggerating about your new identity being the only one I could obtain. I usually get my papers and passports from my connections—" he glanced at Renée, daring her to comment, "and even they gave me a hard time. I had to kill my first contact because he decided he wanted to collect that bounty from the Gestapo. He gave me a broken rib and a stab wound...and I gave him a crowbar to the head."

Renée gasped. "Terrible..."

Penn continued, motioning us to sit closer as if he were telling bedtime stories to children. "If that weren't enough, the second contact demanded an exorbitant amount of money within a day, which he knew I couldn't gather in time, and the third contact only furnished me with the papers because I walked in, pulled the safety pin on a grenade, and threatened to remove my finger from the striker lever. Heh."

"That was reckless." I looked at Renée and mimicked her expression of displeasure. Secretly though, I was thinking of how I would've gone in with two grenades.

"These are desperate times, ladies."

"And how did you get yourself patched up?" Renée crossed her arms.

"A friend did it. You remember Sebastien? The one who got kicked out of medical school."

Renée sighed and changed the subject. "I have to fix up Noelle, and you need to get back to Jasmine. Now, out the back, through the tool shed...you know the way."

Penn planted a kiss on the top of my head. He stood and

approached Renée, leaning in to give her a parting kiss on the cheek. She rebuffed him.

"See how she treats her friends?" He smirked.

"Oh, stop it! Go on, now..." She ushered him toward the door.

"Penn..." I tried to keep my voice level. "Any word from Drake?"

He shook his head. "But don't worry, he knows how to take care of himself."

Yeah, and I wanted to know what else he was taking care of a few days ago. "I hope he had better luck with his contacts than you had with yours."

He laughed. "Let's hope so, or else it'll be as nasty as that Cairo job."

My eyes widened. "The Cairo job? You mean Badru?"

"Drake told me you were with him on that in the beginning."

I nodded and pretended to know what he was talking about. "Of course...how did the rest of it go?"

He wore an amused expression. "I helped him move some money he stole from Badru. Now *that* is what I call reckless."

"Take care, Penn." I smiled, even though I wanted to sit there with my mouth gaping. Why in the world would Ken steal from an Egyptian crime lord? When he invited me down there, he told me that OSS had sent him to obstruct Badru's arms sales to the Nazis. Perhaps emptying Badru's bank account was part of the assignment? Maybe?

Renée nudged him out and shut the door behind him. "Now, let me show you how to fix yourself up."

She beckoned me to sit opposite her and she pulled out a blonde wig, makeup, and other materials she would need for application. I couldn't help but mirror her smile. Her eyes weren't tired and sad anymore; there was actually a glow to them. Though the old man Otto claimed to be even less involved than her, I still admired them both for doing what they could.

"You look like a fire's just been rekindled." I shut my eyelids as she started working on my brows.

"Little things here and there won't ever do for me. It will be everything...or nothing."

"Stay true to yourself." I remembered her words and would never forget.

"Now, when you apply the wig, make sure you apply makeup near the hairline so that it won't look unnatural." She showed me the inside of the wig and some strips of tape. She had me gather up my dark waves so she could place the wig on me. She then explained that she was carefully applying nude makeup near the hairline so that any seams would be undetectable.

"You're good at this."

"*Merci.*" She examined my hair and makeup, and seemed satisfied. "Now, perhaps a little contouring so that the shape of your face will appear a little different."

She paused and turned the volume up on the radio before returning to her work. Part of me wanted to laugh at the oddity of such a situation. Young women my age back in Baltimore, who were doing makeup in their friends' rooms, were usually talking about their sweethearts and listening to some catchy Benny Goodman song. Here I was, listening to an underground French Resistance broadcast and using makeup to disguise myself—so I could infiltrate the University of Paris and extract a Nazi wizard.

"I should've told Penn to send us some of that liquor he's been bootlegging," I said.

At this point, it seemed Renée was engrossed in both her work and the final announcements from Mathieu Perrine. "*And as we come to a close, my friends,*" Mathieu's voice grew somber, "*let us remember all those who have gone before us in the Great Fight. Especially our friend, Angela Wyatt, who we've just learned has perished in Dachau.*"

"Did...he say Angela? Angela Wyatt?"

"What is it, Em...Noelle?"

I felt like someone had stabbed me in the heart. A part of me knew deep down that Stella would not return to our London office, and that eventually Ian would have to cart away her belongings. But why did it have to be Dachau?

"*Mon chéri*, let it out...I can fix that silly makeup later."

My eyes were filled with tears; I let them brim over and streak down my face. "I'm sorry, Renée."

"I understand. Believe me, I understand."

Now I knew why she had those sad and tired eyes. I couldn't help but wonder how many more friends and loved ones I would have to cry over before all this would end.

CHAPTER 7

Renée saw me off in the morning with a tight hug and the most recent Maquis codeword: *Destiny*. I headed out toward the university which had changed in many ways since I last visited three years ago. Much of the artwork which hung in its halls had been stolen and carted away by the Nazis, the atmosphere reeked of distrust and gloom. Any books, magazines, or journals that threatened the unquestioning obedience they wished to instill in the community had long been confiscated and burned. Anyone who uttered a word of protest or raised a question of doubt found himself either cruelly punished or never heard from again.

This explained why the number of students dwindled at the university. Not only did students have to contend with intellectual and political oppression, but some also found themselves and their families starving or even homeless. Groups of refugees wandered throughout the region and supplies grew scarce. If I thought the rationing in England tried me sorely, then the utter want that many people here endured made me rethink it.

I found that most students and faculty kept to themselves and didn't talk to newcomers, and I didn't necessarily blame them. A few Gestapo agents walked the halls from time to time seeking to intimidate or arrest anyone, sometimes just choosing people at random to "teach a lesson to." I needed to make sure that I wasn't one of those people, so I kept my head down and just spent my time in class, taking notes and making observations.

I would have no other chance to be at the university to grab Dr. Heilwig and time was against me. Whoever sent those warlocks after me had learned about their fates, no doubt, and would be sending more. I made sure that I blended in with the students as much as possible while also being aware of my surroundings and keeping an eye out for trouble. Sometimes this was difficult to do, because I'd be tempted to speak out against the pro-Nazi diatribe a professor or two spewed, or break the arm of a Gestapo agent harassing students at times.

Just like the propaganda machine they ran with public newspapers and radio broadcasts, the Nazis sought to communicate everything from their twisted worldview. When I first sat in one of Dr. Heilwig's biology classes, I was struck by his demeanor. I expected him to stare down students as he paced back and forth, forcefully declaring his ideals. Instead, his thin frame carried him across the room like a walking skeleton, and his voice filled the room with a sense of apathy. Within the first hour of class, I walked out after he began reciting how Nazi-approved scientists established the "fact" of the inferiority of certain races in a monotone voice.

The next day, one of my classmates, Isidore, joined me for lunch in a student dining area. He asked me why I had left class so hastily. I didn't know if I could trust him, and so I blamed it on a headache.

"It's unfortunate we don't have a nurse's office anymore…or a nurse, for that matter." He gave a look of displeasure and glanced around our area. With his voice and demeanor, I could've easily imagined him delivering fiery speeches in a political science class instead of turning the pages of a biology book. He seemed out of place here.

"How did the class end? Could I borrow your notes?" I lifted my bowl of soup to my lips and drank. It was all broth anyway.

"Of course." He pulled out his notebook and handed it to me. I placed my empty bowl on the table and wiped my mouth with the back of my hand.

"Are you going to finish your soup?"

"Yes," he laughed. "We'll be lucky to even have bread by next week."

"So, you don't like what's happening here?"

He wrinkled his nose. "You ask a lot of questions."

"Well, genius, that's why I'm in school." I took out my notebook and opened it. "I'm sorry, but I think I left my pencil case in Professor Torsten's room. Could I ask you to..."

"Would you like to borrow my pen?"

"I tend to make mistakes, so I'd better use a pencil."

"I'll grab it, then." He gestured for me to stay seated, and he rose to his feet.

"I promise I won't drink your soup." I smiled.

"It's fine, Noelle. I'll go get it."

Like I said, this was a gloomy and distrustful environment. So why did a cheerful and eager-to-please Isidore suddenly want to be my buddy? When he was out of sight, I flipped through his notebook and checked what he had written. It all looked plain enough, just notes from Heilwig's and other professors' classes. However, I noticed faint underlines of certain letters on each page and realized that it was a cipher. Was Isidore a spy? And more importantly, did he know anything about me?

I grabbed his pen and quickly jotted down the underlined letters in the back of my notebook. When I thought I saw him coming, I dropped the pen and held onto my notebook, hoping that I at least scribbled enough letters to make out a coherent sentence. He approached and held up my pencil case, seeking confirmation. I nodded and beckoned him toward me.

"You are a true gentleman." I grabbed the case and opened it, pulling out one of my pencils. I began copying his notes from Heilwig's last class.

"Where did you live again?"

"Why do you want to know?" I kept copying. I wore an unconcerned expression, although my insides tightened.

"I wanted to be able to call on you and ask you to dinner."

By observing his body language and tone of voice, I could tell he was lying. "I'm sorry, Isidore, but I already have a sweetheart." Well, at least as close as I'd ever get for the time being, and even *he* had a big question mark hanging over his head.

"Did you get everything you needed?" He opened his hand, and I returned his notebook.

"Almost, but it's nothing to fret over. I learn quickly."

"So do I."

"Well," I began collecting my items, trying to ignore the chill running down my spine. "I have to be off now, but thank you for the notes."

I walked across campus and headed for the ladies room where I pretended to primp in the sitting area's mirror with a couple of other girls. When they finally cleared out and I was alone, I took out my notebook and opened it. Breathing in the lingering scent of perfume, I began poring over the letters, trying to create words and make sense out of them.

Simple ciphering was one of the first things I learned as a spy. Usually when someone wanted to break a code, she would use common cipher keys such as the person's name, his favorite food or pet, or a code word. Some codes were harder to break than others, and that's why codemasters existed. After about an hour of trying to decipher Isidore's note, I felt like I would need a codemaster myself. I ran my hands through my hair in frustration and wanted to toss the notebook across the room.

I glanced at the mirror that reflected my angry eyes and pouted lips. In an instant, an idea came to mind. Slowly, I held up the notebook to the mirror, and the message that was written backward unfolded before me:

> *Found her, Marcellus. Will bring her to you, and no one will know.*

Suddenly a gust of wind blew the door open. The lights flickered and died. The room shook, and I ran out with wobbly legs and my heart racing. I looked left and then right, but I only saw a stone-faced Gestapo agent talking with the chemistry professor, Dr. Varenne, at the east end of the corridor. The professor wore a slightly anxious look on his face and seemed to be in some kind of trouble. I couldn't stay to hear what the conversation was about, and I certainly couldn't do anything to help. Looking over my shoulder, I headed in the opposite direction and left the building.

Since my classes were over for the day, I decided to head back to Renée's house. It took me longer than usual to get there because I circled the immediate area and then took a different route just to make sure I wasn't being followed. Isidore's message unnerved me. I knew that I'd heard of Marcellus before, but couldn't remember from where. And why exactly did this person want to find me? He must've sent Isidore to track me. Running to Spain suddenly sounded awfully tempting.

When I made it back to Renée's, she had fixed a modest dinner consisting of vegetables and bread and had it waiting for me. Tonight must have been one of the nights to conserve electrical power, because feeble candlelight illumined the dining room. As I laid my napkin across my lap and grabbed my utensils, I noticed that she didn't bring out her plate.

"Aren't you going to eat?" My fork and knife went limp in my hands.

"I already did." She smiled as the candlelight flickered and shadows danced across her face.

I put my knife and fork down. "This is all there was?"

"I am used to this life. You need your strength."

I sucked my teeth and shoved the plate toward her. "We could've easily split this."

"Do you think, after all I've been through, that this one small meal will make a difference?" She shoved it back toward me.

"Maybe you are a hard woman, Renée." I refused to take the plate. I could be just as stubborn as her.

"Man does not live by bread alone."

"Yeah," I crossed my arms, "well...we're not men."

She shook her head and grabbed the bread roll. "Take the vegetables, then."

I picked at the plate before finally digging in with my fork. I wouldn't put it past her to jump across the table and force me to eat the bread roll. "So...how was your day?"

"The usual. Otto called and we had a nice visit. Agent Karsten hasn't returned."

"Not yet, at least."

"Tell me about your day at the university."

I recounted everything, but left out the part about Isidore. I didn't want her to worry, and I wanted to figure out who he really was before saying anything.

"I'm just about ready to make my move and extract Heilwig. Then...I'll have to report back to London." I felt a slight regret at my words because I enjoyed Renée's company and I was certain she enjoyed mine.

If she felt as disappointed as I did, her expression didn't show it. "Then you aren't reporting to the Gray Tower?"

I shook my head. "Anyone is free to leave when she wants, and believe me, I don't intend to go back any time soon. Besides, I'm not working for the Order."

"Well, I'm glad."

"Why?"

"Because they say the Black Wolves hunt members of the Order."

"I've done pretty well so far." Though I'd piss myself if I had to go at it with a Black Wolf.

She reached across the table and grabbed my hand.

"Sometimes I have doubts, and ask myself, 'what am I doing? Is this all worth it?'"

I squeezed her hand before releasing it. "You're not alone in that."

"Good, because I want you to know that you're not alone. If only there were more people like you, this world would be much better off."

It felt good to hear that. "So you never thought once about just keeping your head down and...keeping your family?"

She bit into her bread roll. "Of course I did, but I didn't do that."

"Why?"

She paused and considered my question before answering. "If we didn't stand and face the enemy, it would've destroyed any possibility of happiness with one another. At least by fighting, we had a chance."

"I'm afraid I'll never have that chance." I told her about Jane Lewis's engagement and how I would probably end up like Stella. I had been holding this in for so long that I felt relieved to finally share my feelings with a friend—either that, or I really needed a shrink.

"Before my husband joined the Resistance," she said, "he was a policeman. He dealt with criminals every day and would come home tired nearly every night. I could tell his work drained him at times, yet we were a comfort to each other. You don't have to end up like your friend. Fight now, so that you can secure the life you want. Be the master of your own destiny."

I understood her words, but it was hard for me to accept them.

It's easy for someone to tell you to go and live as you pleased, and another to actually do it while setting aside obligations, people, and other forces that would steer you down another path.

"Thank you," I said. "If I can extract Heilwig tomorrow and destroy The Plague, we'll all be better off."

"You'll be careful, won't you?" This time Renée's expression did show traces of worry.

"As long as I have friends like you, I'll be fine."

She smiled. "Whether you go by Emelie, Noelle, or whatever codename…never change who you are inside."

We then gladly turned the conversation toward lighthearted small talk, and when we were done with dinner I urged Renée to go lie down and rest while I cleared the table and washed dishes. I felt anxious about how I would confront Heilwig, and whether or not I'd be able to extract him. It wasn't as if I could just walk up to him and politely ask him to come away with me.

In any case, I was at least relieved by the fact that I wouldn't have to see Isidore in chemistry tomorrow. He had the class on a different day. However, it did little to console me since this meant that I only had a day to extract Heilwig. I would have to prepare my magic, arm myself, and finally make my move tomorrow…or die trying.

CHAPTER 8

"Good morning, everyone." Dr. Heilwig watched us all enter and shuffle toward our seats. "I'm sure you saw the note left on Dr. Varenne's classroom door. Unfortunately, he will no longer be teaching with us, so I'll be taking over his chemistry classes."

Several students exchanged looks with one another. Others went pale at the sight of three Gestapo agents entering the room. I probably would've been afraid as well, since they gave us all looks as if we were daring them to shoot us all, but Isidore entered the classroom after them, claiming the empty seat next to me. As Heilwig called out the names of two young women and a young man, they looked toward the rest of us with silent pleas. Finding no help, they grabbed their books with quivering hands and went down to meet the Gestapo agents. I wondered if they had anything to do with Dr. Varenne.

I watched Isidore from the corner of my eye and began to perspire. I feared he would call the agents' attention toward me, which would've been disastrous since I carried two pistols and my golden knife. I figured I might as well do it before he did, so I slipped him a note:

You don't have chemistry today.

Without even using a pencil or pen, he passed back a response that looked as if it were written with charcoal:

I do now. There is someone I want you to meet. Let's be discreet about this, shall we?

He winked at me. I sneered in response. Dr. Heilwig stood at the front, speaking with the Gestapo, and they allowed one of the girls to return to her seat. I passed another message to Isidore:

Can someone help me? I need to get out of here.

Signed,
Isidore

He looked at me as if I were insane, but I gazed straight ahead and my hand shot up in the air. "I wanted to make the agents aware of the young man sitting next to me. He's been passing suspicious notes."

He gave me an incredulous glance and rose from his seat, but one of the agents drew his pistol and ordered him not to move. Isidore complied and let the agent search him. When he found the note, he ordered him outside the classroom and shadowed Isidore, with finger ready on his trigger. After a few minutes, the second agent guided the remaining young man and woman through the door, and they all left down the hallway.

I slouched in my chair, relieved that I had bought myself a little more time. Isidore would either kill them once they got to a private interrogation room or convince them he was a warlock. He said no one was supposed to know and that he wanted to be discreet. It seemed that the Gestapo weren't the only ones after me and I'd have to find out why.

Dr. Heilwig finally managed to capture our attention, and acting as if nothing were amiss, he instructed us to open our notebooks. We pretended to listen to Heilwig's lecture on Dmitri Mendeleev's development of the Periodic Table. Everyone else was probably wondering if the Gestapo agents would return.

Every few minutes I caught Heilwig staring at me like I was an oddity. It made me a little self-conscious, and I questioned if my blonde wig was slipping off. I sat there and considered how I was going to subdue him and take him with me. When class ended, I made sure to be the last student to leave. I tried to stay and speak with Heilwig, but he eschewed me and shut the door as soon as I stepped outside.

The thought of Isidore returning within minutes, in a murderous rage, nearly made me sick with dread, so I picked the lock on the door and let myself back into the classroom. I spied Heilwig sitting at a table toward the back of the room. For a few moments, he stared at his talisman ring, which I could taste was made of gold. I could also sense an enchantment that protected against another wizard's body magic. He had what looked like a diary sitting on the table in front of him, and he held a thin iron rod that he performed a Sublimation spell on.

Instead of using a ritual knife to create his symbol, he moved his fingers through the air. I saw luminous traces of the symbol in mid-air and it both awed and frightened me. I sometimes wondered what it would've been like to become an Elite Wizard like my father, or Brande. Obviously Heilwig's skills were greater than mine, and it would be nearly impossible to overwhelm him with magic as I had originally planned. So, I did the next best thing—I pulled out my two pistols and pointed them at him.

"What's going on?"

"Sorry, Dr. Heilwig, but I need to take you with me."

"Who are you?"

"I'm not a damned Nazi, but I *will* shoot you if you try to run."

"What do you want?"

"I need you to come with me, before *he* gets back."

"Do I know you?" He began staring at me the way he did earlier.

"My name is not important." I eyed the iron rod he dropped. It disintegrated into powder and turned into a dark gas that rose into the air. Alchemists cast this spell to ward off evil and restore their minds.

He saw that I wasn't frightened by the spell. "You're an alchemist too...trained by the Gray Tower...like me?"

"Yes." I gripped my weapons even tighter. So, the Tower supposedly trained him; I hated those types of rogue wizards, because almost all of them ended up becoming warlocks.

It seemed like something connected in his mind, and he looked at me as if he knew me. "But...do you know why you're an alchemist?"

"I was born this way?" Sometimes people said crazy things when they had guns pointed at them.

"I'll go with you freely then, if you answer one last question I have."

This was getting interesting. "What is it?"

"Are you Carson's daughter?"

I almost dropped my guns. "How do you know who I am? Is this some kind of trap?"

My arms went limp, but my legs still worked. I turned and fled the room, sprinting down the hallway and suppressing the urge to scream when I saw him right behind me. I kept running and nearly knocked over a few students who gave me frightened looks. I made a right turn at the corner and pressed on, seeing that my path was clear. I skidded and came to a halt when I saw none other than Nikon Praskovya coming toward us from the opposite direction. I glanced in Heilwig's direction, paralyzed with fear, but to my astonishment he stepped in front of me protectively and kept his gaze on Praskovya as she strode toward us with a grin.

"I knew sooner or later the Ally dogs would come sniffing at the bait," she said. "All the better that it was you."

Since Praskovya's words were directed at me, I gestured for Heilwig to step down, and I stood firm.

"Still upset about Belgium, I see." My fingers gripped my pistols.

"Not in the slightest."

"Shouldn't you be on the Soviet border? Why are you still working with the Nazis when they've betrayed your country?"

She laughed. "Isn't yours still neutral? Why are *you* here? Besides, you should know that at the end of the day, all that matters is survival...and money. I chose the winning side, and you could've done the same, but you were weak. And to think, all that talent had been wasted as a slave of the Gray Tower."

She drew her revolver and I charged her, striking her hand and making her drop her weapon. I would've gladly used my pistols, but I didn't want Heilwig caught in the crossfire of our gunfight. I blocked a few of her incoming strikes, slipping to the floor when she finally landed a blow. As my guns went flying out of my grasp, I swung my leg and tripped her, and then I was on her in a straddling position, hands gripping her head. All I needed was physical contact to enact a mind control spell, much like the one I performed on Karl Manfried the night I landed in Paris. Even if it sapped me of most of my energy, I was willing to do it if it meant subduing her.

She screwed up her face in concentration as she fought back

against my spell. She clutched my wrists and tried to pry my hands loose, but I held on even tighter. She suddenly dropped her arms—and, out of nowhere, pointed her revolver at me. I made a sweeping movement with my hand to deflect her shot, and the bullet missed my head by a centimeter. I hated when she used telekinesis.

She made a quick jab and hit me square in the face. It threw me off balance, and she followed up with a left hook. I rolled with the punch and quickly got back onto my feet. She also stood, but didn't make another move. And she didn't need to—Heilwig struggled in vain against Isidore, who held the professor in a headlock.

"Let's end this!" Praskovya signaled to Isidore, but he did nothing.

"I need to take her to Marcellus...alive." He effortlessly held on to Heilwig.

"If she can't fight her way out of this, then she doesn't deserve to make it to Marcellus."

Of course, she *would* say something like that. We had been fighting and thwarting each other ever since she turned on SOE and joined the Russian Liberation Group. I actually admired her when I first started, but one evening, while on assignment together in Belgium, she confessed her treachery and asked me to follow along with her. When I refused, she tried to throw me out of a window.

As Isidore gazed at me, I could tell he was concentrating on a spell. A ring of fire suddenly surrounded me in mid-air and came crashing down, but with a flick of my wrist I drew a Circle of Healing on the floor in front of me with my knife. Since Circles of Healing were activated by fire, the flames fell and rejuvenated me instead of destroying me. I felt stronger, faster, and even my vision was clearer. When Isidore saw what I did, he quenched the flames and inhaled a long breath that made the entire corridor grow ice cold. I almost slipped on the floor as I backed away, and the temperature dropped so low that I could see my breath in short puffs. I could barely move.

Isidore pushed Heilwig toward Praskovya, leaving them both shivering, and slowly approached me. My arms and legs froze in place and my throat constricted as I tried to speak. As I felt my heartbeat decelerate to a dangerous pace, my eyelids grew heavy, and I struggled to breathe. I forced myself to stay focused. I used all my might to regain even a little movement. I still gripped my knife in my hand and stood ready to use it as soon as I could.

"Do you surrender now?" He reached for my knife.

With a low grunt, I flexed my fingers, and even though my arm hurt with icy numbness, I slashed at his hand, quickly carving a reversed Fixation symbol, an upside down five-pointed star, on his palm. He threw me back with a roar. I skidded across the floor and my golden knife clattered against the ground.

"I told you to kill her." Praskovya pointed her revolver at me.

Isidore raised his wounded hand to his lips and blocked her shot. "No, Nikon."

Her eyes narrowed, and she stood her ground. "Then you're dead."

Isidore's gaze went between Praskovya and me, and he doubled over in pain. His skin rippled like waves of water. I still lay on the floor, freezing and struggling to breathe normally. I couldn't turn my face away and had to watch my reverse Fixation spell at work. Fixation spells turned volatile substances into solids, so it wasn't difficult to imagine what a reverse Fixation would do. Praskovya immediately sent Isidore flying down the hallway, screeching and protesting the entire way, until he exploded. I felt a splatter of blood and bone fragments hit me from behind, and I groaned in disgust.

Heilwig must've used the commotion to lay his own spells, because the next thing I knew, he sent a gust of wind against an adjacent wall. The wind ricocheted off the wall and nearly spun out of control. It caught Praskovya and pinned her against the ceiling. The blast was so strong that she struggled to breathe.

I didn't understand why Heilwig couldn't just directly force her down the hall with Air, but when I saw a gold band around his neck peeking from beneath his shirt, it all became clear. If Praskovya had placed that imperium collar around his neck, then he could never directly cast a spell against her.

Heilwig rushed toward me and knelt, drawing a luminous triangle and then a second one with a horizontal line toward the top: the alchemical symbols for Fire and Air. A warm breeze filled the corridor, and the cold began to subside. I finally felt the warmth return to my body, and I was glad to be free of the freezing spell that would've killed me. My limbs ached as I coughed and tried to draw in breaths. He laid a second Air symbol, but held off its effect.

Praskovya rose from her knees, wiped the vomit from her chin, and cocked her revolver—she aimed straight for my head. "You will not cast any more spells, Veit."

Heilwig held his hands up in the air to show his compliance. "Don't shoot, Praskovya. You heard him—Marcellus wants her alive. I'll go with you to the laboratory."

"Then get away from her."

He took small, slow steps toward her, hands still in the air. With each step he took, the final Air symbol he had created in front of me grew stronger. Suddenly, Heilwig reached into his pocket and withdrew a dark blue stone. Before anyone could react, he tossed it onto the Air symbol and activated a Transfer spell then collapsed to the floor.

I shouted his name as I got caught up in a whirlwind. I tried to reach him, but a blinding light surrounded me and took me away.

The next thing I knew, I was face-down in a field next to a road. As I stood and glanced around, I realized it was the same field I had first landed in here in France. I dusted myself off and winced at the aching throes my body went through in response to

Isidore's ice spell. My mind was in no better shape, still being a little hazy, and then there was the confusion that now plagued me.

Heilwig seemed to know my father and was probably telling the truth about being trained at the Gray Tower. But why had I never heard of this until today? The Nazis forced him to make those chemical weapons and teach those classes as a way to play as their bait. This began to look more like a rescue mission than an enemy extraction.

I never would've thought to see this day: Ken lied to me, and a disgraced wizard saved my life, probably at the cost of his own. The moment he activated my teleportation with the blue Transfer stone, I saw Veit suffer a stroke and permanently lose half his magical strength. This could never be remedied or reversed, and he'd never be the same again. I only heard of alchemists using Transfer stones in the direst circumstances. For whatever reason, he must've felt it was of the utmost importance to protect me and get me out of there.

I walked toward the road and shielded my eyes from the sun, scouting for any trekkers. I heard the rumble of a motorbike in the distance growing louder. My thoughts went back to Heilwig and how he tried to protect me, which meant that perhaps he wasn't all what the dossier said he was. Either way, I'd have to find him. I needed to reach him before they considered him useless because of the physical and magical harm he did himself in casting that Transfer spell. I needed to reach him so I could find out about my father...what if Heilwig knew where he was?

Since I had burned that letter my dad left me, Heilwig was now the only tangible link I had. He left a clue and said that he would go to a laboratory, but which laboratory? Was it even in France? A bit of despair took hold of me, but I disliked quitting at anything, and I absolutely hated to lose—especially to Praskovya.

"Do you need a ride?" the motorbike rider looked no older than twenty. He pulled off his helmet and ran his hand through his dark hair.

"Thank you, but I think I'll walk."

He eyed me for a few seconds before saying goodbye and slipping his helmet back on. He started his bike and drove down the road, making a sharp left turn at the crossroad. As I began walking back toward the city, and I tried coming up with a plan. I had no idea where this laboratory was, so I would have to follow the trail of the chemical weapons which would surely lead me there. I'd made up my mind—I needed to speak with a Maquisard, a member of the Resistance, who regularly received an influx of intelligence. I halted my steps and turned in the opposite direction, away from Paris.

The broadcaster Mathieu Perrine stayed in the town of Mantes. I needed to find him and enlist his aid.

CHAPTER 9

I made it past the city gate just before curfew began. The bells of Notre Dame clanged in a crescendo that reverberated throughout the town, and the scent of the murky Seine filled my nostrils. William the Conqueror had burned much of the town to the ground a few hundred years ago. Yet, that didn't stop it from being rebuilt. I supposed that spirit of tenacity inspired people like Mathieu to join the Resistance and keep fighting. Though I knew I could find him in this town, I didn't know which house or building he broadcasted his nightly shows from. I had no friends or contacts in this city, and worst of all, I just realized that I had lost my knife back at the university.

I could still do magic without it, but my knife was a ritual tool, a conduit of energy and concentration. I had specifically requested that it be made of gold because the types of alchemical spells I liked to cast flowed with more power and harmony when I used the precious metal. The Gray Tower gave it to me as a parting gift when I left.

"Excuse me." I slipped past a woman and her child and snaked my way through the small crowd. I arranged my clothes and smoothed my blonde wig, all the while thinking of where I would hide if I were Mathieu.

Some people headed toward the church, while others approached the shops, begging for scraps. A few of the town dwellers ushered some of the refugees toward their homes. Some slipped inside their buildings, locking their doors behind them. A tall woman stood outside the local inn, handing out cups of water to those who needed it. I approached and accepted a drink.

"I'm sorry this is all I could offer." She took the cup when I finished and gestured toward the partly open doorway. "The inn is full."

"Thank you." I turned and headed in the direction of the church, ignoring the hunger gnawing at my stomach. The drawn faces passing me, looking like those of ghosts, and the energy of this town, writhing with tension, made me feel like I wasn't in the Mantes I had known. It all certainly changed from when I had first arrived, fresh out of college, and met the wizards who invited me to join the Order.

Brande would annoy me whenever he tried to turn a conversation into how I should return to the Gray Tower. Sometimes I suspected that he only visited me because they directly sent him. Now, having seen what alchemists like Heilwig could do, perhaps it wasn't such a bad idea after all.

I had joined the Order partly out of curiosity, but mostly because I wanted to explore these abilities I had been born with and to participate in my father's legacy. Within my first month of testing, they had placed me as an alchemist, and I learned body magic along the way.

"Inside, everyone!" An older man stood at the foot of the crowd, waving his arms, while a boy pointed toward the trekker approaching town.

Everyone rushed to wherever they could so they'd be out of the way. I wasn't too keen on breaking curfew either, so I continued making my way toward the church. I paused when I spotted the woman and child I had seen earlier. Some creep walked a little too closely behind them and grabbed the woman's bag, nearly ripping her arm out as he wrested it from her. The woman protested and he knocked the little girl to the ground as he darted in my direction.

"What's wrong with you?" I growled through clenched teeth as I caught his arm and tripped him with my right foot. He stumbled to the ground, and I grabbed the bag. He looked ready for round two, but the look in my eye told him that he'd better not try.

"Thank you...thank you." The woman cradled her daughter in her arms and accepted the bag from me.

"Let's get into the church." I ushered her along when I saw the familiar glare of the trekker's headlights. Two SS officers jumped out.

We rushed up the church steps, and as I entered through the west doorway, I could smell the sweet scent of incense burning and see the flicker of candles in one of the apses. The stained glass windows grew dimmer with the progressive sunset, and as I made it further into the church, I noticed that the altar lay bare. A long white banner that hung across the sanctuary quoted 1 Corinthians 2:16: *For who hath known the mind of the Lord, that we may instruct him? But we have the mind of Christ.*

The Order of Wizards promised to protect the Mind of God, or the Akashic Record...whatever one wanted to call it. We believed this was the Knowledge of the Universe, and only the most powerful wizards had limited access to it. The coven of Black Wolves lusted for it, but the Order stood in its way because we knew that full access to the Akashic Record would bring disaster on both the wizard and humanity as a whole.

This was why Drifters, wizards who could drift in and out of time and access the entire Akashic Record, were considered illicit by the Order. Personal virtue didn't matter—if you were a Drifter, you were anathematized and as good as dead. Not even being a member of the Order protected you. The Gray Tower executed the last three known Drifters a long time ago.

I quietly made my way past a handful of refugees who gathered in the church. For these people, the war was as real to them as it was to me. I couldn't imagine the devastation of my home being destroyed and being left with nothing. While many cities escaped bomb drops and gunfights, sadly, not all did. It looked like the parish priest had no problem welcoming people in from the chaos. The refugees slept in pews, prayed, or sat and conversed in hushed voices.

I caught the eye of a young priest who emerged from the sacristy. He probably thought I had been harassed and beaten by the SS, because he eyed me with a mix of pity and horror. He approached and instructed me to join him in a secluded corner.

"Are you hurt? What happened to you?"

Though I doubted any Gestapo agents lurked among the refugees, one never knew. "May I make a confession, Father?"

He nodded slowly and pointed toward the nearest confessional. I went inside and waited, clearing my throat and trying to think of what to say. I wasn't a Catholic, so it felt odd to me sitting in that small private space. Anyhow, I wasn't really there for a confession. I needed rest, and my next lead to finding Mathieu Perrine.

"May God, who has enlightened every heart, help you to know your sins and trust in His mercy." He patiently waited on the other side of the screen.

"Father, I need help. I have to find Mathieu Perrine."

There was a long pause. "Who are you?"

"My name is Noelle." I wrinkled my nose at the fact that I had to abandon "Emelie." I would miss that codename.

"No, who are you? In the sight of God and within the protection of the Seal of Confession, tell me who you are."

I didn't know why, but I shuddered. "I'm...a lost person, trying to find a way to help right some wrongs."

He said nothing for a few seconds. "And that is all we are asked to do, one step at a time and one day at a time. Why do you need Mathieu?"

"Because I need his help."

"How can I trust whether or not you have good intentions?"

"You can't...but don't you believe in having faith?"

"I also believe in responsibility. I have a responsibility to my parishioners and those refugees."

I sighed. "I've read about that Polish priest sent to Auschwitz for his defiance...and the Dutch Carmelite too. Sounds like those men were willing to not only speak about faith, but also do something."

"True."

"And the codeword is *destiny*, Father."

"Thank you, I was wondering when you were going to get around to that."

"Look, why don't you just point me in the direction of one of his relatives' houses?" This guy was as evasive as any spy I'd ever met.

"That would be difficult, young lady."

"Why?"

"Mathieu has no living relatives in this town."

I rolled my eyes. "Anything that could lead me to him, Father."

"Do you know his real name?"

"No."

"Then let me properly introduce myself. I am Father Alexis, also known as Mathieu Perrine."

I didn't know whether to laugh or to just get up and walk out. "Father..."

"The decision to believe me is completely yours to make," he said in that voice that was familiar to me and to so many others. If he wasn't Mathieu, he was damned good at imitating him.

"Well, Father...it's good to meet you. Now, do you have any food?"

Father Alexis placed a small bowl of ratatouille in front of me, compliments of the rectory kitchen. I smiled and thanked him then removed the blonde wig that had miraculously remained on my head for this long. He watched with amusement as I laid the false hair aside and began eating my meal.

"I presume you're an SOE agent?"

I nodded. "I'm trying to find a factory where chemical weapons are being stored. The ones they use for The Plague. I'm hoping it could lead me to the laboratory where it's being developed."

"There are at least twelve in this region."

"Is there anything you've heard recently? Any information you've received from the Maquis?"

I continued eating as I watched him rise from his seat and head over to his workstation. We sat in a hidden room within the rectory, behind a set of wooden panels in the dining room. Father Alexis's secret room held a stash of food and medical supplies, maps, icons, a Bible, and, of course, his radio set which he used nightly to broadcast.

He went rummaging through a drawer and pulled out a notebook, which he then opened. He ran his finger down one of its pages, and his gaze went back and forth between the page and his set of icons hanging on the opposite wall. As I finished off the last of my meal, I continued observing him, realizing that whatever information he kept was coded, and his icons were his ciphers. I wouldn't be surprised if he was a codemaster, just by looking at the elaborate system he used. I then turned my thoughts toward the last broadcast he did as "Mathieu Perrine."

"You know that broadcast you did, the one where you spoke of Angela Wyatt at the end?"

"Yes, I do." He returned and sat across from me with the notebook closed, though his index finger kept place.

"Her real name was Stella...she was my friend."

"You have my condolences. Her sacrifice will not be forgotten."

My eyes burned. "I appreciate that."

He reopened the notebook and showed me the code he deciphered. He picked it up from one of England's BBC broadcasts. The translated message indicated that Vélizy-Villacoublay was an area of great interest to the Allied forces.

"A factory is there." He ripped out the sheet of paper and folded it, no doubt saving it for a fire.

"I don't want to impose further, but is there anyone willing to take me near there? They could drop me off outside Vélizy." The town stood south of Paris, and it would be a strenuous bike ride, provided I was even lent one to use.

"Are you sure you don't want to rest? And don't forget that it's past curfew."

I bit my tongue in order not to curse in front of him. "Then I'll go as early as I can in the morning. Would someone take me?"

"Bernard is a Maquisard who lives just beyond the city here. I can give you directions to his house and a codeword so that he'll know I sent you."

I couldn't help but eye him with admiration. "Now I can see why those people came here for refuge." I rubbed my eyes and thought of how perfectly I would fit in with the people sleeping in the pews. No one looked as disheveled and exhausted as I did.

"And I can see why it's important to never lose faith, and to keep fighting." He gave me a silent blessing. "I don't know you, not even your true name, but I pray you remain safe and complete your task. If you ever need anything, you know where to find me. Now, I believe it's time for my broadcast."

"I can't believe you're Mathieu Perrine." I shook my head as I said this. I had always imagined a burly man at a radio set, with a thick mustache and somber face.

He went to his workstation and turned on his radio. "What were you expecting?"

"I expected something else." I watched him turn a knob on the radio set and adjust the frequency to get his transmitter ready.

"Last year the SS came into town, and according to them they wanted to let us know that our country had given up, that it failed us. A young man who spoke up said that he did not give up—and they shot him. The next day, to ensure no one else spoke out, they lined up five youths in front of the church and asked me to choose two of the five to go free..."

I could see the pain still in his eyes. "What did you do?"

"That was the problem. I did nothing. How do you judge who deserves to live or die? They were all murdered, and I walked away feeling helpless. I couldn't look anyone in the eye after that. Then, I built this room as an act of defiance. I planned to hide people from the Nazis, like the Resistance fighters."

"But you ended up broadcasting?"

He smiled in response and spoke into the receiver, his voice an octave lower than usual. "Good evening, fellow Maquisards, Allies, and all who love justice and freedom. As we begin, let us remember the value of faith,"—he turned to look at me—"and that it is not just about preaching it, but also living it..."

I worded a silent "thank you" to him and slipped out. I didn't fancy the idea of sleeping on a hard wooden pew, but there were a lot worse places I could be tonight. I came back into the church and took a pew close to the sanctuary, next to an old woman. She reminded me of the witch from the *Wizard of Oz*, sans the green skin. However, she had a friendly smile and offered to share her blanket with me, so I warmed up to her quickly.

I thought about Rénee and how she would start to worry about me. She didn't have a phone, so I couldn't make a call to let her know I was fine. I would see her again within a day or two. At the very least, I would find a way to get a message to her.

As I sat there with the old lady's head on my shoulder, I smiled at the little girl and her mother who I had helped earlier. They were settling in a few rows ahead, and it made me wonder where they came from and if they could ever go back. The SS might've thought that as long as they bombed people's houses and slaughtered innocents in the streets, that no one would fight back, but *I* still had some fight in me—and I was going to take it straight to the Nazis and their weapons factory.

CHAPTER 10

"I don't like it." Bernard shook his head and frowned. "I don't care if you say you are a wizard. We shouldn't be sending in women like this, especially to such a dangerous place."

I gave him the evil eye, but decided not to say anything. I grew even more irritated when I nearly hit the roof of the car a couple of times as we ran over a few bumps in the road. "Do you think you could *not* give me a concussion before I reach Vélizy?"

"See? Can't even take a car ride, yet you're going to sabotage a factory. What sense is there in that?"

"I can stop your heart from beating and cause major explosions with my spells. I'd stop talking if I were you."

He snorted. "My great-uncle was a Philosopher. The Gray Tower made him leave early. He locked himself in his room and kept writing out equations until he buried himself under the weight of all his papers! I hope you're not crazy like that."

"Not in the least."

"We hadn't seen a wizard in the family since then," he said, shaking his head. "Do you suppose your kind is dying out?" He gestured with his right hand when he saw me raise an eyebrow. "I meant no offense."

I shrugged. "I don't know. All I know is that the world's off-balance."

"I'll agree with you on that."

We passed Paris around 10 a.m., and Bernard drove at a leisurely pace toward Vélizy-Villacoublay. I was about to ask him to stop the car and let me walk from there, but he suddenly slowed and parked the car on his own. There were two other civilian cars ahead of us, and they had also stopped. The Nazis had set up a checkpoint with two trekkers, and about four men from the German Armed Forces were present. Further down the road, I thought I saw an armored car.

"Here, Noelle. Put this on." He handed me a silver ring and placed a second one on his left ring finger. I got the hint and slid the ring onto my finger. I stretched and yawned as I reached toward the back, grabbing a shawl and pulling it over my head. I didn't know who was still out looking for a dark-haired girl with my old code-name. To my surprise, I felt a pang of sadness at abandoning that name, but like Renée said, it didn't change who I was inside.

One of the civilian cars ahead of us passed through the checkpoint and two of the soldiers went to the car in front of us and began their query. The other two watched while toting their rifles.

"Have your wits about you, woman." Bernard wiped his greasy face with a handkerchief and sighed.

"I'll tell you what, try having your wits about you when you run into a Cruenti. This is nothing."

"What's a Cruenti?" He put on a false smile and rolled down his window when he saw one of the soldiers heading toward us.

The soldier looked bored as he stopped at the window and leered at me. "Where are you headed?" His hands rested on top of the car; he cocked his head to the side and awaited an answer. His partner stood a few feet away with his hands nonchalantly folded behind his back, probably ready to draw a weapon at any moment.

"Good morning." Bernard reached into the glove compartment and showed him some papers. "My wife and I are headed into Vélizy-Villacoublay."

"On what business?"

"We wish to visit Saint Denis church."

Well, at least he didn't say we were vacationing or staying with a relative.

"You came all this way just to go to some church?"

I spoke up. "You see, my husband read somewhere that if you pray at the altar at Saint Denis church, that it would cure you of impotency."

The right corner of the soldier's mouth twitched when he saw Bernard go red. "Maybe you shouldn't have married such a fat old man."

"That's what my mother told me." I shrugged my shoulders.

"You don't object if a man beats his wife, correct?"

The two soldiers farthest ahead let the car in front of us pass. They called out toward our interrogator. He waved his hand and responded to them in German, then leaned back in to speak with us.

"Just remember that the curfew still applies, and the bounty's still being offered if you're interested. Just report any suspicious persons or activity to us."

"Understood." Bernard nodded solemnly.

"Can't believe these bastards have got me minding grandmothers and impotent men. I'll be glad when the SS gets here." He said this under his breath in German, apparently not thinking we heard or understood.

"Thank you." Bernard smiled. The soldier waved us through and rejoined his companions. Through the rear-view mirror, I could see them doubled over in laughter.

"Not bad, Noelle." Bernard wore a wide grin.

"Is that a compliment?" I smiled back at him.

"Underneath that middle panel in the back, there's a bag with some weapons and supplies. Take whatever you think you need."

"Thanks."

"Are you sure you don't want me to come?"

"Father Alexis trusted me with you. I couldn't risk you getting hurt."

He furrowed his bushy brows and looked ready to argue. "Well...never be afraid to call on me, *mon chérie*."

"I won't be."

Camaraderie and dedication like this kept spies like me going. I spent most of my time living other lives, going by other names, and not really having a place to call home. Yet, when I found myself surrounded with people like Jasmine, Renée, Father Alexis —heck, even Penn—I felt like I'd found a place where I belonged; physical borders or distances didn't matter.

Before I parted ways with Bernard (who planned to head further south before cutting across the Seine and going back up north), he left me with a few gifts: a Fairbairn fighting knife, a leather fold with a variety of small knives and daggers, a radio transmission jammer, and a set of pencil fuses. With disappointment, I decided that my steel knife would have to double as my alchemy knife. I still carried my red garnet lipstick, but I wasn't sure if I had left my emerald spectacles back at Father Alexis's secret room or somewhere in the car. I didn't have the time or patience to go looking for them, so I secured everything else I needed and said a final goodbye to Bernard before walking the last mile into Vélizy.

～

Usually in the early afternoon, one could see children frolicking in the Vélizy fountain and locals bustling about the neighborhood. However, most people stayed indoors as much as possible these days, nervous about the heavy presence of the German Army. The towers of the Vélizy factory loomed at the edge of town, surrounded by the heavy mechanical rumble of armored cars and a tank. I decided that visiting the local hospice, where visitors could purchase a room and a hot meal, would afford me a place to linger until nightfall. It could also serve as a means to gather information about the factory's layout, if one of the factory workers was there. Clearly, the smoke that billowed from the factory's towers was all for show—the only real work being done consisted of guarding the stockpile.

The effects of the deadly chemical, nicknamed The Plague by Ally soldiers, could be seen on the half-eaten faces and maimed bodies of former fighters who sat in the streets of Vélizy. Some of them bandaged themselves like lepers and sat clanking the change in rusted cans in hopes of receiving more. Others were too distraught to care about their appearance, or in some cases, preferred to use it to shame a benefactor into helping them. I shuddered at the thought of how many innocent bystanders were unfortunate enough to get caught in the crossfire of The Plague. At least the soldier went in with training and a gun.

"Have pity on me, miss." A young man approached—one of the ones without wrappings. A few wisps of blonde hair clung to his balding head, and his skin had a gray tinge. His dry lips parted slightly as he spoke, and though he did wear a jacket, I spotted acid burns running down the side of his neck.

I acknowledged him with a quick nod and promptly handed him a few francs. I made sure not to touch his hand, but it wasn't out of fear. I wasn't about to forget that an alchemist had carefully crafted it to destroy the body on contact. The soldier was lucky enough to survive whatever had hit him. Maybe he had been far enough from the blast to not be immediately obliterated, but it didn't mean The Plague wasn't still working on him and slowly killing him.

"You're afraid of me...aren't you?" He took the money and clenched his fist. Two of his fingers were missing.

"If I were afraid, I would've ignored you like those two people ahead who just passed you by."

He stared at me, and his left eye gleamed. "I'm Timothy."

"I'm Noelle." I crossed my arms just as he made a move to shake my hand.

"So, you're *not* afraid?" He withdrew his hand.

When an alchemist altered and manipulated material to create something new or give it its own magical quality, he infused it with his magical energy. Most of the time this was harmless, but with effort, you could sometimes trace an object or potion back to its creator. However, when you had an alchemist creating a deadly chemical used to eat away hundreds of soldiers like a rampaging monster—well, you didn't necessarily want to go fiddling around with things like that without taking precautions.

"How are you holding up, Timothy?" I wondered if he had any family.

"Well," he pocketed the money, "I can hardly hold down any food I am fortunate enough to buy, and I don't sleep anymore. Shall I go on?"

"I'm sorry." I wished I could say something else, but nothing I could ever say would restore him. Everything I knew about Heilwig's chemicals was in that dossier, and it suddenly became flesh and blood when I had to stare the results straight in the face.

"And where are you going on this fine day, Noelle?"

"The hospice. I'm looking for work."

His eye gleamed again. "Be careful."

"Thank you." I bit my lip and felt a cold knot in the pit of my stomach. He stepped aside to let me pass, and I walked by, feeling like a boulder had been set on my shoulders.

No sooner than I took a few steps, I had to stop once more when the SS officer, Karl Manfried, approached. I was taken aback because he had apparently fallen into some type of disgrace since I last saw him. He no longer wore a uniform, but instead dressed in tattered and dirty rags. He reeked of alcohol, dirt caked his hair, and he had more than a few bruises. Although he drank from his small liquor flask as if it contained the Elixir of Life, he still retained awareness and stood at full height.

"A few francs, for a German soldier who abandoned rank, and refused to cast his lot with his wicked brethren." He slipped the flask into one of his pockets and stood directly in front of me.

Well, at least the lying jerk didn't seem to recognize me. The other officers probably found him still under the influence of my mind control spell when they sorted out the explosion at the Paris office. They must've given him a good beating before stripping him of his rank and casting him out.

"Uh...yes...here." I didn't know why I was giving money to this man. In fact, I should've just kept moving. However when someone looked so beaten down and pitiful, you just didn't want to kick him when he was down. Besides, it didn't look like he would do harm to anyone anytime soon.

"Thank you." He took the money with one hand and quickly grabbed my left arm with the other.

"Let go of me," I said.

"I remember you...you're the fake Russian spy from that night." His grip tightened, and he pulled me closer.

Great, all I needed was to draw attention to myself. "If you remember me, then that means you also remember what I can do. Care to try me?"

"Let go of her!" Timothy shoved Karl and looked ready to punch him. I was relieved that I didn't have to fight Karl in the middle of town.

"Don't mind me." Karl backed away and took out his flask. "I'm just chatting with an old friend."

"Do you know him?" Timothy positioned himself between us.

"No. I don't." I scowled at Karl.

He took a swig from his flask. "Careful, Tim. She'll bewitch you too."

Timothy shook his head and faced me. "I apologize for him, he's a crazy drunk. Shall I walk you to the hospice?"

"Hospice, you say?" Karl eyed me with interest.

I shook my head. "I really don't want to be too much trouble. I should go."

I gently touched Timothy's arm in a parting gesture. Even through the shielding of his jacket, I could feel the presence of the poisonous magic still eating away at him. It felt horrible.

"Tim...everyone...look! Look at the witch!" Karl began waving and gesturing, trying to grab the attention of anyone in the vicinity.

I grabbed him by the scruff of his neck and grunted. "What did I tell you earlier?"

"That you didn't want to be too much trouble." His smile looked like a sneer. "I'll take you to the hospice."

Timothy objected, but I cut him off. "It's all right, he's just a crazy drunk who wants to get a few more francs out of me. He can walk me there."

"Are you sure?"

Hell no, but Karl would scream bloody murder if I didn't let him escort me. I'd hit him with a spell once we reached the hospice. "I'll be fine. Thank you."

I glared at him one last time as he walked alongside me down the street toward the hospice. I could already see the beautiful two-story cottage just ahead.

"You're awfully quiet, witch."

"I'm not a witch. Why do you want to go to the hospice so badly?"

"Where do you think I get my drink from?" He swished the liquor around in his flask and took a final gulp before slipping it back into his pocket.

"Why don't you go back to Germany?" Surely he wasn't planning on remaining a drunkard in the town of Vélizy for the rest of his life.

"They'll hang me or shoot me if I return home like this. I'm better off here, at least until the war ends, when no one will remember or care." He smiled at a couple of children passing by, and they went scurrying down the street.

I looked back and saw that Timothy was gone, and I gave Karl a sidelong glance. "What are you going to do, then?"

"Why do you care?"

"I don't...I'm just making conversation."

"I have a little girl. Once the war is over, I'm going to see her."

"Then take this." I gave him some more francs. Call me crazy, but I was a sucker for dads reuniting with their children.

"I..." he seemed at a loss for words. He hesitated, giving me a strange look.

"Well, here we are." I opened the gate and walked down the paved pathway toward the front door.

"*Scheisse...*" he hunched over and vomited.

I ran up the steps and opened the door. I turned to face him. "Not that I care, but you really ought to leave that liquor alone. You'll want your little girl to see you sober and all cleaned up."

He cursed in German. "Just leave *me* alone, witch. You make me ill."

"Not until you promise you'll be quiet," I told him in a low voice.

He stood and wiped his face with the back of his sleeve. "I promise. Just don't bewitch me again."

"Hey...where are you going?"

He shouldered his way past me to get inside and went straight for the bar. I shook my head and sighed. I went in and took in the view of the large common room which had a fireplace, bar, and tables and chairs set up for those who wished to lounge or play chess. The scent of spicy soup and roasted meat caught my attention as I took my seat in a dim corner, but at that point I really wanted a drink, so I ordered a chilled champagne cocktail.

Out of the corner of my eye I watched Karl get his flask

refilled, and I wondered if at any second he'd go into another frenzy. I noticed a group of patrons lounging on a long sofa by the fireplace. Their backs were turned to me, but I could tell there were three men and a woman. Two of the men wore berets, which Bernard had told me enabled a Maquisard to identify himself to another without arousing suspicion. I sat in my solitary corner thinking of how I would grab the attention of the two Maquisards. When my drink arrived, I kindly thanked the hostess, but she declined payment and said that the men on the sofa had paid for me. Still, I slipped her a few extra francs and asked her about the men by the fireplace.

"I don't know much," she said. "They arrived here a week ago. They haven't caused any trouble though, and as long as they pay their room and board, I'll not complain."

I eyed her with sympathy when I saw her frown in Karl's direction. "I thought perhaps I've seen them somewhere before. Thank you."

She smiled as she took another franc from me. "If I find out anything more, I'll be sure to tell you."

I drank half my cocktail before the plainclothes man, a dark-haired handsome fellow who introduced himself as Marc, asked me to join them. One of the Maquisards pulled up an extra chair for me and smiled.

"Good afternoon, welcome to Vélizy-Villacoublay! Are you a visitor as well?" The Maquisard who guided me to my chair flashed me a warm smile.

"Yes, I'm looking for work."

"There's not much to be had, I'm afraid." The other Maquisard, who looked to be in his fifties, took out a pipe and lit it.

The woman glowered and looked me up and down. "The factory is not hiring, if that's what you were thinking." She wrapped her arms around Marc. Her body language, manner of dress, and the fact that there weren't "any jobs to be had," led me to conclude that she was a prostitute.

"What are you good at, *mon ami*? Perhaps we can help." The younger Maquisard folded his hands and gave a serious look.

I raised an eyebrow. "Well, I'm afraid I'm not good at whoring."

The Maquisards kept their laughter to a low rumble, while Marc looked unconcerned. The woman glared at me and shifted away.

"With such a quick wit, I'm sure you can do many things, isn't that right Pierre?" The Maquisard inhaled from his pipe and blew out a puff of smoke.

"Yes, Rodrigue...indeed."

Marc leaned in and kissed the woman. "I'll see you tonight at dinner. Now, run along." With one last indignant look thrown in my direction, she stood and stalked toward the steep staircase that led to the guest rooms.

"*Mademoiselle.*" Rodrigue extinguished his pipe and tapped the top of his beret. "Do you recognize this?"

The whole setting just felt odd to me, and their characters seemed unsavory. "Yes, it's a very nice beret."

"Don't be coy, you know what it means." Marc sidled next to me.

"I'm sorry, but I don't know what you are getting at." I gave him a sidelong glance when Marc stroked my cheek.

"We are Maquisards," Pierre said. "We can help you with whatever you need. Whether it's money, a place to stay...is there someone you need to get out of jail? Just tell us."

Suddenly I felt lightheaded, and my stomach lurched. I stood to leave, but Rodrigue's hand shot out and grabbed my arm, forcing me back down. I scanned the room for help and saw the hostess with a frightened look on her face as she stood behind the bar pretending to clean wine glasses. Karl watched us from his stool at the bar. He looked like he was in pain.

"You don't look well." Marc's hot breath was on my neck. I shivered as I felt a sensation that I hadn't experienced since that night at Éclat—this man was a Cruenti. He probably sensed traces of magic emanating from me as well.

Although I kept a stoic expression, inside I wanted to scream like a madwoman. The growing terror combined with the sickening feeling in the pit of my stomach made me swoon.

"Do you think she's a Maquisard?" Pierre asked in a hushed voice.

Marc's response was firm and resolute. "She's coming with me."

I wanted to vomit and proclaim that I'd take my chances with either Pierre or Rodrigue. I tried to counter the drug in my system with my body magic, but the drug dazed me to where I couldn't completely purge it. I grew more ill by the second.

"If you ask for more than ten, I'll cut your tongue out." Rodrigue stuck his pipe back in his mouth and pulled out a wad of francs.

Karl approached, and refused to look in my direction. "I…I think I made a mistake."

Pierre laughed. "What mistake? You don't make mistakes. You find them, and you bring them to Marc. Understand?"

Karl looked at the floor and scratched the back of his head. "I haven't used it until today. I must've read it wrong. She's not what you're looking for."

"Let me see." Marc gestured toward Karl, and he tossed him the flask. I could see a small script carved toward the top, and for a moment the words glittered with several colors.

"I…I'll take her outside if you want—"

"It works just fine," Marc said. "Even if it didn't, I could still tell. Just like she can tell what I am."

"Watch out!" Rodrigue nearly choked on his pipe and ran for cover, but Karl aimed his revolver and shot him in the back. Before Pierre could even get out of his seat, he got a bullet in the chest.

I tried standing again, but my legs collapsed beneath me and I hit the floor. Marc sprang to his feet and seemed to jump into the air. The sofa blocked my view, but I heard a few more gunshots and then a physical struggle. I quickly reached into my side pocket and unsheathed my steel knife. I carved a symbol into the hardwood floor: a triangle with a horizontal line going through the top, and then a second one, except it was upside down—Air and Earth. The symbols barely held because of my weakness, but I went ahead and fed every last bit of energy into them. I heard the hostess scream. There was a hard thud on the floor.

"Karl!" I hushed my heavy breaths and listened.

Nothing.

"Hey, Karl!"

I heard slow and deliberate footsteps coming in my direction.

"Marc, what did you do to him?"

I shrieked when Karl's head landed next to me. I turned away from the gruesome sight so that the image wouldn't be branded into my mind, and I felt worse than if I had touched a thousand Timothies.

Marc came around the sofa, his mouth and chin dripping with blood. "Nothing, compared to what I'm going to do to you."

He raced toward me and I released the energy I had built up. He immediately froze in place because of the Earth-Air symbols. He struggled at first, but after realizing that it was futile, he decided to attack me in other ways.

"It's unfortunate I had to eat your little hero."

"You didn't have to kill him..." I felt both rage and sickness. Cruenti usually left people without powers alone. They preyed on wizards.

"When you lose control of your spell, that'll be the least of your worries." He licked his lips.

I forced myself onto my hands and knees and backed away. Marc laughed. If I weren't drugged and sick to my stomach, I'd probably try to blast him away. What was he doing here? He wasn't an ordinary Cruenti; I had never run across one with the ability to mask his powers like that.

I groaned when I saw Karl's body near the sofa, but kept moving because I felt like I would lose consciousness. When the doorway seemed just within reach, I decided to try standing on my feet again. My legs and arms shook, but at least this time I managed to stand. Just as I made it to the exit, Ken swung the door open and grabbed hold of me. I collapsed into his arms as he took me outside, where Bernard already had the car running. I would've torn myself out of his grasp, asked him what he was doing here, and why Bernard was with him, but I was ready to faint.

"What did they give you?" Ken opened the car door and squeezed in after me. He took off his coat and withdrew a small case that held four different vials of liquid from one of its pockets.

"I don't know...they put it in my cocktail." Although I counteracted the drug enough to remain conscious, it didn't spare me from other side effects.

"I know that look. It was probably chloral hydrate. Here, take this and get the rest of it out of your system." He opened one of the vials and tilted it toward my mouth. I still didn't know what he was doing here, and it couldn't have been just a coincidence that he found me here and now.

I turned my head away and rejected the vial. "I don't need it."

"Come on..."

"But I—" before I could finish my sentence, he poured the vial's contents down my throat.

Bernard hit the accelerator and took off, not holding back his invective. "Those pathetic excuses for men back there were traitors working for the Gestapo. I'm sorry, Noelle. Those weren't Maquisards."

It was nice to hear him say that in a sincere tone. My chest tightened, and I felt a pang when I thought of Karl.

"You'll feel better after some rest." Ken pushed my hair back as

I pulled his coat to my face and vomited. When I was done, he slid the soiled coat onto the floor.

I closed my eyes and slowed my breathing. Ken helped me sit upright and offered me a canteen of water. I wiped my mouth and took a few gulps, then handed the canteen back to him. So, it really was an antidote that he gave me. Maybe I was just paranoid, or maybe I had misunderstood Ken's words that day. Maybe he had been mad at Penn because he would have to go out for a second time to find his contacts, and maybe he had taken Badru's money for a good reason.

"What are you guys doing here?" I asked.

"That car that my Boss wanted me to take a look at—turns out it's the Vélizy factory."

"It's not a real factory." I shook my head. "It has Veit Heilwig's chemical weapons."

"I just found that out. I couldn't decode that message Penn gave me, so I had to go to a codemaster to get it deciphered. The problem is, the only codemaster I trusted in this area was sitting in a jail up in Rouen."

"You went all the way up north?"

Ken nodded. "So I get there, and I find out that the guy had been guillotined."

"Ouch..." I frowned. I supposed the SS wanted to break up the monotony of firing squads.

"But I found out he left three notebooks of ciphers with his assistant before being arrested."

"Where was the assistant?"

"Erm...in jail, but he was in Mantes."

"Wait, didn't you start off in that area?"

"I know, makes you want to punch something, doesn't it?" Bernard laughed. "He'll probably end up punching me."

"You two know each other?" My gaze went between Ken and Bernard. I wondered if the older man even knew "Drake's" real name and if they were close friends.

"Do I know him?" Bernard shot Ken a quick glance. "If it weren't for me, Drake wouldn't know how to make it down the street in Paris."

Ken smirked. "Bernard's one of the first Maquisards I ever met. He thinks because he pulled me from a burning car, that I need to be looked out for."

Bernard gestured toward the backseat. "Lucky for you, I saw those spectacles in the back, Noelle. I don't meddle with wizards' possessions and needed to bring them to you."

"Thank you, Bernard." I faced Ken. "Now, are you going to tell me about the assistant?"

"I found him drowned in the Seine River."

And I thought *I* was having a frustrating day. "So, how did you end up decoding the message?"

"I went to another codemaster—Mathieu Perrine."

I could just imagine what a meeting between them would look like. "You've met Mathieu?"

"Yeah, and it looks like you did too. It didn't take long to figure out you had passed through, so I headed out this way, and that's when I ran into Bernard. We came out here when he said he needed to get your emerald spectacles back to you. When I saw you in the hospice with that warlock, I knew I had to get you out of there quick."

"Those spectacles were real emerald?" Bernard eyed us with interest.

"Don't get any ideas, old man. Remember, you don't mess with wizards' possessions?" Ken placed his arm around me and I finally began to relax.

"I'm glad you were there," I told him with a serious look in my eye, "but next time, you might not want to rush into the middle of something like that." Marc would've torn through Ken just like he did Karl Manfried.

Ken threw me an incredulous glance. "What are you talking about? You needed help. You couldn't even walk on your own."

"Just be careful," I said. Sometimes I wished he'd take a step back and analyze what was going on in a situation rather than rushing into something because he felt it was the right thing to do.

"It's good to have you back, Drake—it'll be like old times. And I'm glad we found you, Noelle."

"I'm glad you're both here." I reached for Ken's hand and held it tightly, secretly wishing that "here" was anywhere other than Nazi-occupied Paris. I would've felt like an idiot if I had confronted Ken or accused him of anything.

"I'm glad you're alive." He squeezed my hand in return.

"Where are we going?" I leaned into him.

"A Maquisard safe house." Bernard slowed the car. "Tonight, we're going to hit the factory."

"I'm coming too. It's the only way I'll find the laboratory I'm looking for."

"You need rest first." Ken frowned at me.

Bernard pulled up to a large house just southwest of the factory. It had no gate and looked like it might have once been a beautiful country house. As soon as we stepped out of the car, a Maquisard woman greeted us. A young man who didn't even look old enough to drive came out and took Bernard's keys.

The two exchanged a few words and Bernard patted the young man on his back. "Take care of it, will you?" After he watched the young man drive off, he turned to face me. "Well, whether you like it or not, you're stuck with me."

CHAPTER 11

I awoke with a start. My rest was more disturbed than anything else, but at least I had slept. Darkness permeated the small bedroom and I sat up and reached for the lamp on the nightstand next to the bed. Though my body ached from weariness, all I could think about was the Vélizy factory going down in flames.

As Ken lay asleep next to me, it made me reflect on the question of how many more years, or even weeks I could last? Stella was my age, and her remains lay scattered at the gates of Dachau. She could have lived a normal life, found a new husband, and started a family. And here I was, Noelle, Emelie...and whoever else I've pretended to be; I've barely escaped with my own life, and tonight I would be putting it at risk again by going to the factory.

"Ken...are you awake?"

"Yes."

After a few long seconds, I prodded him with my foot. "Wake up."

"Do you need anything?" He turned to face me.

"I was thinking about some things."

"What is it?"

"Do you ever plan to quit spying?"

"When the war's over with, yes." He sat up.

I snorted. "And when do you think that's going to be?"

"Listen, a couple of sources told me that the U.S. is likely to join the Allies by the end of the year. The Navy's already getting into skirmishes with the Japanese, so this is all going to be over soon."

I hoped his sources were right. "Do you enjoy this life?"

"If I weren't doing this, I wouldn't have met you."

A flicker of a smile crossed my lips. "I'm tired."

"We all get tired, but that's a good thing."

"Why?"

"It means you're still human. If you could go through all this without feeling, thinking, or questioning, then what the hell are you?"

"Do you feel like you're missing out on life? Even the simple things? I think the last film I saw was *Wizard of Oz*. I mean, when's the last time you've been to a cinema? And I used to read all the time when I was at Radcliffe—"

"Yeah, I know...I stole a copy of your file, remember?"

"Of course." I also stole a copy of his within three days.

His grin faded as he stared at me. "Last year, after the Cairo job, the Boss gave me another assignment. I went to Amsterdam and delivered a parcel schedule to the Resistance leaders. They needed to know where to pick up the food we were dropping throughout the country. They needed to feed themselves because the Nazis were taking everything. People were eating wild roots and grass, cats, dogs...anything they could get their hands on."

"You never told me about that." I sat up and wrapped my arms around him. Hearing about the Cairo job bothered me, but I didn't have it in me to ask him about it just yet.

His eyes grew cold. "I delivered the parcel schedule, and then I was supposed to report back to the Boss. Instead, I went with the resistance fighters on a couple of sabotage missions. When it was over, I felt invulnerable, like I really did something. But then a week later, on a car ride across the border, I noticed a whole line of those same men I fought with, tied to fence posts, with their bellies slit open. The Nazis wrote 'Terrorist' across their chests in their own blood."

"I'm so sorry." I couldn't find any other words of consolation, and just held him tighter.

"After seeing that, I felt like it would've been better if I had never come at all. I started questioning everything, and I felt..." he sighed. "But when I was back in the States, OSS forwarded me some letters addressed to my codename. They were from friends and family of the men who were killed. It took me a few weeks to gain the courage to open the damn things and read them."

"And...?" I planted a kiss behind his ear.

"The letters said they wanted to thank me. Could you believe that? They even said they had the strength to survive and move forward. I thought...I thought their letters would say that they hated me."

I kissed him again. "And when you saw how they really felt, you asked yourself why you shouldn't have the strength to continue as well?"

He nodded. "I know what it means to be tired, and there's nothing wrong with that."

With a heavy heart, I considered his words and played out his story in my mind. Sometimes I wanted to quit because it all felt like a burden that was just too heavy to bear. I admired Stella, who refused to let her husband die in vain. Renée—she possessed that quiet strength that had eluded so many.

Deep down, I knew that the one thing I truly hated was losing people, because I lost one of the most important people in my life when I was just a child. Could I be as brave as those two women? My mother once told me, "Know what you can do, and what you can't...and thank God if you have the sense to know the difference." Somehow, I wanted to survive all this, and not just as an empty shell living to see another day. If there was one thing I had learned, it's that when you've been involved in this for too long, you ended up broken. I would rather die than see that day. Or better yet, I would want to retire and have a few neat stories to tell my grandchildren one day.

I heard a knock on the door. "Come in."

"All rested up, I hope?" Bernard entered the room holding a hot mug of tea, looking as if he managed to curl up somewhere and sleep as well.

"Yes. We need to show Noelle a map of the factory." Ken went over to the nightstand and pulled out the drawer. Reaching into the vacant spot, he withdrew a sheet of paper. He unfolded it and handed it to me, gesturing for me to examine it.

I studied the map and committed it to memory. There were two security checkpoints that we would have to bypass before reaching the factory building itself. The first checkpoint was a barricade placed at the road which broke off from the main road and led to the factory grounds. The second checkpoint stood at the gates. The steel gates enclosed the factory building, which had two westside entrances and one eastside emergency exit. The former enamel factory stood three stories high and had a basement area.

"Our plan is to go in and have you and Drake neutralize the weapons. The Maquisards will be our backup if anything goes wrong." Bernard finished his tea and gestured toward the Maquisard woman, who came in with a box full of items. She sat it next to him and left.

"What about the armored cars and the tank?" I hadn't forgotten about them.

"They're not going to risk firing on the factory." Bernard rummaged through the box. "And I have a few men who are going to be dealing with them, if needed. Do you still have that radio transmission jammer I gave you?"

"Yes." I also retrieved and handed him my emerald spectacles.

"They could probably use these as well. Whoever wears these can see in the dark."

"Thank you." He placed them into his pocket and reached deep into the box. He withdrew a black case. He opened it and presented the knife inside. I could taste the light metallic essence of the silver within the weapon and delighted in it, although I still preferred gold. I reconciled myself to the fact that untainted silver would be an immense improvement from steel.

Ken grabbed a uniform that Bernard handed him from the box. "All we have to do is get in, take care of those chemical weapons, and get out. There's no time for fooling around."

"We're going in as SS officers?" I caught a wad of black garb that Bernard tossed toward me.

"I have identification for all of us." Bernard gestured for me to start getting dressed. "God help me, this had better work since we can only use these credentials once. I'm going in as Fritz Aldarich, and you're going to be our nurse."

"We should also keep our eyes open for anything that can lead us to their research laboratories in the region." I examined the nurse's uniform, which came with a black dress, white-collared shirt, a matching cape, and headdress.

Bernard threw on his cap and coat. "We deciphered a message that said Fritz Aldarich is inspecting the factory tonight. As long as we neutralize those weapons before he comes, we'll be all right. I'll see what I can do about the laboratories."

Ken finished dressing and kept fiddling with his armband as if it itched. Bernard grabbed a suitcase secretly laden with weapons and tools. Once I finished putting on my nurse's uniform, we all gazed at each other. If we wanted another day of "cheating death," as Lyder would've put it, we could not afford to make a single mistake.

We pulled up to the first checkpoint, where the diverging road leading to the factory was barricaded. Several German soldiers and trekkers stood before us. The Maquisards lurked further down the main road, just far enough to not be detected, but close enough to rush in if we needed them. We followed one of the soldier's instructions and turned off our headlights, waiting for him and a second soldier to approach.

"Identification, please." He collected our credentials and inspected them. His partner shined his flashlight on us and examined us with an expressionless face. I kept mine as calm as possible, knowing that many Maquisards were imprisoned or tortured in the process of stealing and counterfeiting papers and identities for missions such as this.

The soldier with our credentials took the papers back to his booth to examine them in detail, and two other soldiers came forward with their flashlights and weapons ready. Just ahead, an armored car faced us, and a second one patrolled the vicinity. The tank roamed on the other side of the factory grounds.

He came back and handed us our papers. "You're early—we were expecting you two hours from now."

"Look," Bernard glared from his passenger side seat, "if it were up to me, I wouldn't have come at all to this backward town. However, since we come on the express orders of the Führer, I want to quickly get this done."

"You're aware of standard safety procedure?" The soldier directed his question toward Ken, who was in the driver seat. Apparently he wasn't in the mood to speak with a foul *Ortsgruppenleiter*.

"Of course," Ken answered in German, following Bernard's lead. "The weapons are 'as is'?"

"You'll have to ask Lieutenant Korbin...he's just ahead." He saluted us and returned to his booth, signaling toward the other men to set the barricade aside and for the armored car to let us drive past.

We drove down the narrow road and approached the second checkpoint at the factory gates. This time we were instructed to park our car off to the side of the road and present ourselves at the gate. Ken and Bernard flanked me as we walked toward Lieutenant Korbin and his guards. He saluted us, and we saluted him in return.

"Good evening, *Ortsgruppenleiter* Adalrich. I'll be your escort throughout the factory and can answer any questions you may have."

"Very good." Bernard handed him our papers. "You may call me Fritz. As you can see, I brought along my assistant, Josef, and our nurse Hilda."

Korbin's gaze went between the papers and our faces. "May I ask why you need the nurse?" He handed us our papers.

"It seems you failed to examine all my information." I opened my bag and displayed its contents. "I've also been trained in advanced chemical science and will be collecting samples of the chemical agent. As volatile as it is, we still have to ensure its integrity."

He viewed the chemistry kit with interest. "Is it true, those chemicals were made by a wizard?"

"It seems you need to be sent out into the fray more often." Ken peered into Korbin's eyes. "I've seen it melt men's flesh and expose bare bone. I've heard soldiers cry for mercy with their last breath while the spell consumed them. I don't think the devil himself could have made anything more virulent."

Korbin's face blanched and he quickly motioned for us to follow him through the gate entrance. "How much more do you expect the generals will move? We've already used half."

"If we can weaken the Allies this easily in three months," I answered. "I predict we won't need much to finish the task."

Two guards stood at the building's double doors just ahead. Korbin hailed them as they saluted us, and we passed through the doorway unmolested, gazing at the stars above as we stood in the open courtyard of the factory. From where I stood, I remembered that to my right were the two westside exits, and to my left I'd find the emergency exit if I needed to use it. Dozens of soldiers stood sentinel on the balconies of the second and third stories, either facing the courtyard or pacing up and down.

Bernard pulled out a notebook and pen, trying to ignore the intimidating sight. "Lead us to the weapons, Korbin."

Korbin took us into a small room on the first floor that allowed access to the basement level. I could sense a ward on the reinforced door. Korbin unlocked the door and ushered us in. When the lights flickered on, we saw that the basement was bigger than we had thought, and the stockpile of chemical weapons stood in the middle of the room, about two hundred "cubes" of materials stacked high, forming a pyramid.

The fact that they packaged it this way made me certain that the chemical agent was in powder form. I needed to test its physical and magical composition, and if I could, swipe a sample. However, it would all mean nothing if I couldn't neutralize it.

"You'll have to be careful with it," Korbin told me as he went over to a locker and took out a pair of warded gloves.

I took out my own pair of gloves. "Just leave me to my work."

Bernard pointed toward some notes posted on the locker. "You see those procedural rules? I think they ought to be posted right outside at the door, not on the storage locker."

Korbin walked him over toward the notes. "Since whoever would come to test or transfer the chemicals would have to come to the locker first, I thought this would be the proper place."

Bernard trailed off, going down a list of changes he wanted implemented and grabbed the notes off the locker and went through them. He was probably looking for that research laboratory I needed.

As Ken stood as lookout near the door, I set up my warded chemistry set on a table in the corner and took out my silver knife. I carved a fortified symbol of protection around the seat I'd be sitting in—a plaited symbol that looked like a three-leaf clover.

I put on my gloves and went over to the pyramid to grab one of the cubes from the top. All of the packaging was secured with a ward, but the chemical itself was another matter. I brought it back over to the table and sat within my protective symbol. I snipped open the plastic bag and frowned at the stench already assaulting my nose, but it didn't stop there—somehow, the black grainy powder stirred on its own and spread as if a wind had blown it. I used one of the beakers from the chemistry set to trap it.

I could already feel the powder graze against the beaker and try to rise into the air. It made me wonder if their wards were strong enough to completely contain this. I fed more energy into my own protective symbol, and the chemical settled back down. It almost felt alive; it just moved and swirled on its own. I could even feel it push against my protective magic and pulsate like a beating heart. I would seriously have a problem if this stuff broke through and ate my face off.

With trembling hands, I took my silver knife and made three smaller plaited symbols on the surface of the table. I transferred the powder over to the symbols, dividing it into three piles. I already knew that heat catalyzed the chemical into what we called The Plague, and now I could feel its grainy texture that resembled a darker version of cane sugar. I scooped some of the powder into a warded vial, which I then sealed and dropped into my pocket.

I flashed a nervous smile at Ken as he paced back and forth, listening at the door and making sure Bernard kept Korbin preoccupied. Now that I had the chemicals separated into three distinct piles, I placed a few drops of Aqua Fortis on the first one. The powder turned red and fizzled, but the substance didn't decompose or transform. I almost gasped when I saw the powder inch its way on the table top toward the border of the protective symbol and began to weaken it. I gripped my silver knife again and carved an upside-down triangle symbol for Water (I figured that I would try the opposite of what catalyzed the powder), as well as a crescent moon, which would reinforce any spells done with the silver knife.

Since I tasted no metallic essence in the powder, it meant that some type of protein was present and that it could decay. After placing a few drops of Aqua Vitae on the next pile, I carved a second upside-down triangle, but this one had a cross sitting on top—the spell of Putrefaction. If this one didn't work, I'd have to try to get us out of here without getting shot down by the German Army.

The powder fizzled with the effect of the water and the spell, and the powder made one last push against my protective symbol on the table and broke it. A small cry escaped my throat, but I fell silent when the powder turned black-green and decayed before my eyes. Korbin and Bernard finally came over to watch. I held a match to the putrefied powder.

"Has anyone touched this?" I made my tone sound aggravated.

"N-no," Korbin shook his head. "We've all been keeping protocol. Is something wrong?"

The powder went up in flames and disintegrated without incident. I had neutralized the chemical, and Korbin was none the wiser. "If you value your life, you will tell me who meddled with this."

Korbin knew nothing of alchemy, how the chemical was made, or how it worked. By accusing him or his men of tampering, I was shifting the focus from what I was doing and turning it on him.

"I swear to you, none of us have." He turned to Bernard in a silent plea.

"I believe there is no reason to question Lieutenant Korbin." Bernard rested his hand on the man's shoulder.

"However," Ken approached with a stern expression, "you should go ask your men what they've been doing within the past two weeks."

"Of course." Korbin saluted and rushed past Ken. He went

straight for the door and headed upstairs. I shot Ken an annoyed glance—why did he send Korbin out?

"Please tell me you know how to destroy this stuff." Ken shut the door and locked it. He reached for his pistol.

"It's going to take almost all my strength, but I can do it. Why did you make Korbin leave?"

"There's a commotion going on up there. If the real Fritz Aldarich's also arrived early, then we have trouble coming."

When we heard the footsteps of a group of men come down the stairway, and Korbin's voice demanding us to open the door, Bernard drew a small radio transmitter from inside his coat. He clicked it on and repeated a single phrase: "This is Papa...it's time to put the baby to bed."

I sped around the pyramid, carving my water and moon symbols into the floor. Then, I came back around and splashed my Aqua Vitae all over the packaged chemicals and onto the symbols, trying to ignore the banging outside the door and concentrated on repeating the neutralization.

"Go stand by the door!" I shouted toward Bernard and Ken. They'd have to be as far away from it as possible. "As soon as I neutralize the chemicals, be ready to open it."

I carved another plaited protection symbol and a single large Putrefaction spell at the foot of the pyramid. I fed all my energy into devouring the chemicals. Ken swung the door open, and the loud hisses and smoke billowing from the stockpile caught Korbin and his men off-guard. I heard screams of horror as we were all lost in a temporary blindness, and I heard the guards retreating from the basement shouting a warning to the other soldiers that we had activated the chemicals.

"Let's get out of here." Bernard ran toward me and grabbed my wrist.

I coughed as some of the smoke rushed toward my face and flew up my nostrils. I tried looking around for Ken, but I could hardly see anything, and Bernard would not let me loose. As we ran upstairs and into the room that would lead us back out to ground level, my legs felt weak and my arms began to shake. The Putrefaction spell required a lot, though I knew I needed to hold on longer so that we could make it out of the factory alive.

"Go on!" Ken shouted behind us as he propped the basement door open with his foot. "The Maquisards should be here."

"Come up, Ken!"

"I'll catch up! Just go!"

With reluctance, I stepped ahead of Bernard and opened the ground level door just a bit, and the scene was absolute pandemonium. Maquisards and German soldiers gunned each other down amidst three separate gunfights, and no one gave reprieve to the injured who were caught in the crossfire. The Maquisards took the first level and created a barricade near the entrance. They also took the east side.

The German officers trapped on the second and third floors returned gunfire, sniping anyone who crossed their path. When someone launched a grenade into the courtyard, causing the gunfire to cease and forcing many to take cover, I saw our chance to run straight for the exit. We quickly made our way through the courtyard and dashed toward the double doors.

"This way!" A young man, who hastily introduced himself as Claude, ushered us past the barricade and led us through. He shot two soldiers with his rifle, and Ken and Bernard also fired when a few stragglers emerged from the west grounds. We made it through the gates but instinctively flinched when we heard the tank on the other side of the factory fire a shot. We picked up our pace when we heard it rolling north toward us.

"What happened to our car?" I ran alongside Claude as I gazed at our vehicle, now engulfed in flames. Just a few feet away, the second tank stood still, with nearly seven bodies of Maquisards and two German soldiers lying on the ground.

"Don't worry." Claude motioned for us to head down the road

toward the first checkpoint. "I have a car down the road waiting for you, now go!"

"Tell them to pull back now," Bernard said. "We've done what we needed to do."

Claude remained with us until the car was in sight. He had parked it just behind the barricade that now stood deserted. Claude handed Ken the key and bid us farewell as quickly as he had introduced himself. He turned and headed back toward the factory, and all I could think was, if he were anything like me, he'd buck Bernard's order to retreat and continue fighting.

"Bernard, did you find out anything about the laboratories?" I ran with them toward the car, away from the gunfire and smoke of the melee.

"I didn't find much, but you're going to want to look at Dijon, Reims, and Nice." He looked at me apologetically, almost as if expecting me to be angry.

In truth, I was glad to at least have this lead. Despite the chaos at the factory, destroying the chemical weapons gave me a sense of relief, since it meant no one else would have to fall victim to them. At the same time, I knew I would have to pinpoint the exact location of the laboratory in order to make it to Heilwig.

We reached the car, but suddenly halted when another car pulled up beside it. I immediately grabbed Bernard and Ken, pulling them backward. The way I held their arms and pulled them away told them that something was wrong.

"Noelle, who is that?" Bernard's gaze fixed on Marc, who stepped out of the second car.

Ken recognized Marc and drew his gun. "Get another spell ready."

I immediately laid a spell without a word, though by this time my body felt like it was on fire and my mind could barely focus. Although I did as he said, the spell I placed down wasn't an offensive spell, but an Air spell.

"Step on the glowing symbol," I commanded them.

"What does it do?" Bernard backed away as Marc approached. There would be no use in trying to send Marc flying away—he'd only be back in a few seconds.

"It'll protect you. Now, both of you do it quickly." I felt horrible lying to them, but I'd rather them be angry with me for sending them away than dead. They backed onto the symbol, and as soon as they touched it, a blast of air shot up and sent them flying in opposite directions into the nearby trees.

As I stood ready to cast another spell, I tried sizing Marc up to see if I was a match for him. I mentally reached out, but quickly recoiled when I felt his toxic magical energy emanating toward me like a heat wave. I didn't know if he had let his guard down or if he wanted me to feel the breadth of his power, but it made me queasy to know that he had gorged on over ten wizards.

And if I didn't kill him, I'd be next.

CHAPTER 12

"They didn't matter anyway. I only wanted you." Marc came within a few feet of me, probably sensing that my magical strength had waned. When he saw that I didn't make a move to cast a spell, he came closer until he stood right in front of me. He peered into my eyes—and I stared right back, despite feeling so vulnerable.

"I'm no one important."

"Are you sure about that, Miss George?"

"What did you call me?" I felt a nauseating shock run through me like an electric current. He made me think of the other Cruenti and the warlocks that had attacked that night at Éclat. Despite my surprise, my anger began to rise as I realized someone had betrayed me; whether this traitor worked within SOE or the Maquis, I swore I would root them out.

"I know who your father is, and I believe you're worth tracking down."

"Marc...You're Marcellus..." With a quick movement of my hand, I tried to stab a reverse fixation symbol into him like I did with Isidore at the university, but his hand shot out and grabbed my wrist, twisting and squeezing it until it cracked. I shrieked in pain and dropped my knife. I balled my fist and swung a right hook, but he grabbed that wrist as well. As I began to work my body magic on him, I spoke to him as a distraction.

"Who told you about me?" I pushed the pain from my mind and concentrated on feeling for any weak points in his body.

"A friend of yours..." He pulled me against him, his eyes gleaming with greed. As he lowered his head and breathed in my scent, his lips grazed my neck, and I acted.

I sent a rush of energy into him that would've stopped his heart and killed him. Instead, I only had enough strength to interrupt his natural rhythm and make his body jolt. Blood spewed from his nose and mouth, and he roared in pain. I wasted no time in tearing myself loose and delivering a high kick to his head. I grabbed my silver knife, and with quick methodical flicks, drew a large triangle for Fire. As the air around Marc began to spark and crackle, several flames formed in mid-air and came crashing down on him, but he quickly repelled them.

When I saw that my spells were becoming less effective because of my fatigue, I scrambled toward the car without looking back. I fumbled around and cursed under my breath when I realized Ken had the key, so I ran over to Marc's car, started it, and sped away. As I swerved onto the main road, I kept my right hand on the steering wheel and carefully began feeding small bursts of energy into mending my injured left wrist. I cried when I felt the bone reset, and when the torn sinews beneath refused to heal all the way, I wanted to curse again. Suddenly, an explosion from behind hit the car, sending me spinning out of control.

I hardly had time to brace myself for impact. I erected a weak protective shield when the car slid in its final spin and the rear end collided with a tree. The crash made a deafening sound, and for a moment all I could see was a terrifying darkness. When I forced my eyes to focus, I felt my shoulders stiffen and blood drip down the side of my face. My heart raced as I slipped my silver knife into my uniform pocket and leaned to the side to empty out the glove compartment. I found a short dagger made of steel and a revolver. I took the gun.

My legs folded and kicked when Marc jumped on me from the driver side. He grabbed my legs and tried to pull me outside, but I shot him in the chest. He backed away and disappeared. Just as I sat up, his hands came crashing through the passenger side window and knocked the revolver out of my hand. He wrapped one arm around my neck and the other tore away my nurse's headdress. I tried to pry his arm away, but he was intent on strangling me.

Taking the chance that his avarice outweighed his rage, I managed to tell him through stifled breaths, "If you kill me…like this…my blood will…be no good."

His moment of faltering was all I needed to grab the steel dagger and drive it into his neck. I heard a bone-chilling gurgle as he let go of me. I reclaimed the revolver and crawled through the driver side, thinking that I had at least bought myself another minute since he'd have to dislodge the knife and regenerate. I started to run when I heard an eerie sound in the air that made me freeze in place. It started off as a large whoosh, and then I heard a guttural sound as if someone, or *something*, was trying to speak.

My legs numbed and I dropped to my knees. With unsteady hands, I checked how many bullets were left in the revolver. I couldn't die, not tonight. I took a shot at the dark figure in the air. It blotted out some of the stars in the sky. I missed, and in vain, I shot my last two bullets at it.

I leaned forward on my knees and clenched my teeth as my stomach cramped. My chest tightened as I heard a loud screech that made the air fluctuate and push me completely to the ground. My body was numb. All I could see and taste was the cool soft earth. I didn't even flinch when Marc caught up to me and pulled me to my feet. He stood behind me, gripping me around my waist so that I couldn't break away. His other arm crossed my shoulders, and for a moment I thought he might try to strangle me again.

"Look at it, Isabella." He moved forward with me, toward the Black Wolf that had landed. "And people have the gall to say Cruenti are abominations."

The Black Wolf wore all black garb and a silver hood that covered most of its face. I could see the bottom of its nose and mouth, which made me sick to look at, because it reminded me of a bat's.

"Don't..." I dug my feet into the ground, trying to impede Marc from bringing us closer. There was no way in hell I was going near that thing, at least not without a fight.

"Perhaps I should introduce you." He pushed me forward again.

"No!" I shouted, as the Black Wolf hissed at me. Marc gestured for it to keep its distance.

"Black Wolves trade most of their humanity for their powers. Look at him: he can barely speak, but he's very cunning and strong enough to use his magic to kill his target."

"Are you any better?" I still writhed in pain from my injured wrist. "One minute you want to hunt me down and capture me, and the next you want to kill me. You're losing it already, aren't you?"

Our reason governed our logical decisions, sat in judgment as our conscience, and made up an essential part of what made us human. Cruenti warlocks all eventually degenerated and lost this faculty.

"I am above the Wolves, Isabella. So is Octavian. We'll never become like them."

The Black Wolf crouched to the ground then crawled toward us with unnatural movements of its limbs. It didn't even bother to walk upright anymore. I sank down in an attempt to get out of Marc's grasp, but it was useless. When the Black Wolf came close enough, I kicked it in the face as hard as I could. It screeched and tried to bite my foot off.

"This one's mine!" Marc swung me halfway out of reach.

The Black Wolf crouched again, clicking its mouth open and shut. A dark red Circle shot up around us, one I never saw before. It enclosed us all inside so quickly that it felt like I was suffocating.

"What did I tell you?" Marc said to the Black Wolf as he raised his arm and formed a gesture with his hand. The Circle broke, and the Black Wolf began crawling on all fours again, slowly circling us.

"What do you want from me?" I asked, thankful I could at least still talk with Marc.

"Where's Carson?"

"I don't know."

"We'll know soon enough. He'll come for you if he knows I have you—then it'll be settled."

"What are you talking about?"

"When your father disappeared in Rome, several warlocks boasted about finishing him off. I killed them all, and thought, if they couldn't beat me, then they sure as hell couldn't beat Carson George. I knew he was alive, and it was only a matter of time before I figured out that Carson wasn't hiding from the Black Wolves, but from the Gray Tower. He's a Drifter."

"You psychotic...is that why you took Heilwig? Because of my father?"

Damned liar. Manipulator. I refused to fall for his mind games.

"I took Heilwig because Octavian wanted him to make those weapons for Hitler. Octavian still isn't even convinced that your father is a Drifter. I just wanted Veit so I could rip his throat out and steal his powers. He wasn't meant to survive this anyway, and I will have him in the end. But you don't have to die here. You can come meet Octavian yourself."

"And be used as bait for my father?" Or worse, Octavian's dinner?

The Black Wolf came toward me again. It opened its bat-like mouth, but this time Marc shoved me forward. I screamed, "All right! I'll go!"

Marc spoke to the Black Wolf with a grating voice in a language I didn't understand. He must've given it a command, because the Black Wolf backed away and then flew up into the air and left us. While Marc had been speaking to the Wolf, I had gathered every last ounce of my remaining energy to attempt another spell on him.

I acted and went for his heart again, but with a roar he repelled me once more and threw me to the ground. I landed hard and had my breath knocked out of me, but it didn't stop me from grabbing handfuls of his hair and diverting his teeth away from my neck. I punched him as hard as I could.

The earth beneath us suddenly quaked, and the ground exploded. I felt a tingling sensation in my toes that rose up my legs, then my back, and all the way up to the top of my head. The air changed; it smelled different, and for a moment, it grew dense at my fingertips. I only reacted that way when an elemental wizard did magic.

"Brande..."

Everything seemed to unfold in slow motion. Marc turned and caused sparks to dance in the air until they merged and formed flames around Brande. The fire came crashing down on him, but he only absorbed the flames and sent them flying right back toward Marc. He shielded himself from Brande's reciprocal spell, but I had already created a Circle of Healing with my silver knife and welcomed the fire.

The bright white flames encircled me, and the roar of the curative blaze raged in my ears as it drowned out the sounds of battle. My full strength returned, and my physical injuries were healed. When my restoration was complete, the Circle of Healing subsided and disappeared.

Marc pulled out two searing red daggers. He hurled them toward Brande, and as the daggers went flying, Marc also forced a nearby tree to come plummeting down onto him. One dagger missed, but the other had grazed Brande's arm. He barely kept the tree from crushing him by commanding the soil to rise and form a barrier. Marc swung around and came toward me, but I activated an Air symbol and sent him flying back with a gust of wind. He rose to his feet and lurched backward when a man with a silver sword came from the same direction Brande had—and nearly decapitated Marc.

I immediately rejoined the fight, rushing toward Marc. He still fought with the swordsman, and I positioned myself to strike at him. He quickly backed away from both of us, knowing good and well that if he tried to block my strikes, that he would be vulnerable to the swordsman.

"Leave us, sorcerer!" The swordsman made a sweeping arc with his sword and diverted a spell of blindness that Marc sent whirling toward us.

Marc grunted with frustration when he saw he was at a disadvantage. He retreated, evaporating into a black mist and leaving an ominous air about us. I turned toward the swordsman, and our gazes met. I noticed for the first time that he wore a Roman collar.

"Gabriel di Crocifissa, at your service." He inclined his head and sheathed his sword. With a single gesture, he quenched the remaining flames that began burning the surrounding foliage.

I tentatively shook his hand. "I...don't think I've ever seen a sword-wielding priest."

"Gabriel is not your typical priest." Brande approached, slightly hunched and moving as if he ached all over. He had a cut above his left eyebrow, and he slowly flexed his left arm where the dagger had grazed him. He would've lost that arm if the weapon went straight in. Even though he used body magic to close the wound, it still caused him pain.

"I thought you were back at the Gray Tower." I wrapped my arms around his neck since it seemed to be the only body part that didn't hurt. I gave him a hug, standing on the tips of my toes because of his height.

"I was south of here in the Provence region. I told you it would be more difficult to make it back to the Gray Tower."

"Well, I'm glad you were still in France. I didn't know how much longer I was going to last."

"What were you doing here?"

"I destroyed those weapons that the alchemist Veit Heilwig had made, but the factory was a dead end, and I can't find the laboratory he's in. And Brande, the Nazis were forcing him to make those weapons. Why didn't anyone ever tell me Veit had trained at the Gray Tower?"

"Brande! This way!" Gabriel ran ahead and flagged down an approaching car. I could tell by his excitement that he recognized the driver.

"Where did you find him?" I asked, walking side-by-side with Brande toward the car. I gazed into his clear gray eyes and wiped some dust and dirt from his dark hair.

"I ran into him in Salon-de-Provence. He had disguised and embedded himself among Mussolini's men. He's coming to the Gray Tower as an emissary from the Vatican."

We greeted the young woman in the car and got in. Gabriel sat in the passenger seat, exchanging a few words with her and introducing us as the car pulled off. "Brande, this is Adelaide, an SOE agent. Her father is a dear friend of mine."

Brande said hello once more before letting out a sigh and slouching in the backseat.

"I'm Noelle, I'm also SOE." We exchanged smiles.

"Pleased to meet you. When I heard Mathieu Perrine's broadcast tonight, I came out patrolling the area. I've never seen so many SOE agents and Maquisards on the move."

"Tonight turned out to be an important night," Gabriel said as he turned toward me. "I hear you've brought down another factory."

"With plenty of help." I smiled at Brande. He had fallen asleep.

"Where do you need me to take you all?" Adelaide asked.

"I need to go back to Paris—to Renée Apolline's house." I would be wasting my time going back to find Ken. Knowing him, he'd already be headed to Renée's in hopes of meeting me there. We had agreed to always regroup at our last safe house if we ever got split up.

"I will go with you, then." Gabriel's gaze met mine in silent affirmation of his intent to stay with us.

I began to wonder why.

CHAPTER 13

Adelaide hung on Father Gabriel's every word as he recounted how he had managed to disguise himself as an Italian soldier and avoid getting shot in the head by the army. She kept her eyes on him the entire time—which wasn't good since she was still driving.

"Are you a spy for the Vatican?" I leaned forward and stared at him from the backseat.

I found him intriguing, but at the same time I was wary of him. The Gray Tower and the Church had a long history together, dating back to the Middle Ages. Sometimes they got along well, like old drinking buddies, and then at other times, they'd break out into a brawl. The Gray Tower exposed a few spies from the Church in the past, so I didn't think my question was far-fetched. I surmised that the only reason the Masters would allow Father Gabriel to step foot on Tower grounds was because he possessed magical abilities and would be an interesting riddle to solve. Who trained him? Why? And were there more like him?

"I'm here to offer spiritual comfort to the Maquisards. I also intend to help strengthen the relationship between the Vatican and the Gray Tower." He smiled at me from the passenger seat.

"So, you don't consider yourself a wizard?" I tried to keep my expression neutral, but I could barely adjust the look of curiosity I wore.

"I tend to view 'wizard' as a term used for those trained by the Gray Tower. Since I am not trained by the Order, I refrain from using that term."

"Who trained you?"

"My abilities are a gift from God."

Brande stirred and lightly touched my cheek. "Have you rested?"

"No, I'm not tired. The Circle of Healing helped."

"Good. Where are we headed?" His hand dropped, and he yawned and sat up.

I glanced at Gabriel as he once again engaged Adelaide in conversation. "I'm going to Renée Apolline's house. Your priest friend wants to come too."

Brande sighed. "I promised him that I'd escort him to the Gray Tower, so it seems I must follow."

As we neared the winding road that would take us up to Renée's house, the thought of my father's note came to mind. I wasn't sure if Brande knew anything about my father, or if he had ever heard anything from other wizards. Though Brande and I were the same age, he had trained in the Gray Tower before me. In fact, when I had accepted my invitation to train with the Order, Brande was one of my first instructors.

The only thing that really bothered me was that if you didn't fit into one of their pre-determined categories, they would ask you to leave with the status of a lowly Practitioner. It always irritated me how the Order had its designs for everyone's duties...for everyone's lives. Brande might have been fine with letting them groom him to one day replace Ovidio, the Head of the Order, or even one of the Master Council Wizards whom we called "The Three," but I had different plans for my life.

"Can I ask you something?" I slid closer to Brande and lowered my voice. Adelaide and Father Gabriel still spoke with one another.

"What is it?"

"It's about my father. Did you ever hear anything about him?"

"Only that he was highly esteemed and one of our best Elite Wizards. He was a Philosopher."

"Anything else?"

I placed my hand over his, feeling for any signs of nervousness or deception. He stiffened a little, but then slowly turned his wrist and caressed the back of my hand with his thumb. He paused when he realized what I was doing.

"Don't do that." He withdrew his hand.

It was terribly difficult to work body magic on a wizard already adept at it.

"There's something else, isn't there?" I peered into his eyes.

"I don't think..."

"I know he's alive. He left me a note, and a warning." When he showed no sign of shock, I knew he had been aware of this fact.

"Isabella—"

"You could have at least told me. That's what a *real* friend would do." I glared at him and slid back over to my side.

"There are things that you don't understand, and it wasn't my place to say anything."

"Is that what your damned Masters told you? Can't you think for yourself?" I didn't know how, but I was right back in his face. I stared directly into his eyes, daring him to utter a lie or turn away.

"I thought I could protect you."

"From what?" My heart sank as I recalled my father's note. He too, spoke of protection.

"Carson was—"

"Stop the car!" Gabriel threw the door open and was out of the car before it even came to a complete stop.

"Otto!" My shout was a mixture of a scream and a groan. My chest tightened with dread as I got out of the car and rushed toward the old man. He lay sprawled on the ground in front of his house, blood streaming from his mouth and nose. A young man knelt over him, convulsing with sobs.

"What happened?" Adelaide ran over and knelt beside the young man.

"They killed him...they killed him." He steadied his breathing as Gabriel laid his hands on Otto and began praying. My heart sank when I recognized the young man as his son, Lucien.

"Wait...Renée..." My legs moved in the direction of her house before I could even complete my thought.

Another young man came heading toward us from the opposite direction. At first I thought he was injured, but when he lurched to the side and doubled over and heaved, I froze, and a cold empty feeling took over my mind, as if this were a bizarre dream.

"What's going on? Who are you?" Brande approached the man and grabbed hold of him, making sure he didn't keel over or run.

"I'm Ernest. I'm a friend of Lucien's. I went to check on that lady and...you don't want to go up there."

"Renée!" I suddenly had the will to move again. I dashed toward her house, already feeling as sick as Ernest was. I called her name again, not caring if my screeches alerted the entire neighborhood. I just knew I had to find her, even if I wouldn't like what I found.

"Stop! Don't you see those lights down there? Trekkers are on their way, and it's almost past curfew." Brande threw his muscular arms around me, but I pivoted just in time to push him away. I continued running.

"Renée!" Why was I rushing toward despair and horror?

"Isabella, stop!" Brande was on me again, but this time I felt his magic at work. My muscles involuntarily relaxed, and my limbs went limp. I slumped to the ground, weeping out of anger and helplessness. My worst fear had come true...I failed her.

"I have to go to her." My pleas went unheeded.

Brande scooped me up in his arms and brought me back to the car. The darkness in the sky began to recede as dawn broke. "I'm sorry," he said.

"It's because someone's betrayed us." How else would they have known? There were too many secrets, and too many of them in the open for the enemy to see.

"Then we'll find them." He set me down.

Lucien and Ernest were already in the backseat of the car, and Ernest had to restrain his friend from jumping out and running toward Otto's lifeless body. Father Gabriel urged us to split the group and meet elsewhere. Adelaide sat in the car, trembling and raking a hand through her shoulder length hair. In a high-pitched voice she kept asking us where we should go, and I thought of the only other place Ken would go if he weren't able to reach Renée.

"We'll all meet at the Red Lady's house, Adelaide."

"But I thought she doesn't..."

"Just do it. Take Lucien and his friend. You'll have to go around the long way so they don't catch you."

She raked her hand through her hair again. A few strands snapped and got caught in her fingers. "Okay. We'll meet you there."

As she sped off down the road, I gestured for Brande and Gabriel to follow me. "We'll have to go through Renée's backyard. She has a tool shed that connects with an underground tunnel. We can come out through the chapel once the road is clear."

We picked up our pace when we heard the trekkers come up the road. When we made it to Renée's, I noticed that her front door was ajar and not a single light flickered inside.

But she shouldn't be left alone in the dark...

Fresh tears welled up and I felt sick to my stomach. We ran down the walkway that led to the backyard then went into the tool shed. As we went through the underground tunnel, all I could think about was how I could've helped Renée and Otto if I had arrived earlier.

When we reached the end of the tunnel, Father Gabriel asked, "How long do you think we should wait before going up into the chapel?"

"I'll let you know. I've done this before." I glanced at Brande, who produced a small flame that hovered above his open palm. He stood silent yet attentive, and eyed me with a somber expression.

A part of me wished that Father Gabriel would've accompanied Adelaide and the others in the car. I didn't feel comfortable talking about certain things with Brande in front of Gabriel. I still didn't know what the priest's intentions were, or if I could trust him as an ally. All I knew was that two people I cared about had been murdered, that there was very little information to lead me to Heilwig and the laboratory—and I was running out of will power, and time.

~

The sun began its ascension into the morning sky when we knocked on Jasmine's front door. The maid gave us an eyeful when she answered, and it dawned on me that I still wore my bloody, tattered SS nurse's uniform. I was still in shock over Renée and could hardly speak, but I let out a grateful sigh when Penn came to the door and welcomed us in. Gabriel took it upon himself to explain that Adelaide and the others would be coming soon, and Penn assured him that he would prepare for their arrival. Gabriel then asked leave to go upstairs and rest.

Brande and I followed Penn down the wide, art-decked hallway and into the immaculate living room where Jasmine liked to receive her guests. She sat on a plush sofa, wearing a silken white robe and drinking coffee as she read a newspaper. I expected her to be caught off-guard, or even a little perturbed at our unannounced arrival. She preferred her home to be off limits. However, when she caught a glimpse of me, she set down her coffee and newspaper and rushed toward me, pulling me into a tight embrace.

"Oh, Emelie..." She broke away to greet Brande and hugged him, but quickly grabbed hold of me again and guided me toward the sofa.

"Jasmine...I didn't know where else to go."

"Honey, don't worry about it." She sat next to me, still holding me close. "Lydie! Bring out some breakfast for my friends."

Brande sat in a chair across from us with his head bent. His posture was in an almost contemplative pose. He did that whenever he felt troubled, and for a second I thought of saying something to help put him at ease, but then my anger got the better of me and I said nothing. I just couldn't put aside the fact that he had kept knowledge of my father away from me. He knew my past, and he knew how I felt about it. I began to wonder what he would have to gain if he slipped the wrong person my name and information. Was it him?

"Renée is dead." I lowered my head when I said this to Jasmine. I felt responsible and ashamed. "The Black Wolves know who I really am. We can't trust anyone."

Jasmine's lips trembled, and she shook her head in disbelief. Tears formed in her deep-set eyes. In that moment, we just sat there, unable to speak, trying to sort through our thoughts and sorrow. Lydie returned with a serving cart and placed a plate of food in front of me. She then set up a tray next to Brande and did the same for him. He thanked her and reminded her to send something upstairs for Father Gabriel. Penn emerged from the kitchen with a pitcher of water and a couple of glasses. He poured some water and offered it to us, but we declined.

"Are you sure there isn't anything I can get you?" Penn wore a pained expression. Although Renée used to chide him for his bootlegging ways, she always welcomed him into her home, and he cared about her as well. I wondered if Penn was disappointed in me for not saving her.

"We're fine." Jasmine blew her nose into a handkerchief and offered another one to me.

The doorbell rang, and Penn started toward the front. "By the way," he nodded in the direction of the kitchen before heading toward the hallway, "your sweetheart is in the nook in the back having breakfast."

"Ken's here?" Just as I stood, he came through the doorway. I rushed toward him and threw myself into his arms. I made sure to be careful, since his right arm had been bandaged, and he walked with a limp.

I planted kisses on his lips, cheeks, and forehead. We said nothing, and we didn't have to. We just held each other for what seemed like an eternity, and we found comfort in that. It gave me the strength I needed to repeat to him what had happened to Renée, and he held me even more tightly while murmuring words of consolation.

"Well," Jasmine stood, "it sounds like we have a few more guests coming in. I think you need to introduce me to these people you have up in my house, Brande."

I kissed Ken again and tightened my embrace. From the corner of my eye I saw Brande rise from his seat and quickly look away as Jasmine walked with him. Before Jasmine turned the corner, she gave me a sidelong glance. I felt a little guilty, because I knew what it was for.

I did very well at pretending I was unaware of Brande's affection for me. When I was younger and in the Gray Tower, I did have a crush on him, but nothing came of it. When I left and returned home before going to England, he finally expressed his feelings, but then, at the time, I didn't want anything to do with the Gray Tower or anyone associated with it. I ended up ascribing it all to mere infatuation on both our parts and left it at that, assuming he would do the same.

At times I felt that he was on the verge of contradicting this, whether it was a single look, the tone of his voice when he spoke to me, or the way he grew silent if I ever mentioned Ken. Because of that, I made sure to be as considerate as possible, but I wasn't going to hide the fact that Ken and I adored each other. We were drawn to one another since we first met...since he...stole a copy of my file...

Ken looked directly into my eyes. "For a moment, I thought you wouldn't make it."

"Where's Bernard?" I loosened my hold on him.

"He fell through the trees and got knocked unconscious. I had some Maquisards take him back to Mantes to see a doctor. Now, would you mind not sending me away like that?"

My stomach tightened, and I pulled away. He was good—I'd give him that. To make me feel foolish and shy away from doubts and questions, and to be in the right place at the right time to make it seem like he had saved me and had been looking out for me. I even bought his sob story about his Amsterdam mission.

"Kenneth, remember that conversation we had before we went into the Vélizy factory?"

"Yes." He reached for my hand, but I rebuffed him.

"Everything was a lie, wasn't it?" Renée's face flashed in my mind. I would never see her again.

"What are you talking about?" His jaw dropped, and he stared at me.

"So did you leave my file lying around somewhere? Or did you sell it?"

"Are you insane?" He looked hurt, and it made me hurt too, but damn it, he was trained to be a good actor, and to make people believe who he was and believe his words.

"I'd feel better if it were blackmail, at least that you were forced to do it and really didn't want to."

"Did that warlock hit you with some kind of crazy spell? If I'm a traitor, then why the hell would I be risking my life fighting by your side?"

I ignored his question. "After I neutralized the chemicals at the factory, why did you stay behind in the basement?"

"To take a last look at those notes and documents in there. I wanted to see if I could find anything about the laboratories."

"What about the Cairo job? Why did you steal money from Badru? Were you rogue, or playing dirty?"

"That *murderer* built his wealth on the blood of innocent people, so I took his money away and gave it back to its real owners."

Great, now he wanted to play Robin Hood. "Well...did you leave a copy of my file—"

"No I didn't—"

"And someone saw it—"

"I destroyed it—"

"Then how do our enemies know—"

"I feel bad about Renée too, but if you want someone to blame, then start with the people who killed her."

"Then what about that day we were at her house and Penn came by? You lied about going to see your contacts. Who did you go see?"

"I'm not a traitor."

"Answer the question." I reached forward and caressed his cheek. Not out of affection, but because I was ready to stop his heart from beating. It would be easy.

He narrowed his eyes. "You think you know everything, don't you? Well, at least I know where we stand."

"Just answer me." When I saw him slip his hand into his pocket, I sent a quick tendril of energy straight to his head. He convulsed and cried out in pain as he fell to his knees.

I stepped away. He gasped but kept his hand in his pocket. It seemed to strain him physically, but he finally revealed what he had kept hidden—a ring box.

"Oh, Ken..." I groaned as he carefully set the box on the floor in between us.

I moved toward him so I could touch him and reverse the body magic, but he raised his arm to ward me off. He slowly rose to his feet, with his face screwed up in pain, and faced me.

I almost choked on my words. "Do you see why I wanted out? Why this had to be my last mission?"

"No, I don't." He flexed his right arm. "This isn't you. What happened to you?"

"I got tired."

"And I wasn't good enough?"

"I'm sorry." I grabbed his hand. I was glad that he didn't pull away. Now all I needed was for him to come with me. I'd be willing to endure his resentment and his distrust. I'd give him all the time he needed. All I wanted was for him to agree to leave with me.

He shook his head. "You gave up...you're giving up on everything."

"I gritted my teeth in frustration. "I'm not giving up."

"Oh, that's right, you call it *retiring*."

"There's nothing wrong with retiring!"

"I'm seeing this entire war through to the end. I'm sorry that you couldn't."

My jaw tightened. "This is supposed to be my last assignment. And, there are things I have to take care of with my family."

"Are your mother and brother all right?"

I nodded. "They're okay."

He sighed and retrieved the ring box. "Good."

"Ken..."

He opened my hand and handed me the box. I clutched it and tried to speak. No words came forth.

"Maybe this was all doomed from the start, and maybe I was just too blind to see it."

I deserved that, though it felt like a slow and painful death. "Goodbye, Kenneth. You deserve better."

He kissed my forehead. "I didn't want better. I wanted you. Take care of yourself."

As he pulled himself away and headed toward the coat closet, he instructed one of the maids to deliver a final thanks to Jasmine for her hospitality. I stood there feeling like the crappiest person on earth. Part of me wanted to take off and chase him, to throw myself into his arms again and promise to stay with him and make amends. I regretted that it wasn't the part of me that won out, because I just stood motionless, like a coward, and only when it was too late and I was alone, did I utter: "I love you."

～

"I remember one time when I had to smuggle an important map from the Maquis leaders to our OSS friends in Spain. They booked a show for me in a nightclub in Madrid where someone was going to meet me. Anyhow, I've known people to memorize entire maps like this, but I told Renée that I didn't have time to memorize the whole thing and I was too damned nervous to try. She said, 'Jasmine, you are *La Dame Rouge*—use that to your advantage.' So, I ended up at the airport with my luggage being checked by Nazis and I was awfully scared. I made it through and made it back again from the other side without a problem.

"When I saw her again, she looked so proud and asked me, 'How did you do it?' She probably thought I had taken her advice and used my celebrity to walk right by the searches, but instead I told her I wasn't into the whole smooth talk psychological games. Just give me a secret, and I'll take it with me to the grave, but don't have me playing spy. I told her that I took the map with me...and had sewn the thing into my undergarments! She looked at me like I was absolutely certifiable, and she never let me forget it. I've come a long way, haven't I?"

I laughed so hard that I had to set my wineglass aside. "I can imagine the look on her face...I didn't know you two were so close."

"Yeah, we had some wild times." Jasmine sniffed, and her smile faded. "Now I know what she meant about being tired of all this shit. I'm tired of seeing people die. Anyhow, are you going to tell me why your sweetheart left so early?"

"Ken isn't my sweetheart."

With a sullen expression I took another sip of Château. Maybe he was right about us being doomed from the start. Maybe he didn't know me as well as he thought he did. Ken knew little about this other world I belonged to. He only knew I was an alchemist and respected my training, but he had never seen or experienced everything I had, and, whether I liked it or not, I would always have ties to the Gray Tower. People like me tended to have enemies, secrets, and lousy luck when it came to holding together a marriage, especially with a non-wizard. Even my parents, as perfect and romantic as they were, at times argued about my father's work with the Order. One day it had gotten so intense that all I remember was my mother screaming at my father. He had ushered me toward a car and driven me away.

"Honey, save it for someone else." Jasmine languidly stretched on her bed and threw me a glance. "I was so sure you were going to marry Blondie that I had already bought a dress to wear to the wedding."

I ignored her comment. I sat at her bedroom windowsill with the window half open, enjoying the fresh air and the view of the stars. We were waiting for Penn to return since he had promised to find out anything he could about the research laboratories. I could only hope Dr. Heilwig was at one of them.

I turned to face her. "Well, what about Penn? Why is he always around?"

"Wouldn't *you* like to know!"

Her expression elicited a small grin from me. I glanced out the window that overlooked the garden. I saw Brande down below, walking and talking with Father Gabriel. The two seemed engrossed in conversation, although he did look up once. I timidly waved at him and he stared at me for a moment before turning his gaze back to Gabriel.

"What's wrong, Emelie…uh, sorry, *Noelle*?"

"I think Brande hates me." I closed the window. I'd be lucky if anyone even wanted to be around me by the end of the week.

"You know that's not true, and I don't want to see you moping around like this. Why don't you go downstairs with Adelaide, or Lucien and his friend? Did you get a good look at his friend?"

"I don't feel like talking to anyone."

"You don't have to talk. I just don't want you to be alone."

"I think I'm sleepy."

"Tell Lucien I'm sorry about his father, and I'll speak with him in the morning."

"Jasmine…"

"Thanks! Close the door behind you."

"All right…one drink, and then I'm off to bed."

"Goodnight."

"Yeah…goodnight."

I went downstairs through the living room and into the kitchen nook. Lucien and Ernest sat at the table downing drinks and viewing a solitary candle sitting at the center of the table. I decided not to flip on the light switch and walked toward them. Lucien stared at the candle's flame, muttering something in French before kissing the tip of his extended fore and middle fingers. He touched the bottom of the candle.

"Rest in Eternal Light, Father."

Ernest imitated his friend's gesture. "Rest in peace."

They looked up as I cleared my throat. "Hi."

"Hey," Ernest gestured toward the empty seat next to him. Lucien just stared at me.

"I'm sorry about your father," I said, still standing. "Jasmine is as well. She said she'll speak with you in the morning, if that's okay."

Lucien bowed his head and peered into his empty glass. "Thank you."

Ernest stood and offered me his hand. "I don't think we've been properly introduced. I'm Ernest Wilson."

I shook his hand. "I'm...Noelle."

"American?"

I smiled in response and took my seat. "And, so are you. Are you with OSS?"

"Somewhat, and I don't mean anything by it, but I didn't know they were sending out lady agents now."

I shook my head. "They're not, I'm an SOE agent."

Ernest glanced at Lucien and asked in French, "How about that, Luce? Ever been to London?"

"Ah," I switched over to French, "so you speak the language of love?"

"Don't encourage him," Lucien said.

"Blame it on my Creole grandmother." Ernest chuckled.

"How long will you two be in France?"

"Long enough to go hunt some Nazis." Ernest sat back with a sour expression. I supposed they weren't the only ones with retribution on their minds.

Otto said they had been on special assignment in Spain. Perhaps they'd be willing to help me out on this one. "If that's the case, then why don't you join me? I'm going after one of their labs. This could be a big win for our side."

Ernest poured another drink. "We've raided one of those before, headed by that Dr. Meier. Those Nazi sons of bitches were experimenting on people."

"The lab I want to break into develops weapons," I said, trying to block out nightmarish images that flashed in my mind. "I don't know what your plans are, but—"

"It won't work," Lucien said as he pushed his empty glass aside.

"We went in with a band of highly trained military men. Who would come with us?"

"Me, for starters, and a few other people."

Lucien sighed. "I don't doubt that you're good at what you do...Noelle...but I'm not sure you know what you'd be getting into. Why don't you go sabotage a factory?"

"I've done that," I said, crossing my arms. I didn't like his tone at all, but I reminded myself to be a little more patient with him, for Otto's sake.

"What kind of weapons are we talking about?" Ernest asked. Lucien glared at him as if telling him not to give me false hope.

"The same ones that took out Ally soldiers on the Western Front. This is the place where they created The Plague." I hoped I could at least get Ernest on my side, though I doubted one friend would go without the other.

Ernest frowned and shook his head. "And where exactly is this lab supposed to be?"

"Penn's never failed me. He's out there getting the information for us as we speak. Once he gets back with what we need, we can pinpoint the lab's location and then head out."

"We'll think about it," Lucien said without looking up.

I wondered if he was just moody or a jerk all the time. "It won't break my heart if you don't come."

Lucien leaned forward. "The lab we raided last year was in Catalonia. It ran underground beneath the Spanish and French borders. Twenty of us went in, and only three came out. A Black Wolf killed half of us within ten minutes. And you want to walk into one of these places?"

"Brande and I trained with the Gray Tower, and Father Gabriel...has abilities too. I think the three of us could take on a Black Wolf."

Ernest blew a low whistle. "I hope you don't take this the wrong way, but we had a wizard leading the group, and it turned out he was more worried about saving his own skin than looking out for the men."

"I'm not that type of wizard—or that type of person."

"But one of your type was the one to lead seventeen men to their deaths." Lucien gazed at me. "He couldn't care less about those of us without powers."

Ernest finished his drink. "The only reason Luce and I survived was because we stuck with each other and knew when to get out. The wizard survived because he magicked himself away."

I really didn't like the direction this conversation was going in. "Listen, I just lost two people who were important to me, who were willing to sacrifice themselves. I'd do the same in a heartbeat; so don't lump me in with whatever you think all wizards are like."

Ernest lowered his gaze and looked embarrassed. His expression told me that he was at least considering my words. Lucien just fell back into his angry stare.

"Like I said, Ernest and I will think about it."

At this point I was done for the night. "Okay then, I'll see you in the morning."

I went back upstairs to my guest room, wondering if I had made the right move in inviting Lucien along. We could certainly use his firepower and expertise, but if he couldn't trust me or even tolerate me, then maybe it would be better for him to stay here and give himself time to grieve over his father.

I thought of Otto and Renée once more, and a numb feeling came over me. I crawled into bed, replaying in my mind how I didn't arrive soon enough to save them. After lying in bed for an hour, the tension in my shoulders finally eased, and with a little body magic, I warded off an oncoming headache. All I wanted was sleep, to at least escape this hell for just a while. Every waking second, all I could think of were the friends I lost and those I felt responsible for losing.

~

I dreamed about my father. I'd had this dream countless times before. It always started with an odd fire that surrounded me but never consumed me. I would be cowering in a small place, probably the tool shed from our backyard. I would scream for help, and as soon as my father opened the door, the flames would disappear and I would feel safe. Then, for some reason, my father would also disappear and leave me all alone.

I was always my eight-year-old self in this dream. I knew that I saw things from the perspective of a child and couldn't fully comprehend what was happening. I had gone through several books trying to find interpretations, but nothing ever made sense.

I awoke with a start and couldn't go back to sleep, so I slipped out of bed and went to bathe. Afterward, I wrapped myself in a robe Jasmine lent me and wondered what to do next. I glanced at the clock—it was 4 a.m., and it seemed everyone but me enjoyed a peaceful rest.

I went downstairs to the kitchen and found the last of the Château chilling in the icebox. I grabbed a glass from the china cabinet, made my way to the little breakfast nook in the back, and poured my wine. I could go from eating fine cuisines in one week to supping on porridge the next, but I figured I might as well enjoy a fine wine while I could.

After I downed a couple of glasses, I decided to use the phone to call home, well, my brother's home. My mother sold the house in Baltimore and moved up to Cambridge with Jonathan and his wife two years ago. I fumbled a bit before finally steadying the receiver in my hand and getting a ring. I patiently waited until I heard my brother's sleepy voice on the other end.

"Hello?"

"Jonathan...it's me."

"Izzy?"

"Yes."

"Where are you?"

"The ambassador has me in France for a while. How are you?" My family didn't know that SOE had recruited me. They still believed I was a hard-working clerk in the office of the U.S. ambassador to England.

"It's nice of you to call, but you do know that it's almost 11 o'clock at night here?"

"Sorry, I forgot."

"Shouldn't you be asleep?"

"I just wanted to talk to you."

"How did you get through without an operator?"

"I put a spell on the phone."

"Really? You ought to come visit Harvard one day."

"No, I'm not going to guest lecture in one of your stuffy classes." I laughed.

"I've got to find some way to get my worldly little sister out here."

"Believe it or not, I'd like to visit soon. How's your wife?"

"Rachel is fine. She's asleep."

"I can't wait to meet her, Johnnie."

"If you call back during the day, I'll be sure to put Mother on the phone."

"I'll try, but don't say anything to her. I don't want her to be disappointed if I can't call back."

"I understand. Are you working with the Gray Tower too?"

"I'm a little busy, but I'll get around to my studies again. Listen...I should go, Johnnie."

"Goodnight, and I want to see you soon. I miss you."

"Goodnight." I hung up the phone and quickly stifled a sob with the back of my hand. I glanced around to see if any food had been left out, since the wine was getting to my head. To my surprise, Brande walked in, but I didn't want him to see me like this, so I lowered my head and poured another glass—yes, I knew, brilliant.

"What are you doing up this late?" I pretended to sip my wine. I knew that if I drank anymore that I'd make myself sick.

"To you, it may be late, but to me, it's early." He leaned over with his muscular frame and took the bottle away, setting it on the counter. He came and sat in the chair across from me.

"So...you're talking to me now."

"Did I ever stop?"

"Did the Gray Tower call and tell you to come downstairs to see what I was up to?"

His jaw slackened. "Jasmine asked me to find you. Penn is here."

"Does he have the information I need?"

"I think so."

"And you and Father Gabriel are coming?"

"Yes." He looked a little perturbed.

"I'll go get dressed then." I rose from my seat. As I walked past, he grabbed my hand. I shuddered when I felt a warm tingling sensation.

"It's...so you won't get sick." He released my hand.

I reached for the cut above his brow. "What about you?"

"I'll be fine."

"No, I insist." I lightly touched the scar and reciprocated the spell he performed on me. I could also detect the pain in his arm where Marc's dagger grazed him. It would probably take a few more rounds of healing to set it right.

It wasn't uncommon for wizards like us who dealt with mentally strenuous disciplines to choose a secondary form of magic like body magic. It allowed us to restore ourselves and provide another outlet for our powers. However, not many went the route of elemental magic. The only other person who I respected as a brilliant elemental was Kostek Ovidio, the Head of the Order of Wizards.

"Thank you," he said.

"You're welcome."

As I turned and headed upstairs, I rubbed the part of my hand where Brande had touched me. I thought about how it made me feel. It amazed me how complementary an alchemist and an elemental could be. He understood how to use and control the natural elements of earth, water, fire and air, and I understood how to use and control the properties of natural elements found in the earth. I could always sense when his magic was at work, and I was certain he felt mine. It made me wonder if we ever united and unleashed our full powers on a foe, what kind of a magical storm it would be.

But no, I don't think we'd be a storm...we would be fire.

CHAPTER 14

Penn confirmed what Bernard had told me last night, that we had to choose among three cities: Dijon, Nice, and Reims. Penn used all his ingenuity, resources, and a few bribes, to find out which of the three hosted the laboratory.

After visiting a few contacts, he had ruled out Nice because he found that the Nazis began pulling key projects away from areas occupied by Mussolini's men. Traitors above all feared being betrayed, and so after the Nazis double-crossed their Soviet allies, their alliance with the Italian government unofficially began degenerating.

Then it was down to Reims and Dijon. Reims stood in a comfortable strategic location for the German Armed Forces, being not too far from Germany itself. It had been accosted and usurped by Germany in the Franco-Prussian War, and the first Great War, so it would feel like coming home for the German Army. The Führer would have been further lured by the history of the town, which boasted of Roman arches still standing from the glorious days of the Roman Empire, kings being coronated in its cathedral, and even of miraculous oils and ancient relics.

Based on all the information, Reims became the apparent

choice. We agreed that as our cover Brande and I were postulants on retreat with Father Gabriel. Since it would have been suspicious in more ways than one for a young woman to be traveling alone with men to whom she had no relation, Gabriel said that I could claim him as my cousin. After enduring Lucien's half-hearted apology, I accepted his and Ernest's offer to back us up. We agreed that they would be dropped off before we reached town so they could come in separately. We didn't want our group to be too large.

Adelaide lent us her car, and Father Gabriel volunteered to drive. I hopped in next to him and took the passenger seat. Brande, Ernest, and Lucien took the backseat. As we headed out on the road toward Reims, I thought about how Ernest's presence would be useful since there would definitely be German Armed Forces protecting the lab, but I wasn't as confident in Lucien. I knew he wanted to come so he could get a chance to avenge his father's death, but in his state of mind, a person didn't always think or act straight.

My thoughts wandered toward Ken, and all of a sudden I felt like turning around and trying to find him. I ignored this urge and turned toward Father Gabriel and began chatting him up as a distraction. However, as soon as I started asking him about his Vatican connections, one stern look from Brande prompted me to make small talk elsewhere. Lucien nodded off and looked like he needed more sleep, and when I noted how much he looked like Otto, I felt sorry for him, because he'd never see his father again.

I hoped that we'd be able to depend on Lucien, and that he would be able to focus on the mission at hand. I'd seen his mood in other people who experienced great loss. They would appear normal for a while, and would even interact with you, then suddenly their disposition would change and they would grow sullen or depressed. It also bothered me that I could taste the toxic essence of cadmium metal coming off him. If I asked Ernest about it and started prying into Lucien's habits, he'd refuse to explain anything and clam up. I decided to ease into conversation with Ernest first, and asked him about how he began working alongside OSS.

"I trained with the Red Tails." Ernest had a proud gleam in his soft brown eyes.

"The Tuskegee pilots?" I shifted in my seat to a more comfortable position.

"One and the same. I flew missions against the Italian army in the Mediterranean, but one day, two of our pilots were assassinated."

"What? How?"

"They got into their planes, and before the planes even took off, they exploded. I guess the enemy didn't like all the damage we dealt. And let me tell you, half of us were scared to get back into our planes afterward."

The car swerved. I gazed at Gabriel for a few seconds. "Were...you just driving on the wrong side of the road, Father?"

He stroked his chin. "It would seem so."

The car accelerated, but it didn't seem to bother Ernest. "We figured we needed to catch whoever was planting bombs before anyone else died. So based on a lead, I ended up posing as a Moroccan businessman in Casablanca."

"Because you trained as a spy?" I glared at Father Gabriel before facing Ernest again.

"No, I was the only fool crazy enough to take the assignment! I was going back and forth between there and Spain. I know enough French to make my way around, and I would pass along things I'd hear from French speakers in the area. No one ever said anything that could lead us to the assassin."

The car horn blared, and we swooped through a crossroad. I looked at Father Gabriel again and frowned. "Does anyone else care that we almost crashed back there?"

"We'll be fine." Brande yawned.

"You want me to finish my story?"

"Sure, Ernest. At this rate, it may be the last one I hear."

"I ran out of leads until I met a spy named Galeno. We kind of became drinking buddies, and one day he told me that he had a lead on the assassin."

"But how did you end up in Spain for so long?" I shifted again in my seat. "Didn't the Red Tails need you?"

Lucien rubbed his eyes and leaned forward. "They called him out for another flight and Galeno was waiting for him. He was the assassin all along, but he's the sick type who likes to play games with his targets. He shot Ernest right out of the sky."

"Faster than Babe Ruth whacking a ball," Ernest quipped.

"You mean the Bambino?" We both laughed when Lucien and Brande exchanged confused glances at my reference to the famous baseball player.

Ernest continued. "Anyway, I landed in Spanish territory and ended up doing side jobs for OSS while I waited on orders from the Red Tails. That's how I met Lucien."

"We're almost there." Gabriel flashed me a smile.

Ernest nodded toward Lucien. "I saved his life three times already. He loves trouble, and trouble loves him."

Lucien gave him a critical eye. "What about that time I saved you from that ambush in that brothel?"

"I told you, Galeno went in there—and I followed."

"Yes, for four hours." Lucien nudged Brande, and to my surprise, he laughed.

I scowled at the idea of him being amused with anything having to do with whorehouses. I turned to Father Gabriel. "Are you going to let them talk like that?"

The priest eyed me as if expecting me to whack him over the head. "Perhaps we should focus our thoughts and conversation on more...immediate matters."

I crossed my arms. "Men..."

The drive took us over an hour, and we dropped off Ernest and Lucien as planned. Before noon, we were taking in the view of Reims' rolling hills and bountiful vineyards. The city was nestled next to the Vesle River and looked splendid beneath the morning sun. I could see why it attracted many people, and this worked to our advantage. No one took particular notice of us as we pulled up to a quaint hostel called Le Fleur and asked for rooms. We gauged our surroundings and noted some German military, and even a few SS officers, moving about the city, but there were so few that I began wondering if we had chosen the right place.

My stomach rumbled with hunger, so I decided to enjoy a nice meal and let one of the guys do the fretting. I thanked Claire, the waitress, who brought us chilled wine and set a large platter of fruit and cheese on our table. With a warm smile, she urged us to take our time browsing, pointing out that the menu listed both German and French dishes. As she left to give us time to decide, I leaned into Brande.

"When you're done with your meal, go to the smoking room and see how Lucien's doing."

"He looks fine, so far." Brande glanced at Lucien as he sat at the bar and started up a chat with an attractive blonde. Ernest ordered drinks.

I drummed my fingers on the table. "We need him, but we don't need him being a wreck."

"He says he wants to fight, and since we can only anticipate what's waiting for us at that lab, I think we'll need both him and Ernest." Brande drank some wine.

"Yeah, well a soldier who wants to go in with blazing weapons, not caring whether he lives or dies, will likely get himself killed." My knuckles turned white from gripping the menu so tightly.

"Is that your concern? People grieve in different ways."

I frowned. "Just find a way to tell Ernest to make sure Lucien doesn't pull a *kamikaze* on us."

"Then perhaps I should speak with him." Gabriel stirred his coffee.

"Fine, I don't care who does it...God, my lunch is already going to be ruined."

"Language, please."

"Sorry...Father."

"What will you be having, then?" Claire brought out a pitcher of cold water and stood ready to take our orders.

"Well," Gabriel took one last look at the menu, "I'm looking forward to the rabbit stew. We're all going to have the rabbit stew, and some Château would be nice. I hope you both don't mind me ordering for you."

I set my menu on the table. "Well, never mind what I might want...continue."

"We'll have crepes, and more coffee too. That will be all."

"My, you must be starving!" She collected our menus. "Where are you from?"

Gabriel spoke up. "I'm leading these two postulants on a retreat. They're deciding whether or not to enter a monastery. This young man is a good friend of our family, and the young lady here is my cousin."

Claire's smile widened. "Well, bless you! I wish you luck. I'll be back soon with your entrée." She left to fill our orders.

Brande grunted when I gestured for him to go follow Lucien and Ernest to the smoking room, where men congregated and smoked their cigars. Once again, I tasted the sour tinge of cadmium in the air, and I spotted Lucien fondling something in his pocket. As I feared, he fell into a mood swing, and became sullen and irritable. I groaned at the prospect of several more mood swings that were sure to come. I was headed over to the bar when I saw a middle-aged SS officer enter. His belted tan jacket, black pants, and immaculate dress shoes, all clued me in to who he likely was.

"Good afternoon, *Stellenleiter* Vester. How are you today?" The balding man at the bar smiled and began mixing a drink for him.

A *Stellenleiter* was an SS local office head. He was most likely the highest-ranking officer here, and if anyone would know about the laboratory, it would be him.

"You know, the usual." Vester took off his cap. "But I must admit, this is far more pleasant than sitting in that moldy office back in Nuremburg."

Several Masters of the Order believed Nuremburg Castle housed the famous occult items and relics Hitler had been collecting, such as the Spear of Destiny and the Grand Grimoire. That belief was reinforced when several attempts to infiltrate the castle were thwarted by over a dozen Black Wolves. Vester must have thought himself important to work out of Nuremburg, and wore his uniform with an irritating arrogance.

I also noticed that he wore a talisman ring with the image of an owl on it; it guarded against body magic. It took me a few seconds to realize that it was Veit Heilwig's ring. I wanted to punch Vester right then and there, but I decided not to miss my opportunity, since he would be my key to finding out where the lab and Heilwig were. I hopped onto the seat next to the blonde and gave her a subtle nudge.

"Hey sister, beat it."

She turned and faced me with an offended look, but I stared her down and she stormed away. The bartender came over and asked what I'd like to drink.

"Just a water please, thank you." I spoke loud enough to draw Vester's attention. He eyed me for a few seconds before closing the gap between us.

"Usually, when people sit at a bar, they want liquor." He stared at my chest.

"Well, I'm not much of a drinker. You see, I'm here with my cousin—that priest over there. He's leading me on a retreat so I can decide if I want to join a convent. I've read about Saint Joan of

Arc and what she did here, and I must say that I already feel inspired."

"That would be a waste. You look no older than twenty five."

Suddenly my urge to punch him returned. I expected him to say twenty, at most. "Should age determine desire?"

"Not at all, my dear. In fact, I find that with age comes much experience. Perhaps, I can teach you a few things."

Not in a thousand years, buddy. "Well, my food is ready."

"How long will you be in town?"

"Less than a week, *Monsieur*—"

"Vester...Simon Vester. Well, I have a prior engagement for the rest of the day, but tomorrow evening I would be happy to escort you and give you a private tour of the city."

"Wouldn't it be better to tour during the day?"

"You don't know this city like I do, darling."

"I don't think I would be allowed to."

"There's no need to worry. I'm not like those other officers. I'm in charge, and I love being here...the food, the countryside, and the pretty girls. I love it! This is so much more amusing than sitting in a stinky old office. I swear I am a gentleman, and you will be safe with me."

"Well, perhaps a small tour wouldn't hurt."

"Not at all, I swear it. Do you like shopping? I think all girls do." He pressed the back of my hand to his lips. "Shall we meet tomorrow at 6 o'clock?"

"Yes...and my name is Noelle." Resisting the urge to gag, I headed back over to my table. Brande had returned from the smoking room, and I took my place between him and Gabriel.

"What was that all about?" Brande left most of his plate untouched.

"I have a date." I fondled the case of garnet lipstick in my pocket. I was saving it for when I really needed it. The talisman ring didn't protect against red garnet, so I would use it on Simon

Vester tomorrow evening so I could find the lab and rescue Heilwig.

※

The guys went out scouting the city. They even looked for any Maquisards who could help with the lab raid. I declined to join them and took advantage of the rare opportunity to lounge at a café. I even went to a small dress shop, where I bought a powder blue dress that caught my eye. However, when I made it back to my room at Le Fleur, I sadly realized that I probably would have no reason to wear it unless I used it as part of a cover.

With the exception of cash, a few weapons, and special items, I didn't carry much on me. I didn't even have much of a wardrobe at home since I hardly resided in my flat in London. Sometimes, when I did return there, I'd go straight to Baker Street and then back to the air hangar.

Regret consumed me as I thought about Ken, and if I had convinced him to leave with me, we'd already be in each other's arms somewhere far away. The only thing that helped me keep my resolve was the thought of Stella, Otto...and Renée. If for nothing else, I needed to finish this for them.

I ate dinner in my room, since the men hadn't yet returned, and I tried to drive away my doubts and sour thoughts through reading. I went to the rickety bookshelf in my guest room and browsed the books inside. I immediately grabbed the Emily Dickinson poetry collection and lounged on my bed. After an hour, I heard a knock on the door.

"Come in."

It was Brande. He had a newspaper rolled up beneath his arm. He acknowledged me with a nod, went straight for the large cushiony chair in the corner, and sat down. He unfurled his newspaper and began reading. "We decided that someone should keep watch here, since Simon Vester turned out to be a man of ill-repute."

Well, with his tall muscular build, he could take on anyone of ill repute. "So, after seven hours, the only thing you geniuses found out was that Simon Vester is a bad man?"

"One night under watch won't hurt. If your plan works tomorrow, we'll find the lab and raid it. Then we'll be done with all this."

"I can take care of myself."

"I know."

"Well, why does it have to be you?" I had the feeling this was all his idea.

"Ernest and Lucien need to maintain their separate cover. They're only here for backup. And, I don't want you badgering Father Gabriel about whether or not he's a Vatican spy. I'm the only logical choice."

He was such a liar. "Oh, spare me your logic."

I grabbed a pillow and flung it at him—without looking up from his newspaper, he caught it with his right hand and placed it behind his head.

"Thank you."

And he wondered why I sometimes kicked him out of my Baker Street office. With a sigh, I rolled over and re-opened the book, scanning the pages until I reached the poem on which my father's message was based. I replayed the words in my mind:

> *Safe in their alabaster chambers,*
> *untouched by morning and untouched by noon,*
> *sleep the meek members of the resurrection,*
> *rafter of satin, and roof of stone.*

I drifted into a quiet sleep, devoid of any dreams of watching my father appear and disappear in a blaze of unnatural fire.

I awoke in the morning with my book still near me, and Brande gone. On my way to the bathroom, I noticed the faint glow of a Circle of Protection around my bed, and despite myself, I smiled. I quickly washed and brushed my teeth, deciding to go with the blue dress I bought. My only other option was the blouse and skirt Jasmine had lent me when I left her house. However, I did put on the thin gold bracelet she gave me as a parting gift.

When I came down for breakfast, I saw only Father Gabriel sitting at the table we had shared yesterday. I joined him and began eating and drinking the meal that Claire set for me. Today he wore a cassock and a cape, no doubt using it to conceal his sword. I understood how he felt about having his weapon on him; even though I still had the silver knife from Bernard, I longed for the one I had lost at the university.

"Where's everyone else?" I buttered my toast and took a bite.

"Lucien wasn't feeling well, so they took him out for a walk."

"I knew it. He's of no use to us like this."

"He lost his father only a couple of days ago. It'll take time to heal."

"I know how that feels."

As soon as I was old enough, I began asking all kinds of questions, and researching any of the old news articles I could get my hands on about my father and his final assignment. I had found out that he had been repeatedly sent on diplomatic missions to the Ottoman Empire at the end of the Great War. The Turkish government began phasing out the Caliphate, and Mehmed VI feared for his life as it became increasingly clear that he would be deposed.

He asked for protection since he cooperated with stepping away from the Empire, and so my father was among those sent to watch and protect. The U.S. got what it wanted, which was a safe transition, a pair of eyes and ears in that region of the world, and the Gray Tower was given access to Mehmed's personal collection of esoteric texts and scrolls spanning centuries. The Order of Wizards wouldn't dream of passing up an opportunity to possess tomes of knowledge from ancient and medieval alchemists.

Of course, wherever there was mystical knowledge to be had, not only did it attract the Order, but also our enemies. The Gray Tower, and my father in particular, proved to be a constant thorn in the Black Wolves' side. When we had learned of my dad's disappearance and apparent death, I was as devastated as Lucien, and understood the heartache and loss. However, with the knowledge that the Black Wolves have failed and my father indeed lived, it gave me a sense of hope—but it also raised even more questions. For a moment, I thought of Marc's accusation of my father being a Drifter, but the idea made me feel ill, and I quickly dismissed it.

"I trust you have everything planned out regarding our friend Simon Vester?" Gabriel drank his glass of milk and patiently awaited an answer.

"I'm going to get him to tell me where the lab is. Heck, he'll even give us a map if I want him to."

"Then when it's time to go there, I'll dress in disguise."

"You mean you don't want a secret Nazi lab knowing that the Vatican is sending in warrior priests to shut them down?" I didn't think I would ever get past that.

He leaned toward me. "I know I should've been at the Gray Tower by now, but I wanted to help you."

"How sweet of you...why do you carry a sword?"

"It's my weapon of choice, like your alchemist's knife. My sword is a relic of sorts, and it holds great sentimental value."

"Hmph." I lifted my glass and drank some water.

"Just think—when you use a gun, bullets can fly anywhere or hit anyone." He raised his hands and wagged his index fingers in varying directions. "However, with a sword, if I want to kill you with it, there's no mistake."

"And how do you reconcile that with being a man of the cloth?"

"I only fight in the defense of others, or if my opponent is a Cruenti. I mostly dispatch them, and Black Wolves."

"You're the oddest priest I've ever met." However, I did like the idea of a Cruenti getting whacked on sight.

"I'll take that as a compliment."

"If you weren't trained by the Gray Tower, then how do you know to control your powers?"

"You assume that the Gray Tower is the only means of learning to do this?"

"Yes, now that you've mentioned it, the Black Wolves also specialize in training people with abilities."

"Lucky for you, I am not one of them."

Although his tone implied no malice, I felt mildly disturbed. Well, I wouldn't say Brande didn't warn me about questioning the man. In any case, despite my resentment toward Brande for not telling me about my father, deep inside I trusted him. If he could trust Father Gabriel, then I was willing to refrain from jumping to conclusions—for now.

"Can I ask you something, Father?"

"Of course."

"How old were you when you first knew of your...gifts?"

"I was nine years old."

"How old are you, Father?"

"Forty."

I gasped and poured myself some Château. "Is that part of your gifts? You look my age."

He shrugged. "Perhaps."

"So...why did you become a priest?"

He studied me for a moment before answering. "When I was young, I had an encounter that I would never forget. I believed that in order to avoid falling into the trap that some wizards have found themselves in, that I should dedicate my life to God and keep constant vigilance."

"So, that's why you go after Cruenti warlocks? Get the devil before he gets you?"

He gave a firm nod. "Does that surprise you?"

"Not really."

Some people made pacts with demons for money, fame, or power. Cruenti made pacts with them for magic, regardless if they were born wizards or not. They satisfied the bond through their Blood Magic, which primarily consisted of feeding off other wizards. Something like that couldn't be done without destroying one's self in the process. The longer one remained a Cruenti, the closer one came to transforming into a Black Wolf. Sure, he would be all magic and still powerful, but his humanity wouldn't remain intact. He'd be an abomination.

A wizard sensitive to the spirit world ended up being the easiest target for these demons. He'd either repel the temptation or, if he proved weak, would suffer from oppression until he finally gave in and became a Cruenti.

I shook these thoughts off and turned my attention toward Ernest, who came in with his arm around Lucien's shoulder. I saw Lucien's face and sighed.

"Look, breakfast is ready!" Ernest pointed toward the food, but Lucien only stared into blank space with red and swollen eyes. They took their seats a few tables away, and Brande came in carrying a paper bag. He looked rather relaxed, and had changed into a khaki shirt and black pants.

"Nice shirt." I gestured for him to come sit next to me.

"Nice dress." Brande took his seat.

"Thank you. I hope your outing this morning was productive." I glanced at Lucien from the corner of my eye.

"Lucien just needed some fresh air. We stopped by the pharmacy and got a few things." Brande handed me the bag, which was probably filled with minerals and metals for me. He always knew exactly what to look for and where to find ingredients, even though he didn't have to do that for me.

"Excuse me." I stood and walked toward the exit. Lightly brushing Lucien's arm in passing, I impressed upon him the urge to come and sit outside and talk with me. He walked out after me, joining me on a bench next to a flowerbed a few buildings down from Le Fleur.

"I know what you're going to say." He stared at me without blinking. "I want to be here, and I want to help."

"Lucien, we need all the help we can get, believe me. But if you're not ready for this, then just stay in the hostel until we're done."

"They killed my father. I'm going with you to that laboratory and, no matter what the cost, I'm going to kill as many of them as I can."

"I know, and that's why I'm afraid you're just an empty shell looking for revenge and not caring about anyone else."

"Don't patronize me." He reached into his pocket and took out a lighter. When he lit his cigarette, the tainted fume of cadmium was even more pungent, and we both coughed.

"It shouldn't require two other adults to take you out for fresh air and walk around. You're a mess…and stop using that lighter or you'll kill yourself. The metal's toxic." I tried to remain calm, but my frustration already had a hold of me.

With a smirk, he placed the lighter back into his pocket. "I'll live long enough to finish this assignment, I assure you. I've already drawn out what the layout of the lab may look like. I wouldn't be surprised if it's the same as the Catalonia lab."

"Good, then once you get your head straight, you can actually be of use to us."

"Assuming this weapons lab is even in this city, and assuming we can handle the guards, be it man or Black Wolf."

"Brande, Gabriel, and I will take care of all the warlocks. You just take care of the German soldiers."

"All right then." He reached into his pocket, pulled out the tainted lighter, and tossed it to me. "If we die, we die."

The lighter made my stomach feel queasy, and I set it aside. "Listen, I only knew your father briefly, but from the moment I met him, all he talked about was you. From what I hear, you're helping to make a difference, and whatever you can do for us is appreciated. I want all of us to make it out alive."

He gave a surprised look. He probably expected a verbal lashing. "I was supposed to take care of him, but he died in my arms...I have nothing now."

"Nothing to fight for, right?"

"Why do you care so much?"

"Because, I can't go through all of this without thinking, feeling...or questioning. Can you? If you think you have nothing to lose, you'll run in there reckless and get yourself killed, and maybe us along with you."

He snorted. "It seems this conversation wasn't completely altruistic."

"You're damned right it isn't, because if anything happens to Brande, you'll regret it."

A flicker of a smile crossed his face, and he shook his head. "You know, he told me the same thing about you this morning. Well, in his version, he said if anything happened to you, that he'd throw me off the Eiffel Tower."

I smiled. "I'm not surprised...we're good friends. So tell me truthfully, are you with us?"

"Yes," he nodded. "I'm with you."

CHAPTER 15

I sat at the vanity mirror in my room, taking down my pin curls and gently running my fingers through my hair. I didn't want to lose my waves, so I took care not to comb too hard, and ended up pleased with the results. I refused to wear perfume, as the thought of Simon using my pleasant smell as an excuse to put his face near me made me cringe. The most important accessory was, of course, my red garnet lipstick. Brande once jokingly called it, "love potion on a stick."

The red garnet stone enhanced one's romantic desire and inclinations, and when ground and mixed in with something as common as a lady's lipstick, would go undetected. One kiss, mixed with my intention and energy, would send the target into a state of mind where he would obey any command and perform any action for the sake of pleasing the object of his affection.

The red garnet lasted longer than my body magic's mind control spell, and with the lipstick, I didn't have to renew the spell so soon or keep physical contact with the person. Red garnet had its benefits, especially if I wanted to reserve my magical energy for other spells. At the same time, it could also be dangerous, because red garnet also inspired aggression and violence.

I would never put this in the hands of an inexperienced or ill-intentioned person, and even *I* had only used it twice before: on a mercenary spy who the London office believed double-crossed our French SOE friends, and a very handsome wizard who had lied about being trained by the Gray Tower and infiltrated the Maquis so he could steal information for the Nazis.

With slow strokes, I applied the lipstick and took a long look at myself in the mirror. Sometimes I imagined myself stalking one of those beautiful Hollywood actresses and working a spell on her so that she would have to tell me the secret of those tiny waists and perfectly sculptured figures. I slipped on my Agate stone ring. Its deep green matched the color of my eyes. Then I slipped on the Bracelet of Vitriol I had made from the supplies Brande brought me. Something like this would fetch a very high price on the black market, and only Apprentices like me knew how to properly make them. I had known some Practitioners to have made decent wages opening their own shops and making all kinds of charms, talismans, and potions. Still, even the best Practitioner Alchemist couldn't make vitriol.

Vitriol was a chemical compound of sulfuric salts. It would be like eggs in the world of baking—highly desirable, used often, and you couldn't make the really good stuff without it. Alchemists used vitriol to transmute base metals into gold (though no one has figured out yet how to make this permanent), and to create weapons and charms.

I carved my salts into little beads, which I then fixed onto the gold bracelet Jasmine had given me. I placed in three red vitriol beads, which would lend me energy, three white beads for mental and physical purification, and black vitriol made from iron, which would provide me with protection from evil yet deal deadly blows to my foes. I decided to set three of each color, because three was a lucky number, and nine was the mystical number for endurance.

I slid my knife into the leather sheath strapped to my leg then slipped into my heels. With a long deep sigh, I fondled my bracelet and headed out the door. Simon would arrive at any moment. I went outside and sat at the bench where I had earlier spoken with Lucien. As the sky dimmed and purpled, I scanned the nearby area. A few couples strolled down the street in each other's arms, and shopkeepers called out to them in an attempt to get a last sale for the day. A couple of German Armed Forces soldiers patrolled on foot, but I didn't see any of the SS officers.

Within minutes, I noticed Simon walk up, and I caught his eye. He looked over to the right, and then to his left, like a sneaky little rat. He approached and took a seat next to me, greeting me with a grin.

"You look...mesmerizing."

"Thank you." I forced a smile.

"Your cousin will not be joining us, will he?" He rumbled with laughter.

"No, it will be just you and me." Why couldn't he at least be twelve years younger? He looked like one of those men that you just knew had been attractive back in his youth.

"He would just spoil our fun. Shall we?" He offered his arm, and I took it.

We walked arm-in-arm down the street, turning the corner at Rue de Vesle, the major street in the city. As the night sky settled and the stars began to peek out, shopkeepers finally closed their doors and pedestrians quickened their pace.

A gypsy, wearing a hooded cloak and raggedy clothes sat on the sidewalk and leaned against the grocer's store edifice. He played a mandolin and would stop to rattle the change in his upturned hat whenever someone passed. One of the passersby caught the grocer in time and paid him for a wrapped meat sandwich, which he threw into the gypsy's hat.

"A franc to spare, sir?" He played a quick tune and gestured toward his hat. I smiled and tossed in the money.

"For god's sake," Simon said through clenched teeth, "didn't I tell you last week to get out of my city?"

"*Your* city?"

"Yes, *my* city, you filthy parasite! If I see you again, I'll shoot you."

"Let's go, Simon." I wanted to hit him with a Putrefaction spell...right in his face.

"We'll stop by Ruinart, Noelle." He buried his face in my hair and inhaled. We began walking again.

"You mean the champagne house?" I shied away.

"Yes, their cellars are caves that date back to the time of the Romans, and the house is one of the oldest in town."

"It sounds wonderful, but I don't drink, remember? And it's getting late."

"It's very mild and smooth, you'll see. It's a wonderful alternative to ale and wine. And don't worry about the time, because I always leave Ruinart open."

"Then perhaps I'll try a glass." I turned my face away so he wouldn't see me scowl.

"Wonderful, darling. Look, there it is."

We approached the champagne house and entered. The host sat us at a candlelit table and Simon ordered the Cuvée for us. The ambiance would have put me in a romantic mood if I had been with someone else. There were both old and young couples enjoying champagne and intimate chatter, and some snuggled in secluded corners. A group of friends sat near the pianist who played a slow melodious song. After drinking a few glasses, I rubbed my white vitriol beads on my bracelet to prevent becoming befuddled from the drinks. Simon, on the other hand, drank twice as many glasses as I did. Perhaps I wouldn't have to use the red garnet kiss after all.

"See those two lovers at that table in the corner?" He pointed toward a young man and woman who held hands and sat closely.

"She seems happy."

"You've never seen them before, but can't you feel what's going on in the air around them? Passion is life, Noelle."

"But one shouldn't be blinded by it." I finished off my Cuvée, secretly envying them. How I would have given anything to be in that woman's place, with someone I loved, gazing into his eyes with such depth and intensity, relishing each touch and kiss.

"Come with me, I want to show you something." He grabbed my hand and led me away from the table, farther inside toward the cellar entrance.

"How far do we have to go to reach the caves?"

"Not far, but we'll not take the stairway down." He went over to a shaft where a double rope hung. It reminded me of a dumbwaiter. The servant boys likely used it in their daily tasks of quickly hauling bottles and supplies between the cellars and the champagne house.

"What are you doing?" I ran over just in time to see him grab the rope and start rappelling down the shaft. He was surprisingly agile and he landed at the bottom with a huge smile on his face.

"Are you afraid to come down? Or will you take the plunge?"

"I'm not afraid." I smirked and grabbed the rope, gliding and rappelling until I landed in his arms.

"For a moment, I thought you would run to the other side and take the stairs." He set me down.

"I have more courage than you think, Simon."

"Indeed."

We walked through a narrow passageway which opened up into the first cave. Rows of wine racks lined up perfectly into organized sections, and sconces with real torches were fixed to the wall, a testimony to the cellar's medieval origin.

"Tell me, what are you thinking of?" He stood behind me and swept my hair over my right shoulder, planting a kiss on my neck.

I rolled my eyes and turned to face him. "How big are these caves?"

"Extremely big, my dear." He held my hand and caressed it.

"Mm, yes...well, tell me about yourself. What do you do here?"

He waved his hand dismissively. "Let's not ruin our moment

with talk of work. I don't have to work today or tomorrow, so why not enjoy ourselves while we can?"

"One last question, then." I could smell the alcohol on his breath, and I saw his glassy eyes redden.

"One last question, my dear, and then no more talking."

"Is it true that there's a laboratory in the city?"

He paused for a long moment, and then guffawed, leaning on me for support. "Oh, Noelle..."

I prodded him further. "The laboratory, Simon."

Suddenly he grabbed a fistful of my hair and shoved his pistol beneath my chin. The hairs on the back of my neck stood, and a quiet cold dread grew inside me. Apparently he wasn't as drunk as I thought he was, and a drunken man with a gun was as unpredictable as he was dangerous.

"Do you work for the Maquis? Or the Americans or British?"

"Does it matter?" I bit my lip, hoping that my response didn't provoke him to shoot me.

"Perhaps it doesn't, since I'm certain you'll never be found."

"You knew I was a spy?"

He shook his head. "But I was going to take what I wanted and kill you anyway."

"You're a rotten bastard."

"A rotten bastard with a gun." He tilted my head back and pressed his lips against mine, kissing me roughly. He pulled back and breathed heavily staring at me as if hypnotized. He was now under the influence of the red garnet lipstick.

"Listen to me," I turned to face him. "I want you to put your gun away."

"Of course." he placed it back into his coat pocket and kissed me again. This wasn't good. A second kiss would make the enchantment even stronger.

I broke away and wiped my lips with the back of my hand. "Now, if you really want to please me, Simon, you'll tell me about the lab."

"The laboratory is a few miles south in the largest cave. All these caves and tunnels run like a maze beneath the city."

"Is Dr. Heilwig there too?"

"Yes."

"If the lab's here, then why aren't there more officers and guards?"

"It would draw too much attention and become a target, like Vélizy-Villacoublay."

"Who's guarding the lab down here?"

"Can I kiss you again?"

"Later, Simon."

The storybooks and films presented the effects of love enchantments all wrong. They portrayed the lover sitting around mooning over his beloved in a brainless reverie, but in reality, he still kept his own will, his own thinking, and his own annoying questions.

"Please, just another kiss."

"All right, but first..." I pushed him away, "first, I want you to find some chalk like the ones the servants use down here. Mark the way to the lab so that I'll be able to find it. Make sure your markers blend in with the old graffiti, so that no one else will notice. When you come back, I'll be waiting."

"And then we'll kiss?"

"Yeah, sure. But, Simon, while you're at home tomorrow, remember not to take any calls or receive any visitors until later that evening. Understood?"

"Yes, this will be between you and me. I promise."

"Good, now go make the marks like I asked." I was nervous about asking him to do anything else, because the more steps to a task, the more opportunities there were to mess it up. Besides, I didn't want to be around for his impatience and aggression to grow stronger. Why did the fool have to kiss me a second time?

He began executing my orders without further question, and I decided to leave him for tonight. I'd get a hold of him later if I needed another important question answered, or even a map. I headed toward the stairway that led back up to the champagne house. I trembled from the adrenaline still coursing through my veins and shook with rage. Had I been a defenseless girl, I would have been violated and dead. How many other women had he done this to?

Simon Vester wasn't just a man of ill repute—he was the devil.

I took a deep breath and left Ruinart, heading back down Rue de Vesle. The streets were cold and empty, and I worried whether or not Simon would grow difficult and even more unpredictable. All I wanted to do now was return to my room and go to bed. I didn't know how late it was, but I didn't care. I just needed to sleep off the angst and frustration of my evening. As I neared Le Fleur, I felt a presence near me, and I slowed my pace.

"How long have you been following me?"

"Since you left Ruinart." Brande came up by my side and fell in step with me.

"The laboratory is hidden in one of the caves beneath the city. We can reach it by going through the Ruinart cellars."

"Where's Vester?"

"Probably still roaming the caves."

"You used the red garnet lipstick?" He held the front door open for me, and I went in.

"Yes." I glanced at him and saw his eyes narrow.

"You could've just used mind control." He walked upstairs with me.

"He's wearing Veit Heilwig's talisman ring, it wouldn't have worked."

A blaze of anger, directed at myself, ran through me when I remembered that I should've asked for Veit's ring while in the cellars with Simon. I unlocked my door and opened it, not bothering to close it since I knew Brande would come in as well.

"You're not hurt, are you?"

"Why do you ask?" I took off my shoes and decided that a nice hot bath would soothe me before bed.

"When you left the champagne house, you looked upset."

"I was, but I'm fine now."

"I'll keep watch again."

"I'm going to take a bath. Can you come back in an hour?" I almost forgot about my knife. I reached for the sheath and unstrapped it, placing the knife on the nightstand.

"An hour, you say?"

"It'll give you plenty of time to tell Gabriel and the others about the lab, and I'm sure you've already planned how you're going to kill Vester, so you can sit and compare notes."

"I'll...see you in an hour."

∼

I must have drifted into sleep during my bath, because I was thrown into another vivid dream. This time, I stood in the Gray Tower, wandering through its unusually desolate halls. Despite the emptiness, I kept hearing echoes and screams; bodies tumbled and magic whooshed, indicating that a fierce battle ensued. I felt sick to my stomach whenever a resounding boom vibrated the entire main building.

I called for my father, then for Brande, but no one answered. I stumbled into the Courtyard of Light and fell against the stone pedestal where the statue of Sophia, Divine Wisdom, stood. Clothed in a marble robe like a Greek statue, she wore a hood that concealed her eyes. Her wings were outstretched like those of an angel, and her right hand held a sword upright, a real sword made of pure gold.

I thought I heard someone call my name; I shut my eyes and covered my ears. An odd sound filled the air, and I couldn't make out what it was. Rain suddenly began to fall, the water splashed against my cool skin and hit the ground in a crescendo.

When I opened my eyes, I was horrified to find that the rain was a shower of blood. With dread, I looked up and saw the face of the statue staring back at me. I heard that odd noise in the air again and gazed into the sky above. A blaze of light hurtled toward me like a falling star, and I shrieked when I realized that it was one of the Three, the one who wore the white robe. With a sickening crack, the Master Wizard expired, impaled on Sophia's sword.

Something ripped me away from the dream. I was in murky darkness and splashing water. It took me several seconds to realize I was awake and still in the tub—and fighting with Brande. He called my name, and his voice seemed far away, like in the dream. I stared into his face, and for the first time in my life, I saw him afraid. My body trembled with stress, and my heart beat at a frantic pace. I thought of the voice from the dream and realized it had belonged to my father. The dream may have been another message from him.

"Look at me...Isabella...look at me!" Brande quickly dragged me out of the tub and sat me on the cold bathroom floor. He threw my robe over me and knelt so he could hold my head between his hands, trying to get me to focus on him.

"I had a dream." I gasped.

"Are you hurt?"

"No, it was a dream."

"What happened?"

"It's my father. He's sending me a message." I put the robe on and stood. I pushed him away when he followed me out and tried to guide me toward the chair in the room.

"I don't understand what you're talking about, Isabella."

"I don't need to sit down! My father's note said he'd see me again. What...what if he's here?"

I rushed toward the door, but he got there first and blocked me. "Are you insane? You're not even dressed. What was that in there?"

"I fell asleep in the bathtub and had a dream. It was more like a vision. A warning."

"But why were you on fire?"

"I...what?" The entire world, in that moment, seemed to stop. I felt like I couldn't breathe.

"When I touched you," he said, holding up the palms of his hands to show me how red they were, "I had to absorb it. It was almost too powerful."

I turned and headed toward the window to look outside, but Brande must've thought I was going to climb out, because he grabbed my arm.

"Please, just sit."

"Let go of me!"

"I'll listen to everything you have to say, but please, sit and talk to me."

I snatched my wrist away from his hold. I stumbled over to the chair, and sat down, my chest heaving and my mouth forcing out the questions I knew I finally needed to ask, but was afraid to.

"Why were you in Salon-de-Provence?"

"What?"

"Why were you in the Provence region?"

"I told you, I was trying to find a way back to the Gray Tower without being detected."

"Cut the crap and try giving me the real answer."

"Isa—"

I held up my right hand in a gesture to silence him. "You—and the Order—knew my father was alive, but didn't bother to help him, or send for him, or tell his family."

"I can explain..." he lowered himself to his knees, reaching for my hand and holding it. I forced myself to ask another difficult question.

"You were tracking my father, weren't you?"

"Y-yes."

"The Order killed an alchemist in Salon-de-Provence four

hundred years ago, and his name was Michel de Nostredame. He was a Drifter...like my father."

I had been making excuses, coming up with explanations, and flatly denying the signs before me. Now, with Brande's admission, I could no longer avoid the truth. Saying it out loud left a bitter taste in my mouth, as if I tasted cadmium again, and I looked at Brande with a mixture of distrust and hurt.

"You know the law, and you know our purpose." He lowered his gaze.

Law and purpose be damned, this was my father. "Whenever you came to see me, you were only looking for my father so you could kill him. You knew he'd try to contact me."

"No, I told them you were off limits."

I pushed his hand away and leaned forward in my seat. "Yeah, whatever. Tell me what happened."

"The Master Wizards gave me the task three years ago and I've been tracking him ever since. There are seven of us, mostly Elites, and two Masters. I finally caught up with Carson in Salon-de-Provence and fought him. I almost had him when Father Gabriel intervened. He mistakenly thought I was..."

"A warlock?"

He nodded. "Carson escaped and I had to explain who I was to Father Gabriel. Once he knew all the facts, he ended up agreeing with me."

All these years I could neither see nor touch my father, and Brande almost took him away from me. "Would you really have killed my father?"

"Yes."

I slapped him as hard as I could. He took the hit without protest or retaliation. "I trusted you."

"Forgive me." He couldn't even look me in the eye.

"You want compassion, even though you wouldn't give the same to my father? Are you your own man, or a creature of the Gray Tower?"

"Please, tell me what to do, and I will do it."

I rose from my seat. He stood with me, finally raising his head and gazing at me through watery eyes. I wanted to scream at him; I wanted to hit him again and tell him how much I hated him—but I couldn't, because I knew I didn't. I understood the law and how important it was to protect the Akashic Record, but it turned into something different when the Drifter who had to die was your father, a man who was nothing but good and honorable. He didn't deserve this.

"So you want me to tell you what to do, huh? Don't you think that's your problem? You've lived most of your life doing what others tell you."

"Please, forgive me."

"I would be lying if I said I did, so don't ask right now." I may not have hated him, but it didn't mean I wasn't infuriated with him. He was the only person from the Gray Tower I still talked to and believed I could trust. If he ever wanted to restore that, he would have to show me that our friendship was more important than blindly serving the Order.

"Is there anything I can do?" he asked.

I looked into his sad gray eyes and wanted to cry. "Choose a side and stick with it, Brande Drahomir...before I kill you."

CHAPTER 16

The next morning I got out of bed and noticed another Circle of Protection had been cast around me. I gritted my teeth and imagined what Brande would do next to earn my forgiveness. Though I wouldn't admit it, in a way I could understand his struggle between doing what he believed was right and what he felt obligated to do for the sake of a higher purpose. After my very first mission in Belgium, Ian had sent me on an assignment to help the Maquis intercept an important train delivery headed into Orleans.

The Nazis had planned to send newly developed weapons from one of their factories for distribution to their allies in the southern region of France. We were ordered to disrupt the delivery at all costs, steal what we could, and destroy or hide the surplus. We had obtained train schedules, maps, everything we thought we would need to get the job done.

The local Maquis group leader had decided that we would blow the train tracks along a particular point in the route, forcing the train to derail. The derailment would stop train travel along that route and other Maquisards would be left behind to alert contacts at the nearest train stations. All of this was done so that unsuspecting travelers in other trains wouldn't stumble upon the derailment scene.

Everything had been going according to plan, except for one fact that eluded us: the Nazis had switched schedules and trains at the last minute, had loaded the weapons into the storage areas of a passenger train, and sent it along our route. When we saw a train headed our way—two hours earlier than expected—we panicked and thought the Nazis would surely beat us to the drop off point. We had already placed our explosives and anxiously prepared ourselves for the explosion. However, one of our scouts had realized the train wasn't a freight train after all. He had gotten a closer look and spotted civilian passengers on board. He radioed us a warning, but this left us with only minutes to decide which course to take.

Would we help the Allies and deprive the Nazis of new weapons, thus saving countless lives in the process, and putting us one step closer to winning the war? Or would we abandon the mission—and contradict our direct orders—for the sake of the lives on that train that were never supposed to be there? I felt torn between both decisions, and either way, someone would die. But like Father Alexis said, how could you choose who deserved to live and who didn't?

I wasn't in charge of the mission and was only there to aid the Maquis leader. I tried to convince him we could find another way to stop the train and take those weapons. He assumed I was just trying to encroach on his authority since I was an SOE agent and not a Maquisard, and I felt he also put less value in something a woman had to say, especially a woman who was new to all of this. He shouted me down and ordered me to act as lookout, just in case the train was being followed or escorted by Nazis, and he didn't allow me anywhere near the tracks. The closer the train came, the sicker I grew.

I tried reasoning with myself that the greater good would be served, and that more lives would be saved in the end. However, when that train derailed and I stood there, watching cabins crash, glass fly, and maimed bodies roll across the ground—well, let's just say when I returned to London, I didn't even bother going to Baker Street. I headed straight home and refused to come out for five days. Jane Lewis had to break into my flat and force me to eat and bathe.

I had a choice between what I was ordered to do and what I believed was right. If given another chance, I would've told the Maquis leader to go to hell, that I was going to disarm the explosives on the tracks, and if he didn't like it, he could blow me up too. I wish I would've done that, even though those weapons would have likely gone into Nazi hands. Instead, I suppressed my opinions and meekly followed orders.

I understood that conflict as well as anyone else, and so a part of me empathized with Brande. Still, I felt he should've used his own judgment and had the courage to choose what he knew in his heart was right. I had failed before, and the sadness and remorse in his eyes last night reminded me of how I felt after the Orleans mission. However, the difference was that I would never be able to ask for forgiveness. They're all dead.

I dressed and went downstairs for coffee, and was glad that I didn't run into Brande. A few other patrons sat in the dining area enjoying breakfast and listening to a radio broadcast. I didn't feel like hearing a false account of how the war was going, so I slipped into one of the corners and had Claire bring my drink.

"Would you like something with your coffee, Noelle?"

"No thank you, I'm not very hungry."

"Maybe just a small bowl of fruit, then?"

"Fine."

I sipped my coffee and picked up a newspaper left on the table by a previous guest. The title on the front page exclaimed in large letters: "Germany is on the Move." The article, of course, praised the efforts of Operation Barbarossa, the German Army's ongoing battle with the Soviet Union, and touted the mass execution of Soviet civilians as just punishment. It also saved a scathing last paragraph for the United States, condemning it for freezing German and Italian assets in America. I believed Ken had been right, that it was only a matter of time before America officially joined the war. There were now confirmed reports trickling in about the U.S. Navy engaging in sporadic battles with Japanese forces in the Pacific.

"Here's your fruit." Claire smiled, placing my bowl in front of me.

"Thank you."

"Also, there's a phone call for you at the front desk."

"From whom?"

"He wouldn't say, but he asked for you."

I excused myself and headed toward the front desk. An elderly man sat there, engaged in record keeping and greeting new guests. He spoke with a couple of men, but when he saw me approach, he gestured for me to come behind the desk and pick up the phone. A thousand possibilities raced through my mind as to who it could be, and when I answered, I regretted that I had come downstairs at all.

"Noelle, my sweet, I did as you asked. The markings in the cave are discreet Roman numerals. Just follow them in numerical order to reach the lab."

"Thank you, Simon. I don't recall asking you to phone me. Remember? I said not to speak to anyone until after tonight?"

"Yes, but I didn't think that would include you. Besides, you promised to wait for me, but when I returned, you were gone. I went home, and all I could think about was you, and all I dreamed about was you. Will you come to my house?"

"No, I won't."

"Then I'll come to you."

"That won't be necessary," I hissed into the receiver.

"You're going to break into the lab, aren't you?"

"I..."

"You could have asked me, since I'm in charge of the laboratory. Tell me what you want from there...and I'll bring it to you."

"I don't think so." This was so frustrating that it was driving me insane. All I wanted from him was key information about the lab, and how to reach it, but it felt like every act of cooperation had a consequence of its own.

"Tell me you love me," he panted.

I turned toward the wall and whispered, "Have you considered that maybe you're not yourself today and that you ought to go lie down?"

"I know how I feel, and I'm more alive than ever. This is the passion I've been waiting for. This is true love."

"You attacked me. I don't think that's true love."

"Then let me make amends. Will you join me for dinner?"

"Eh...midnight?"

"Why so late, darling?"

"Why not?" At least we'd be out of the lab and the hell out of the city by then.

"Very well...midnight. I live in the large estate a few blocks east of Rue de Vesle."

"Great, and remember, don't leave your house. Wait patiently until I arrive."

"Of course." I hung up the phone and moaned. I promised myself that I would never use red garnet again.

∼

Basking in the sun at a nearby park helped cheer me up a little and clear my mind. I sat in the grass near a small fountain, watching a few children fish out coins. When I noticed that one of the boys carried a wrapped sandwich like those at the grocer's store, I offered him a franc for it and took it off his hands. I opened it and polished it off, disappointed that it was only a cheese sandwich and wishing I had eaten the fruit I ordered earlier.

I felt a tingling sensation at the sound of a mandolin playing, but it was so faint that I wasn't sure if it was all in my mind. I asked the boys if they heard anything, but they insisted that I was crazy. They gave up on me and ran away, just as the sound of the melody increased. I listened to the music for a while before following the sound to a copse with looming trees and swaying branches. It was serene and secluded, *a perfect place for lovers to frolic*, I wistfully thought.

As I approached, I saw the same gypsy who had been on the street corner the other evening. His hood shaded his eyes and gray hairs streaked his dark beard. He played the song through to the end, and for some reason it mesmerized me. I settled in the cool grass next to him.

"Good morning, miss."

"Good morning."

"I remember you. I still have the franc you gave me."

"Yes...please, keep it."

"You're not from here." He put the mandolin aside.

"My name is Noelle..."

"No it's not."

I felt that tingling sensation. It ran straight from my shoulders, down my back, and through my legs. My thoughts became murky, and when it became more difficult for me to concentrate, I realized that he had enchanted me with the song.

"Who are you?" I slid my hand down my side so I could reach my knife, wondering why he didn't try to take over my mind with the enchantment. In any case, it would be his last mistake.

"Isabella...do you remember me?"

"No." I shook my head and gripped my knife. It would be too risky to lay a symbol while under an enchantment. I'd have to do it the old-fashioned way and stab him.

"Did you receive my note?"

I gasped and loosened my hold on my knife. "Which note?"

"Do you remember me?"

"Dad...is it you?" My hand shook as I reached for the hood, but he gently held my hand at bay.

"Whoever sees your memories could also see my face. Very few know me by sight."

Although part of me couldn't believe it, and I didn't know how I was supposed to feel, all I knew was that I slowly wrapped my arms around his neck in an embrace, and didn't bother to wipe away the tears that fell. After all these years, I had finally found him again! I was scared this was just another one of my dreams, that I would wake up and find him gone. But the longer we held onto each other, my fear subsided.

"Dad? Can you lift the enchantment now? I promise I won't be hysterical." I wiped my cheeks.

"The enchantment wasn't for tranquility, but for your memory." He took both my hands and held them in his. "What do you remember about me?"

"I always have a dream about you. I dream about the tool shed, and fire all around me. You'd come and save me, but then you'd disappear. Sometimes you would reappear and then vanish again."

"Those aren't dreams, those are memories."

I felt ill. "Was there something else I was supposed to remember?"

"Not now, it's too dangerous."

"I want to help you."

"Find Veit Heilwig."

"What does he have to do with this?" I shuddered when I felt the presence of a strong wizard approaching.

"It seems even as we speak, I'm being tracked." He let go of my hands and stood.

"Before you go, can I ask you something?"

"Yes, quickly."

"Why didn't you come home? We waited for you, and you

never came." For all I knew, I could've asked him for the secret to the universe, but this wasn't Isabella the Alchemist asking, this was a daughter asking her father.

"I'm a marked man, and I'll always be hunted. I would never put my family through that. I sacrificed my presence for your safety."

"I thought you were dead."

"And I felt like I was, being away from you, Johnnie, and your mother. But it was the only way."

He started to leave, but I called out to him. "How will finding Dr. Heilwig help you? I need to know."

"First, he knows the truth about me. Second, he will help you understand more. Above all, he's my friend, and we need him."

"When will I see you again?" I had so many other questions and so many things I wanted to say, and all of them were fighting to be heard. Even though it was likely out of the question, I wanted to at least try to convince him to come home, even for a little while.

"I'll come for you before the end of this year. You need to complete your training."

"Training?"

"You left the Gray Tower too soon, but we can remedy that."

I knew he wanted to help, and I had toyed with the same idea, but seeing him changed everything, knowing who he was changed everything. "I can't go back to those people. Not when they're hunting you like a criminal."

"Either way, you will train. If you want, you can be with me, Veit, and..."

"I miss you." For such a great Philosopher, I swore he just couldn't catch on. Come on, Dad, all I wanted to hear at this moment was that you missed me like hell, and nothing would ever stand in between you and your family again.

He leaned down to kiss me on the forehead. "One of my trackers is near, and he's headed straight toward us. I must go now—he'll follow my trail. Veit knows he is to remain by your side and tell you everything."

He disappeared in a flash, leaving me alone in the copse. I felt empty and sad, the way I did when I was a child and had found out that he would not be returning home. I hoped that I truly would see him by the end of the year, and I would make sure that I'd find a way to be at home with Johnnie and Mother so that they could see him too.

I stood and walked back toward the fountain, reclaiming my spot on the grass. I felt sorry for my father, because he had to constantly fight and run. The trackers were probably already on his trail again. As I thought about our meeting and replayed everything in my mind, I suddenly recoiled when someone's hand touched my shoulder.

"What is ailing you on this beautiful day, young lady?"

"I'm fine, thank you." I turned and gazed into the eyes of an elderly man. He looked like one of the businessmen who frequented the park during the day, with his dark gray suit and silver hair peeking from beneath his hat. His clean-shaven face carried a benevolent expression as he looked down at me. However, my senses went off, and I could feel there was something different about him.

"Whom were you just speaking to?" He kept his hand on my shoulder.

"No one..." I shuddered and tried guarding my mind against his mental invasion. My head ached, and my mind burned as he pried into my memories to look for his answer. I quickly constructed mental blocks. I even concentrated on mundane things like what I had to eat earlier, but he quickly tore through them and opened my mind further. When I continued resisting, he then switched over to body magic in an attempt to bend my will, so that my mouth would speak the words he wanted to hear.

Like I said, it was difficult to perform body magic on a wizard who had been trained in it. I reversed the flow of the spell and sent a wave of energy up his arm, straight toward his heart. He clenched his teeth and reached for his chest, and I fed more energy into the attack, hoping that he wouldn't break the flow and launch an even stronger offense. If I wasn't already sitting in the grass, I would've sank to my knees from the force of the magic going back and forth between us. His hands began to shake and he finally released me, starting to back off.

"You're stronger than I thought, Isabella." He let out a heavy breath but quickly regained his composure.

"Who are you?"

"Leto Priya, of the Gray Tower."

I went cold. "Leave me alone."

"That is no way to speak to a Master Wizard, Apprentice."

"Go to hell."

"Who's the gypsy?" When I said nothing, he continued. "I'm giving you an opportunity to tell me. If I have to, I'll rip your mind apart and lay it bare to find out."

"Get away from her." Brande came to my side and helped me to my feet. As he stood next to me, Leto gazed at us with a stoic expression.

"Brande, how good it is to see you. I didn't think you'd be here."

"I'm here...and I'm with her." He glared at the Master Wizard and took my hand in his. I didn't know whether to be grateful or afraid, but I held on tightly.

"I have reason to believe that Carson contacted her. I think we should bring her in for...questioning."

"No."

"That wasn't a request, Elite. Now step aside." He came toward me, but he paused when Brande moved forward and blocked him.

"Do you have proof, Master Priya? You can't bring in a member of the Order on just suspicion. That is the law."

Leto bared his teeth. "Who do you think made those laws?"

The air grew dense, and I felt electricity at my fingertips. Two other wizards appeared in a whirlwind and landed. As they approached Master Priya, I recognized them and stiffened a little. I had met both of them while at the Gray Tower. The young man was Hotaru, an elemental who came from Japan. The young woman was Mehara, a mentalist from Morocco. Both were Elites.

Since the Masters only took on Elites to teach, and half of the Masters were constantly outside the Gray Tower fulfilling various duties, Apprentices didn't necessarily know all of them by sight. I knew many Elites since they were the ones who had instructed me.

Hotaru greeted Brande and me with a nod, saving a quick bow for Priya. "Master, we picked up his trail a few miles south. Mehara and I followed it, and we caught up to him."

Priya grunted. "Then what are you doing here?"

Mehara looked at Hotaru and then faced the Master Wizard. "Hotaru tried to distract him with fire while I tried to pry into his mind, but Carson had already placed counterspells before we even made our attacks. He had a Circle of Healing with a smaller Circle of Protection inside—"

"Impossible. He couldn't have laid one within the other like that."

Mehara looked afraid to continue, but she went on. "His mind had a powerful seal, so I couldn't get in. We tried to get close enough to use body magic, but we couldn't break the Circles without weakening ourselves."

"You should have signaled for me. That was sloppy of you."

"We did, Master. However...he had already placed an enchantment that prevented us from signaling you."

"And what was my old friend doing the whole time you fought his spells?"

Hotaru spoke up this time, his expression betraying embarrassment. "He drank coffee and read a newspaper."

"Was he disguised as a gypsy?" Priya glared at me.

Hotaru shook his head. "He wore a black fedora and trench coat."

"Go and pick up the trail again. I'll be with you shortly." He watched them take off, and his face once again returned to its immovable expression.

"You seem a little frustrated, Master Priya." I couldn't help but smirk. My father did well indeed. There was no wonder why they couldn't catch him this whole time. I prayed his luck wouldn't run out.

"I'm not frustrated, my dear, I'm simply disappointed. Your father is a difficult man...always has been. I'm sorry you had to learn about him this way, though I dare say it was inevitable." He tipped his hat toward me and then faced Brande. "You and Father Gabriel are expected at the Gray Tower, so I suggest you get there soon. And may I ask, what are *your* plans, Miss George?"

"Kill Nazis."

"Excellent. Perhaps our paths will cross again...maybe in London? My mother was from there, and my father was from India. Carson actually accompanied me there once, a long time ago." He lowered his gaze as if in deep thought, then regarded Brande with one last mysterious look before turning away and disappearing.

I breathed a soft sigh and turned to face Brande. "What you just did for me...thank you."

"We have to be careful. I've seen Master Priya do terrible things to get what he wants."

I didn't doubt that. The Order of Wizards had a noble purpose, stood between Octavian's Black Wolves and the rest of the world, and there were many selfless and righteous people who made up its ranks. However, people often confused this with pure benevolence, and forgot that individual wizards within the Order could fall prey to the vices and faults that plagued all humans. I had seen selfish wizards, cruel wizards, and morally questionable ones—they weren't all under Octavian's control.

"Sometimes I really hate them."

"I hope...you don't hate me."

"I don't hate you." I smiled at him, and he just stood there and gazed at me—well, it was more like he was ravishing me with his eyes, but I wasn't going to complain.

The boys I saw earlier had returned and gathered around us, offering more sandwiches for francs.

"I'll...walk you back to Le Fleur," he said, finally aware of his surroundings.

"Thanks." I waved goodbye to the clamoring children.

Brande offered me his arm, and I took it. As we headed down the street, I kept thinking about the meeting with my father. I raked over each and every detail from his gray-streaked beard to his somber words. *Find Veit Heilwig...* I would find him all right, and he would never have to be forced to make those deadly weapons again. He'd reunite with my father.

Brande opened the door for me and I went inside Le Fleur. Father Gabriel spotted us from the dining area and called out to us, gesturing toward two seats that were apparently saved for us. Lucien and Ernest sat at the bar, drinking and chatting with the bartender.

"We were worried, Noelle." Gabriel poured us water from a carafe. "You shouldn't have gone off this morning without telling anyone."

This immediately killed my mood. I may have forgiven Brande, but Father Gabriel was a different matter. We took our seats, and I diverted my gaze to the cup of fresh coffee and plate of chocolates in front of me. I drank and sat there, avoiding small talk and not making eye contact with Gabriel.

"To the smoking room, then?" Lucien joined us, offering Brande and Gabriel cigars. His eyes were bright and alert, and his demeanor gave off a sense of strength that I hadn't seen before. I supposed he had taken to heart the talk we had the other day.

We stood and headed into the smoking room. The lights gave

the worn billiard table a soft glow, and the lingering scent of cigars hung in the air. After we entered, Brande locked the door behind us then joined us around the billiard table.

"What time should we meet?" Gabriel asked.

"Seven," I interjected, thinking about my unwanted midnight rendezvous with Simon. "It shouldn't take us more than an hour to get there."

"I'll take care of supplies," Brande said.

"Noelle and Brande..." Lucien gestured toward us. "You should take the Ruinart entrance. If the tunnels and caves run beneath the city like a maze, then it's better if we split up and come in from four different directions."

Ernest nodded. "I can come in from the south, Luce can take the west tunnel, and Father can come in from the east."

Lucien faced me. "You don't suppose Simon Vester wouldn't mind allowing me access to the records hall so I can copy a map?"

Sure, it would be like sticking my bloody finger in a shark tank. "I...think I can manage that."

"So, we come in from all four sides." Brande pocketed his cigar. "Who's going to disable the alarms?"

Ernest spoke up. "Whoever's at the main entrance will have to do it. At the Catalonia lab, there were two guards posted at the main entrance with an outside trigger—if you see two men, then you'll know you're at the main door."

"Those men will have to be taken care of immediately. If it's set up like the other lab, there should be between ten to twelve elite armed forces men inside—and a Black Wolf."

I thought about Praskovya, and Marc. "There will most likely be other warlocks there too. I should lay Sublimation symbols when I go in, and when the job's done...or as a last resort, blow the entire place to hell."

"You can hold it off, right?" Ernest asked.

I nodded. "I'll have to rig the electrical system so when I release it all, I can get an explosion, but it's doable."

"Then do it after we find the doctor."

"Then that'll give us a limited amount of time," I warned him. "I can only hold off the symbols for so long."

"I'll help Ernest and Lucien fight off the guards," Gabriel said, "and I can break away to help you and Brande dispose of any warlocks."

"Then I'll see you all at seven." Lucien loosened his collar as if he had just come home from a long day at work. He went over to the wall and grabbed a couple of mounted cue sticks. He handed one to Ernest.

"Brande...Father Gabriel...are you in?" Ernest stuck his cigar in between his teeth. "Noelle?"

"I'm...tired. I should go lie down." My head throbbed, and I didn't care too much for being sequestered in a stuffy room full of cigar smoke.

"Should I keep watch?" Brande moved toward me.

"Hmph." Ernest smirked at us and muttered something to Lucien. Both of them chuckled.

"Sure," I told Brande. "I'll see the rest of you tonight."

"Actually, why don't I play chaperone," Gabriel said, "while the fellows here enjoy their game and cigars. Brande, you haven't eaten today. You must be famished." Gabriel placed his hand on Brande's shoulder to keep him from going any farther and then followed me.

I turned away and scowled. I rushed out of the smoking room and headed upstairs without looking back. When I reached my room, I plopped onto the bed, burying my face in my pillow and praying that Gabriel would just leave me alone.

"I take it you're no longer angry with Brande?" He shut the door behind him and went over to the cushioned chair in the corner.

"He explained everything to me, and I know what happened in Salon-de-Provence. Do you really think what the Tower does to

Drifters is right? *Father?*" I faced him and shot him an accusatory glance.

"Due to the Fall of Man," he said as he gazed straight into my eyes, "most of us have lost what should be our innate abilities and capacities to interact with nature, and to truly see the world as it is..."

"Spare me the sermon. I don't want to hear about how wizards are all abominations."

He continued. "If you'll allow me to finish, I was going to say that there are people both within and outside the Church who strongly exhibit preternatural abilities. Their function is still debated among theologians, but all are accepted as God's children. Though I will say that the Church, along with the Order of Wizards, holds the belief that it would be imprudent, presumptuous, and above all dangerous, for any person to attempt to access what you call the Akashic Record."

Well, that didn't sound too horrible. "So...if my father were here, you wouldn't try to kill him?"

"No, I wouldn't. I already told you why I fight."

"But you wouldn't stand in the way of someone who was tracking him?"

"The Church has never interfered with the Gray Tower when it came to this matter."

My jaw tightened. "Can you please leave my room?"

"As you wish, but before I leave, I would like to share an observation. I hope...you consider the fact that Brande is beholden to the Gray Tower, similar in some ways to how I am beholden to the Church. Be careful regarding your trust in him."

I said nothing else, and I watched him get up and leave. I could tell he was holding something back, and it scared me—but even more, his words angered me because part of me saw the ugly truth in them. Brande was handpicked and groomed to ultimately become the Head of the Order. He possessed all the qualities they wanted, including a fierce loyalty that they presumed belonged only to them. Also, the fact that he came so close to subduing my father, a Philosopher, demonstrated both his strength and acumen, which they also highly prized.

When people thought of traditional philosophers, they would usually call to mind the Greek ancients like Plato and Aristotle, or other masters of logic and argument, or constructors and deconstructionists of entire systems of thought. Among wizards, the Philosopher could very well encompass these, but the most exceptional thing about them was their ability to calculate and predict others' actions and reactions based on observance of human nature and mathematical probability—all with an uncanny accuracy.

I had seen Philosophers walk through war zones raging with fire and blood, avoiding being hit by a single bullet, or eluding the radius of an explosion because they've already projected and determined which type of soldier would perform a certain action, when they'd perform it, and what the result would be. Philosophers had entered rooms filled with heads of state, barely speaking a sentence, and directing the tide of political decisions. They were like master chess players, except the match was life itself. My father could do all these things, and had done them both on behalf of the Gray Tower and the country he loved.

The Order of Wizards had cast him aside though, because his foresight was a little too accurate. The Masters must have figured out that he was more than just an extraordinary Philosopher: he was a Drifter. And when he faked his death in Rome and went into hiding, it only confirmed that he was a dreaded time wizard who could literally predict the future and even access the Akashic Record.

This obviously changed everything, and I wasn't sure what my next move would be. I still wanted to be in the United States before the end of the year, so my father would have to meet me at home. Once I rescued Heilwig, he could come with me, and maybe even teach again at a university, like Johnnie. I really wanted to go home, to my brother and mother, and my sister-in-law who I've never met. I wanted time to heal my mind and body, and I needed time to think about other important matters, like those of the heart.

If I hadn't ruined things with Ken, I would've been planning my wedding. Today, I felt drawn toward Brande, but I knew pursuing him would only complicate things, and besides, I'd feel like I was deceiving myself and Brande if I gave to him something I could easily retract because I still had feelings for Ken. Whoever I ended up with, I would want him to know that I gave myself heart, mind, body and soul, freely and completely. And, I would want the same devotion from him. With that said, I still had the feelings and desires of any other twenty-six year old woman.

And sometimes it was hard as hell.

CHAPTER 17

"Could I interest the lady and gentleman in a sweet glass of Cuvée?" The server, Jean, clasped his hands together and smiled.

"Yes, thank you." Brande looked a little bored, but when he gazed at me, his eyes lit up.

"And would you like me to take your sweater, miss? We'll be starting the fireplace soon, so you won't have to worry about it being as cool inside."

"We're fine," I replied. "And we'd like the Cuvée chilled."

"As you say." He left to retrieve our bottle of champagne.

I stared at Brande, and it was like I was seeing him clearer than ever. Though he rarely smiled or expressed excitement, I could simply look into his eyes and tell what he felt. His demeanor carried a quiet strength that I found reassuring. And then there was something inside him that made his exterior even more appealing; he had an intelligent, compassionate, and wonderful mind that shone through.

I couldn't help but think of how I used to laugh when our receptionist, Bernadine, would fall over him every time he'd come to visit me at the Baker Street office. She would pout her lips, speak to him with a syrupy voice, and find any excuse to touch his hand. Now, if I caught Bernadine speaking to him, I'd be tempted to whack her with a Circle of Silence.

"What time is it?" Brande rested his hand next to mine. We were sitting next to each other in one of the booths.

"Don't worry, we have a few minutes left. Just enjoy the atmosphere."

"Do you like places like this?" He slowly pulled his hand back down to his side.

"Yes," I faced him, trying to interrupt the awkwardness with a typical taunt. "I swear, you need to get out of the Gray Tower more! Do you like it here?"

"I do."

"If you prefer more lively places, then I know this bar in Cairo..."

"I had a lively time just tracking you down in a park earlier today."

"What can I say? I love excitement. It certainly helped me say yes to SOE and the Order." But then the excitement wore off with harsh reality and the mundane, and I got tired.

"If the Order never invited you to join, what do you think you'd be doing?" He sounded more like he wanted to ask himself this question.

"SOE recruited me because they needed wizards," I said. "I'd probably still be working as a clerk for the ambassador, or even back home teaching. How about you?"

"I don't know. I came to the Gray Tower when I was sixteen, and it's all I've known. Even for my formal schooling, they'd invite professors to come in from the University of Prague to instruct younger members. It seemed the younger you were when you entered, the fiercer their grip was on you."

I knew it. Deep inside, even *he* noticed how they manipulated people. "At least I enjoyed a little independence and freedom before I came. I swear if I see Leto Priya again, I'll punch him right in his face—Master or not."

Jean came back with our champagne. "Your chilled bottle of Cuvée."

He uncorked the bottle and filled our glasses. We both thanked him before taking our drinks in silence. Brande asked for the time again.

I sighed when I peeked at the clock on the wall opposite me. "We should head down to the cellars."

I finished my drink and led Brande down the same way Simon had led me. As planned, everyone else took their assigned entrances: Gabriel the east entrance, Lucien the west, and Ernest would come in from the south. I had telephoned Simon earlier so Lucien would be able to go to the records hall and find a map of the city to work with.

We trudged through the winding tunnels, keeping an eye on the markings and going by memory of the map. Most of the tunnels had iron sconces mounted every few feet on the walls, with large candles giving off flickering light. Frescoes with fading and chipping paint covered the ceiling, and, of course, graffiti from past and present. When the tunnel grew darker, we knew we were close to the entrance, and we proceeded cautiously. We peeked around the corner and saw two armed SS officers guarding a steel door. A single ceiling lamp, powered by electricity within the lab, lit their path so they could spot anyone approaching.

I unbuttoned my sweater and let it slip to the ground. I wore a black shirt and cargo pants, with my knife stored in one of my pockets, and my pistol in my holster. My bracelet made with vitriol still hung on my wrist, and I stood ready.

We needed to neutralize the guards before they triggered the external alarm, and then we had to subdue the officer who would be at the front desk before he sounded the internal alarm. Brande increased the heat in the ceiling lamp's bulb, so that it cracked and went out, making the tunnel completely dark. He used this moment of confusion to approach the guards. I heard a scuffle, a confused gasp, and then silence. They were dead at a single touch.

Brande ignited a small flame to give us light as I scraped the black vitriol in my bracelet against the keyhole. The lock instantaneously corroded and fell apart. We opened the door and went through. I immediately grabbed my silver knife and laid a Circle of Silence while Brande forced the guard at the desk toward us with Air. The officer came flying toward us and maneuvered himself so he could kick Brande, but he cut off the spell, and the officer dropped to the floor. He quickly got to his feet and made a quick jab at Brande, who blocked him. They continued fighting as I made my way over to the desk to disable the alarm.

Goosebumps ran up my arms, and my stomach tightened. I could already feel the presence of a Black Wolf here, perhaps two. Brande was smart to conserve his magical energy, since the real battle hadn't started yet.

As I took my knife and began cutting wires and readjusting them, I also thought about Simon and why he didn't tell us Black Wolves were here. He had led me to believe there were only just a handful of German Armed Forces soldiers, and of course, I anticipated the possibility of running into Praskovya and any other warlocks. Although I felt that something was wrong, I knew I had to stick to our plan. Our lives depended on each of us accomplishing our assigned tasks.

I patched up the control panel to the alarm and stood to get a view of Brande. He had subdued the guard, as evidenced by the blood splattered on the floor near the guard's body. Brande stepped over him and approached.

"You can release the Circle now," he told me. "You'll have more energy for the Sublimations."

I nodded and leaned against the desk. We were in the section called "Chamber One," a mid-sized room with only the desk, some maps, and notes hanging on the wall behind it, and two corridors on the right and left sides.

"Give me a boost first." I pointed toward a large grate on the ceiling which would open up into the ducts where electricians and engineers crawled in to work on the electrical system or maintain the venting. I would need to go throughout the ducts, planting Sublimation symbols along the way and readjusting the wiring. When I could no longer hold off the Sublimations, I'd release them, and then the entire laboratory would go up in flames.

I jumped onto the desk and pulled on the grate. It came down with little effort, and Brande helped steady it and set it aside. He climbed on top of the table with me and held onto my waist, giving me the boost I needed when I jumped.

"I'll take the left corridor." Brande paused and listened. We heard voices and gunshots.

I crawled into the duct and let him replace the grate. I moved through, trying my best to cause the least amount of noise. Every few feet, I would carve in a Sublimation symbol, without activating them. When I found some of the wiring I needed to rig, I set to work on those and then kept moving.

I turned a corner and I felt Brande's magic at work. By gauging the strength of his spells, I knew he had run into the Black Wolf. I could hear some of the other soldiers within the lab, some shouting orders and others engaged in a gunfight. I heard Ernest and Lucien taunting them as they shot back at the guards and lured them away from the inner lab areas. Metal ringing and slashing off in the distance, filled my ears—and I thought of Father Gabriel.

Just ahead, I saw a vent that let out into one of the research rooms. The light was on in the room below. I slowed my breathing and approached, peeking down into the room from my hiding place. Dr. Heilwig stood in there, mixing chemicals on an apparatus and storing a blue liquid in small tubes. If that liquid was anything like the black powder in Vélizy, then it would have to be destroyed as well. I was just about to whisper Heilwig's name when I heard a familiar voice address him.

"I think my brother will like this new formula. We'll deliver it in the morning." Marc came into view and walked over to Heilwig, observing him with that same look of avarice he held for any wizard whose blood he wanted to drink.

I grimaced as I recalled the night I had escaped from him. I wanted to jump through the vent and blast him with a spell, but instead, I held myself back and listened to their exchange.

"Then...do you think Octavian will let my wife go free?" Heilwig's lips trembled, though he kept his hands steady. I could tell from the way he moved and spoke that he still suffered the effects of the stroke from the Teleportation spell.

Marc sneered. "After that little incident at the university, you're lucky to be alive."

"What about my wife?"

"I'll talk to my brother, but I want something in return."

"I have nothing, Marcellus."

"I know you're out of the Gray Tower's good graces, so a few dead wizards wouldn't matter, right? I was wondering if you knew any exceptionally strong wizards I could...easily get my hands on. You know, like your friend Carson."

"Even if I did, I wouldn't tell you."

Marc grunted. "Faithful till the bitter end. When will you learn that the Order has abandoned you?"

"I see you've made no progress with Octavian."

"Oh, he'll believe me once I find Carson. We just need to catch him before your beloved Gray Tower does."

"Carson died sixteen years ago."

"Like hell he did. That reminds me, I ran into his daughter a few days ago. She lit me on fire, shot me, and tried to make my heart explode...I like her."

"Well, I pray next time you run into her that she succeeds."

"You insolent bastard, do you want to be stuck in here the

rest of your life? In a room with padded walls so you can't see or hear anything?" He looked ready to lunge for Heilwig's throat.

"You want to talk about living?" Heilwig gritted his teeth. "You're nothing but an empty shell. You wish to kill *real* wizards and steal their powers just to prove yourself better than your brother. Octavian's no better than you, but at least he was born one of us...but you? You're just a pathetic parasite."

Marc's facial expression suddenly lost all amusement. "I should've drained you dry when I had the chance."

"One day you'll get what you deserve, *abomination*." Heilwig shook as he said this.

"Do you want to know something?" Marc grinned and ran his finger across the apparatus as if inspecting it.

"What, Marcellus?"

"I killed your wife yesterday."

"Rosa..." A pain-stricken look of disbelief showed on his face, and his shoulders shook with quiet sobs. My heart hurt for him when he doubled over, almost breathless with grief.

"I convinced Octavian that she really didn't need to live, and after tonight, neither will you." He placed his hand on Heilwig's back. "There, old friend. See? Now you truly have nothing."

"Why her? I don't care what happens to me, but why her?"

Marc grabbed the tube filled with Heilwig's concoction and set it in a dark wooden case with five others. He closed the lid and locked the case.

"It was a pleasure doing business with you, doctor."

"Rosa...why?"

"If you want to end this now, I'll happily oblige you."

The door opened, and an SS officer entered. "Sir, the lab is under assault by wizards."

"Stay with Dr. Heilwig, and make sure no one comes in." He rushed out of the room. The officer went to close the door behind him. As he shut the door, I scraped my enchanted bracelet against the grate like I did the Chamber One door, and the vent's cover corroded and fell out.

I quickly dropped in and struck the guard before he could pull his weapon. He stumbled backward, slightly dazed, then steadied himself as he threw several punches. I blocked and dodged, and made a chop to his neck with the blade of my hand, emphasizing my lower wrist, where I knew the black vitriol would touch him. He screeched and clawed at his neck as he backed away. He fell against the wall, blood gushing, and a dark corrosive substance eating way at his flesh.

"Dr. Heilwig!" I ran toward him and grabbed hold of him. I wanted to say something...anything about his wife. I didn't know if Marc was lying or not, but the pain on Heilwig's face showed that he had at least believed him. "Do you remember me?"

"Of course, from the university. What are you doing here?"

"I'm Isabella, Carson's daughter, and he sent me to take you out of here."

He stared at me when I tried to pull him along. "What about Marcellus and the Black Wolves? And...Praskovya?"

"Praskovya's here?"

"Her, and about four Black Wolves."

I wanted to curse. I thought at most there'd be two Black Wolves, not four. "Stay here while I scout ahead. If I'm not back in five minutes, get into that duct and crawl through to Chamber One. If you need to...there are Sublimation symbols along the ducts. I'm sure you'd know what to do with them."

"I can fight, too."

It would break my heart to tell him he couldn't help. He didn't have the necessary reflexes, and he still wore the gold imperium collar around his neck, which meant that his spells were limited; he could do nothing against Praskovya. "Dr. Heilwig...I don't want to take that chance. My father said to find you, so I need you out of here and in those cellars."

He nodded. "Please, don't tell me you came alone."

"Don't worry, I have an Elite with me, two military men, and a priest."

"Are you sure you don't want me to—"

"Please, just do what I told you."

I made him close and lock the door behind me before scouting the immediate area and deciding to head left, down the corridor. I heard two gunshots and a man painfully shrieking.

Thankfully, I could still feel Brande, though the force of his magic wasn't as fierce as before. I checked several research rooms just to make sure they were empty, and when I came out of the third one, I saw a Black Wolf approaching. This one was the most human looking one I had ever seen, though his eyes shone an eerie red and his skin was as pale as a corpse.

Before I could make a move, he gestured with his hand and paralyzed me. Like a flitting spirit, he was right in front of me, having only been down the hall a moment ago. The only thing that kept me from panicking was the fact that one of my Sublimation symbols had been carved into the duct right above us.

Just as his skeletal fingers reached for my neck, I released the Sublimation symbol and caused an explosion. As fire and shrapnel came flying down, I regained my ability to move and quickly dipped low, crouching beneath him so that he would take the brunt of the hit. He let out a deafening shriek, and the vibrations of his voice turned into an invisible force that slammed me to the ground.

I quickly made my next move and drew my pistol, shoved it beneath his chin, and took a shot. He lunged toward me and sank his teeth into my right shoulder. I cried out in shock, but my vitriol bracelet kept me from feeling the pain. Another Sublimation symbol down the hall released, and an explosion erupted. I prayed none of my friends were down there and got caught in the fire. I forced myself to stay focused, knowing that with each slip up, I could blow us all up before we even had the chance to escape.

I held the Black Wolf at bay with my forearm and scraped the black vitriol against his face. As he roared and pushed himself off of me, I jumped away and ran down the corridor. I lost hold of another Sublimation symbol, and a second explosion nearly caught me from behind. The hallway blackened with smoke and heated up like an oven. When I heard the unintelligible tongue of the Black Wolf, probably cursing me, I ran into the nearest research room and hid behind the open door. I didn't have time to close the door or else he'd notice, but I made sure to breathe as quietly as I could.

Through the crack between the door's hinges, I could see a German officer walking in with his rifle ready, but he didn't venture too far into the room. We both heard feet dragging, and that awful guttural voice. The officer turned around and started screaming in German, "Stop! I'm on your side!"

A few rounds went off and his gun flew to the other side of the room, clattering against the floor. I heard the Black Wolf grunt, then I heard teeth grinding, and what must've been the tearing of clothes, flesh, and bone.

I wasn't going to stick around for that monster to corner me in the room, so I dashed over to the abandoned rifle, picked it up, and shot the Black Wolf in the back as he hunched over his prey. Though bullets riddled his body and my black vitriol corroded half his face, he still stood there alive, though clearly weakened. I ran toward him and kicked him in his head, then drew my pistol again and shot. I almost stumbled over him and the officer's mangled body. When the Black Wolf backed off and began regurgitating a black liquid and human bones, I ran away.

I forced my magical hold on the Sublimations to remain stable as I rushed down the hall. I couldn't afford to unravel individual symbols anymore—not when it caused two or three other symbols to unintentionally fall apart and ignite explosions. When I thought I heard Praskovya's voice, I made a right turn and headed toward Chamber Three. I grunted and held my breath as I stepped over mutilated bodies; one of them definitely looked like a Black Wolf.

I went down the next corridor and crossed over to a storage area with crates. In a large open space I saw Praskovya fighting in hand-to-hand combat with Ernest. I knew her fighting style well, and I could tell she was toying with him. Ernest probably didn't know that she was telekinetic and could kill him at any second without him being aware of what hit him.

"Praskovya!" I hoped that my shout would distract her enough for Ernest to back off, or at least land another blow to stun her. However, she simultaneously faced me and sent Ernest flying into a crate. Then she sent a reinforced crate that hung above him to come plummeting down.

I took my silver knife and quickly drew the symbol for Air. A blast of wind rose from the ground and met the falling crate just as it was about to crush Ernest. I managed to control and guide the crate so that it avoided hitting Ernest, and instead it headed straight toward Praskovya. She ducked, rolled, and with a flourish of her hand, sent me flying toward the other side of the room. I quickly got back onto my feet, expecting her to follow up with a physical attack, but she had disappeared.

"Ernest, are you hurt?" I ran toward him, all the while thinking how odd it was that she left so quickly. It wasn't like Praskovya to run.

"I'm all right." He shakily sat up and gazed at the ceiling, apparently in awe that the crate didn't land on him.

"Ernest," I handled him as tenderly as I could. "I think your arm is broken."

"Well, I still have one good arm. Just give me a gun." He yelped and winced when I tried to examine his injured arm.

"Here, take this." I slid my bracelet off and gave it to him. "It'll dull the pain and protect you. Don't go anywhere until one of us comes for you."

"Where did the Russian babe go?"

"I don't know…" I cursed under my breath when I realized Praskovya's intentions. As I shouted my instructions to Ernest once more, I raced down the corridor, retracing my steps, in hopes of reaching Heilwig before Praskovya did.

It took me a few minutes to make it back over to the research rooms, but when I arrived, Heilwig was gone. I noticed the case holding the formula was lying on the counter. I hid it in one of the drawers, sealing it with an alchemical symbol that would only open for an alchemist.

"Noelle, this way!"

"Simon! What are you doing here?" I could barely conceal my startled gaze. Didn't I tell him to stay at home?

"Hurry, love. This way!" He frantically gestured, and I followed.

"Have you seen Praskovya?"

"Yes, she's looking for Dr. Heilwig. I think he escaped."

I breathed a sigh of relief. Maybe he went through the ducts after all. "Who's still around, Simon? Can you tell me?"

"I saw a man with a sword fighting Marcellus, and a young man in a gunfight with a soldier, but this is all so chaotic."

"Simon, do you have any more written formulas or important records?" We turned a corner and approached Chamber Six.

"Yes, I keep it all in my office. Do you need them?"

"It would make me very happy to have them." I would eventually have to activate the rest of my Sublimation spells, and afterward there wouldn't be anything left to save or take away from the laboratory.

"It's down here." He led me further down the hall, to a door near the end with his name on it. He unlocked it and let me in.

With no time to spare, I ran over to his desk and began grabbing papers, notes, and anything else that would be of use to SOE and the Allies later on.

"Were you looking for something in particular?"

"No, just…anything significant." I folded the papers with haste and stuffed them into my cargo pockets. I instinctively looked up when I heard the door shut. Simon stood against the door, revolver drawn and pointed at me, a cold look in his eye.

"Simon, this isn't the time to play games. Put that away and help me."

I flinched when he fired a shot. The bullet whizzed past my ear. I instinctively brushed my finger against my Agate stone ring, which helped deflect bullets, but it didn't make me impervious to them.

"We need to talk, Noelle."

"Well, it seems the red garnet spell finally wore off."

"No, I still feel the same. How many times must I tell you my feelings are genuine?"

The door opened and Praskovya came in. she wore an expression of mild shock, but smirked when she saw me in my predicament. Simon ignored her and spoke to me again.

"I went out today and saw you this morning at the park. I saw you with *him*!"

"I—"

"Quiet." His lower lip trembled, and his eyes bulged. "Why...why couldn't you be that way with me?"

"Mister Vester," Praskovya said, "just shoot her and get it over with. We must find Heilwig and go."

"Stay out of this, Nikon."

"Simon." I kept my voice level. "You're still under the enchantment, and for it to last this long, you must've fed into it."

He dismissed my statement with an indignant look. "Remember that couple we saw in Ruinart? And remember the question I asked?"

"Simon..." the next gunshot grazed my right arm, and I flinched as I sucked in a quick painful breath. A small stream of blood traveled down and dripped from my fingers. Though my legs quivered and my arms felt weak, I tried my best to not appear afraid. Showing him fear would only embolden him and make him feel more powerful.

"I asked you if you remembered."

"Y-yes, Simon. I remember them."

"The way they looked at each other...it was the same way you two looked at each other. Now, I did everything you asked, so why don't you love me?"

"If you want me to answer," I said, "put the gun away. In case you haven't noticed, I've laid Sublimations throughout the lab. If you shoot me, this entire place will explode."

"Sir," Praskovya spoke slowly, apparently not wanting to provoke him in his instability. "Don't shoot. Our first priority is finding Heilwig."

His eyes bulged again. "Oh shut up, Nikon! If you would let a man touch you every now and then, maybe you'd understand what I'm talking about, instead of reacting like a heartless bitch."

Simon's gun flew out of his hand and into Praskovya's. She shot him right in between his eyes—and then she shot him three more times before he even hit the ground.

"You're out of bullets, Praskovya." I thought I'd remind her since she had turned the gun on me.

"Then let's play a game, Isabella." She dropped the gun. "Let's play...who can find the doctor first?"

She sent both the desk and me flying toward the ceiling. I braced myself as I hit the roof and grunted in pain when the desk crashed against my back and knocked the breath out of me. Loose papers flew and encircled me like a tornado, so that I could barely see. When I landed with a crash, she had already gone out the door. I rose to my feet, back aching, and limped over to Simon's body. I slid Heilwig's ring off his finger and placed it on my own, then headed out the door toward Chamber One.

I ran as fast as I could, taking every shortcut I could remember. If Heilwig wasn't distracted or withheld, he should have followed the symbols carved in the ducts and be at the Ruinart entrance, if not already in the caves. As I raced through corridors and Chambers, I noticed the eerie silence permeating the laboratory. Worry caught hold of me, but I pressed on, remembering what my father had told me. I needed to bring Heilwig to safety, and he needed to remain by my side.

After whisking through one last corridor, I finally arrived where I began, in Chamber One with the solitaire desk and the maps on the wall. I clenched my teeth when I remembered the six vials in the drawer, and hoped that I wouldn't forget them before I ignited the place. When I heard the fall of footsteps coming in my direction from the corridor that Brande had taken earlier, I used my knife to enclose myself in a loose circular formation of symbols representing the four elements: Earth, Air, Water, and Fire.

I pivoted and swept my foot across the symbols, feeding them with energy. I would only be able to do this once, or else I wouldn't be strong enough to hold off those Sublimations in the ducts. I drew my pistol and waited. Sure enough, Praskovya came striding into the Chamber with Heilwig in tow. She held a colt revolver to the back of his head, and the case with the six vials was nestled under her other arm. Heilwig must have attempted to retrieve the case when Praskovya surprised him.

"It appears I've won." She gestured with a quick nod, ordering me to drop my weapon.

"It isn't over yet." I placed my pistol on the ground and stood with hands raised.

"Which do you care about more? Is it the doctor, or this formula that could destroy thousands of more lives? Which would you take?"

"Are you offering me one or the other?" I tried to figure out what her angle was.

"Yes."

"Please," Heilwig sank to his knees and crossed his hands behind his head. "Take the formula. They've already used me to spread their evil doctrines and to kill, and I selfishly went along, trying to save my Rosa. I shouldn't have done this."

"If I were you, I'd take the formula, Isabella. He's outlived his use to everyone, even the Gray Tower." She cocked the revolver.

"Why don't you take both, Praskovya?"

"Because you've laid Sublimation spells and would be willing to kill us all to keep me from taking him and the formula. However, I'm willing to compromise. We could at least walk away with something."

"I don't—"

"I know you just as well as you know me, and I think you're tired of all this. Isabella, what better way to return to London than in victory? You've done your duty, and if you continue, you'll only end up like me."

Okay, maybe being broken wasn't the worst thing that could happen to me, but I knew I'd never become a turncoat like Praskovya. "No. I'm not going anywhere. I've already got samples of the original formula, and they're on their way to the British by now. The Allies would figure out sooner or later how to counteract the new one."

"Wrong. Again. The products at the Vélizy factory were carefully crafted decoys. The real stockpile is here."

My stomach tightened and my right hand involuntarily trembled. All I could think about was the trouble I had gone through at Vélizy, of victims like Timothy and all the lives that were risked and lost. If the decoys took most of my energy to work on and neutralize, then I wouldn't even have a chance if I tried to replicate the neutralization with the real stockpile. How much more powerful were the real chemical weapons? The Plague was powerful enough to destroy the entire world.

I gulped. "Well, I guess that's all the more reason for me to bring this place crashing down on us, Praskovya."

Hopefully that wouldn't be the case for my friends and me. I could already feel my hold on the symbols weakening, and my hand shook again. When another Sublimation gave way and an explosion could be heard from one of the chambers on the other side, my stomach tightened and I tried not to think about how I may have just killed Ernest or Lucien.

"I don't plan to die today," Praskovya said, "and neither do you. Let's be reasonable." She slid the case over toward me, and it halted between us.

"Take it." Praskovya shoved the gun in between Heilwig's shoulder blades. "Serve the greater good, and you can go back and tell SOE that you've saved thousands of lives by retrieving the formula."

Her words triggered my painful memory of that Orleans job. That pig Maquis leader said it had all been for the greater good, and he boasted of how we had saved thousands of lives, if not millions. But he did it with blood on his hands...on my hands too. No, I wouldn't leave Heilwig to be shot in the head or eaten by Marc so that I could boast about how I served the greater good. I'd find a way to get both him and the formula.

"I want Heilwig."

She waited so long to respond that I thought she'd refuse. "Get up, and go to her."

As soon as Heilwig rose to his feet, I set off my Air symbol and mentally guided the strong gust of wind toward Praskovya. I knew she'd try to shoot Heilwig in the back. She flew backward, hit the wall with a crack, and fell to the floor. Heilwig grabbed the case and dashed toward me.

Praskovya jumped to her feet and fired a few shots at us. I ran forward and deflected two bullets, though the action made my grazed arm sting and run with more blood. I shouted for Heilwig to keep running and head for the Ruinart cellars. When I heard the front door open and shut, I felt a surge of confidence and energy. At least Heilwig made it out.

"Bravo, Isabella." She slipped her gun into her holster with an arrogant grin. "But there is something you've forgotten."

"Go ahead, enlighten me." I stood ready to activate all four symbols and wreak havoc.

"Where are your friends?"

"I'm not playing your games anymore." Though I spoke these words, fear grew inside me. Where were they? And why couldn't I feel Brande?

"Perhaps Marcellus is feasting on their blood." She smiled. "But not Drahomir, I sent the Wolves after him."

I hated the fact that my emotions had the better of me in this moment, and I especially hated that she knew exactly where to strike. The fury within me began to burn.

"Where's Marc?"

"I don't know, but you should go look for him."

"I think you're lying." My chest tightened, and my stomach ached. Now I knew how Heilwig had felt when he heard about his wife. I prayed they were all safe, especially Brande. Defeating a few Black Wolves on your own might as well have been like raising the dead with a snap of your fingers.

I fired a shot to distract her, knowing she'd use her powers to halt or deflect the bullet. I rushed her and pistol-whipped her, and she reciprocated with a middle-kick to my rib, to which I countered with a right hook. We both backed away, heaving and limping. When I heard Ernest call my name from the left corridor, my heart leapt, and I quickly delivered another strike, which she, in turn, blocked. She broke away and fled toward the corridor on the right. I was ready to follow her when I turned to see Ernest and Gabriel, hauling an unconscious Brande in between them, and Lucien trailing after them, using a makeshift walking stick to support his gait.

"What happened to him?" I ran toward them and switched places with Gabriel, placing Brande's left arm across my shoulders, supporting him.

"It was a couple of Black Wolves." Gabriel's right cheek was swollen, and the cut under his left eye bled. "I tried to heal him, but whatever spell hit him...the Circle of Healing didn't work."

Ernest held onto Brande from the right, almost oblivious to his own injuries because he still wore the bracelet. "Tough guy. He went up against all four Black Wolves."

"That damned vampire bit me." Lucien scowled as he rotated his left arm. "Then he said I wasn't his type."

"That was a Cruenti warlock," Gabriel said as he sidled next to him and helped him walk. "And without his head, he'll never bite anyone else again."

I felt Brande's cheek against mine, and I grew alarmed at how cold it was. His face felt like a block of ice. What did those monsters do to him? He still breathed, but his breaths were so slow and laborious that it seemed he would stop at any moment.

"Brande, can you hear me?" My heart sank when his eyes didn't open. Not a single movement, not even a groan of pain. He was unresponsive and silent.

Ernest looked at me. "I'm sorry..."

I shook my head. "No! We need to help him." I took a deep breath and tried not to panic. He couldn't die...I wouldn't let him.

"What can we do?" Lucien asked.

The only thing I could think of was the bracelet. It was charged with enough power and protection to at least keep Brande breathing. "I'm sorry, Ernest, I'm going to have to ask for the bracelet. It's the only thing that'll help him right now."

"Sure." He slipped it off and slid it onto Brande's wrist, but began shouting in pain and cursing. He refused to let Gabriel take his place, and insisted that he had endured worse as a soldier.

My hand trembled again. I felt the ties holding back the Sublimation symbols unravel. "Let's get out of here so I can blow this place up. Heilwig's waiting for us in the cellars."

We painstakingly snaked our way through the cavernous tunnels. When I knew I couldn't hold on any longer, I released the Sublimations, and a large explosion quaked the caves. As we neared the tunnel that would take us straight to the Ruinart cellars, I noticed a trail of blood on the floor. The amount wasn't copious, but it still made me anxious, and I asked Gabriel to take my place while I ran ahead to find Heilwig.

I entered the cellar and scanned the floor, following the drops of blood to a corner not too far from the stairway. Heilwig sat on the floor, breathing with his mouth open, and leaning against a rack of champagne bottles. He had placed the case across his lap and held his hand over his left side, trying to stem the blood flow from his wound. Praskovya's third bullet had hit him, and I cursed her, hoping that she had died in the explosion.

"Come on, let's cast a Circle of Healing together." My body ached with exhaustion, and I knew I couldn't do it alone, but if we combined our energy to cast the Circle, we could both be healed of our injuries and weakness.

He shook his head. "It's too late for me."

I knelt beside him. "My father said we needed you. I need to take you to him, and with your help, we'll be closer to winning the war. Please, hold on."

"Take the formula, Isabella."

"Why don't you hold on to it? You're coming with me." I tasted my salty tears as they rolled down my cheeks. The more he slipped away, the more I felt I was losing my chance of finding answers and of helping my father in any significant way.

He winced and moved his hand away from his wound. He activated a symbol in his lab coat, an upside down triangle within a circle, with a second circle and triangle within those—the symbol of Secrecy.

"You don't need me, Isabella, but you do need this." He reached into his coat where he activated the Secrecy symbol, and pulled out his diary. It was the same one I saw him use at the university.

I took his diary with trembling hands. "Please don't die."

"Your father knew the risks, as well as I did. Tell him to gather the others."

"What others? I don't understand."

"Do you think he orchestrated this all alone?" He coughed up a handful of blood.

"Is there anything I can do for you?"

"Marcellus?"

"He's dead."

"Then tell your father..." His facial expression relaxed, and his mouth fell open as he exhaled his final breath. I placed my palm over his eyelids and shut them before slowly removing the case from his dead grasp.

"Isabella..." Brande still had to be carried by Gabriel and Ernest, but he was at least conscious again. He looked like he wanted to rush toward me, but he could hardly move.

I took the case and diary in my arms. I slowly approached them, trying to hide my own disappointment. "I couldn't save him."

"At least you have the formula." Lucien's eyes were filled with pity. "You've just saved many lives."

I glanced at Dr. Heilwig one last time. "I think he would've wanted it that way."

I hoped that he was finally at peace—him and his Rosa.

CHAPTER 18

After resting for a few days at Jasmine's house in Paris, Lucien and Ernest had said their goodbyes, as their leave time had come to an end, and they needed to report back to Spain. They had also wanted to take up the task of searching for the spy-assassin named Galeno, who had shot Ernest out of the sky, and still posed a threat to our pilots running missions near the Mediterranean. Brande and Father Gabriel stayed an extra day, but they knew better than to further test the Order's patience and would have to leave soon. Also, Brande still suffered from the mysterious spell the Black Wolves had hit him with. Neither Father Gabriel's nor my own Circles of Healing could help. He would need the healing of the Master Physician at the Gray Tower.

Father Gabriel and Brande planned to leave in the afternoon, and I also prepared to leave, dreading my upcoming debriefing with Ian in London. I would feel better if I were able to return with both the formula and Dr. Heilwig. I thought of my father and whether or not he'd be disappointed with me for losing his friend. For me, that would be worse than telling Ian about the particular failures of my mission.

I wondered when my father would see me again this year, and

if he had planned on letting my mother and Johnnie know he was alive. Most of all, I questioned how much longer he could outrun the Order. Michel de Nostredame had tried burning his books so as to not leave a trail, and had built an admirable reputation as a prophet and healer with the Catholic Church, which, at first, made it extremely difficult for the Gray Tower to strike him down. However, when his secretary, Jean de Chavigny, went to his master's workroom on the morning of July 2, 1566, he found Michel—the famous Nostradamus—dead in a standing position.

Your father knew the risks, as well as I...

Heilwig's words burned in my mind. I recalled Master Leto Priya, and his cold disdain. How many of the other tracker-wizards were like him, scouring the earth and mercilessly hounding my father? Why were they even compelled to? Simply because a person *could* do damage by using his powers as a Drifter didn't mean he would. Still, I wouldn't deny the strong possibility of irresponsible actions or corruption as a result of having the power to lay bare the Akashic Record. After all, Octavian and his Black Wolves had sought that power for a long time, and I'd rather die fighting to keep it out of their hands than to let them have it.

As I reflected on all this, I fondled Heilwig's talisman ring and paced through Jasmine's garden. The bright tulips and fresh scent of hyacinth appealed to my senses, but they did nothing to soothe the turmoil inside. I had the diary tucked under my arm, and I settled in the grass with it, crossing my legs. I was so busy tending Brande that I hadn't the chance to sit down and delve into its pages.

Just as I was about to open it, a shadow overcast me, and I looked up to see Brande. He stared down at me a moment, then sat next to me and slid my bracelet onto my wrist. I set the diary aside and instinctively rubbed the bracelet. I definitely would have found a way to get it back if he had gone off to the Gray Tower with it.

"Thank you." I smiled. "I almost forgot about it."

"I should be thanking you." His gray eyes looked tired, and his skin was unusually pale, especially in contrast to his dark hair. He seemed to exert much of his energy just to sit upright.

"Consider us even." I patted his freshly shaven cheek.

"I...want to help you and your father."

I gave him a dubious glance. Although it must've taken a lot for him to stand up to Master Priya, I didn't think he was ready for this—and, Father Gabriel's warning also came to mind. "Could you really go against the Gray Tower?"

He reached for my hand. "When we were in the park that day..."

"The Order isn't going to let you go, not without a fight, and I'm already in the middle of a scrap with them. For now at least, you should go."

"But you asked me to choose a side."

"And you were willing to risk your life for me. That's all I need to know. Do what's necessary at the Gray Tower, and keep your eyes and ears open."

His eyes told me otherwise, but he said in a firm voice, "I will."

"Take this." I gently pulled my hand from his grasp and took off my Agate stone ring and handed it to him.

"Don't you need it?"

"If you ever need to get a message to me, then send the ring and I'll know it was you."

"Will you ever come back to the Tower?"

"I won't say it's impossible."

"Then, if you need me for..."

"I know."

I smiled at him as he stood and headed toward the house, but I called out to him when I remembered something. "Could I ask you a question...before you go?"

"Yes."

"It's about Jasmine's side operation, with hiding and transporting people. You're the one who's been helping her, aren't you?"

He nodded. "How did you know?"

"I've talked to her about you, but I had never introduced you to each other. When we came here from Vélizy, she knew you on sight and greeted you by name."

He smiled a little. "Imagine that...I actually did something on my own, without the Gray Tower getting involved."

He went back inside to say his goodbyes to Jasmine and Penn, and I couldn't help but eye him with even more admiration than before. Perhaps there were a few more things I needed to learn about him. Though I believed he sincerely wanted to help me, it didn't mean his loyalties weren't divided, and that's what concerned me.

In some ways even *I* still felt entangled with the Tower. It seemed no matter how much I disliked the Order and tried to keep my distance from it, the Tower still somehow found its way into my life and showed me why I needed it. If I were going to be of use to my father and even go against the Black Wolves, I would need to be more than just an Apprentice. But would the Gray Tower even welcome me back, now that I knew who my father was? And if I were invited to return, would it only be to use me as a pawn?

My father said I could possibly train outside the Tower, but I doubted he could teach me much while on the run, and at some point he'd have to find an Elite or Master Alchemist to take over the advanced stages. I grabbed Heilwig's diary and opened it, wondering if in fact the key to my training was inside.

The first thing I noticed were a few pages of notes written in Turkish. An odd map opened across the next two pages—if I could call it a map. It had no obvious real world correspondence and looked like a layout of the constellations in the sky. There was a thirteen-sign zodiac, names like Eratosthenes and Ophiuchus, a prominent eight-spoke wheel, and the number 23.5 written near the center of the page.

I wasn't even sure where to begin with the names and symbols, and I had never studied Turkish, so I would have to find a way to interpret the text. However, I did go into the house and grab a pen from the kitchen so I could write down in one of the margins, "Ottoman Empire?" since I remembered that people spoke Turkish there, and my father had gone there before he disappeared.

I went into the living room and settled on Jasmine's plush sofa, ready to take more notes and continue reading. I heard the rumble of a car engine outside, and Jasmine speaking in a singsong voice. I curled up with the diary in my lap, releasing a slow breath when I turned the next page and saw that Veit had switched over to English. My name was written in large red letters, which intrigued me, but when I read his instructions to cast a Locus Circle, my fascination turned into fear.

A Locus Circle would help me build a memory palace, a dream-like state that I would step into in order to view my memories. But what could be so deeply hidden in there that Veit would be crazy enough to have me do this? Sometimes Locus Circles blurred the line between dreams and memories—and nightmares. Many wizards have stepped into these only to end up trapped in their own psychological prisons, driven mad, while others' bodies gave out on them because of the stress or fear. Even in the Gray Tower, you had to be given special permission to cast this spell.

I stopped right there, conflicted over whether or not I should go any further. Even though Veit had died helping my father and me, I didn't think he would want me to hurt myself just to understand everything in his diary. My shoulders tightened and I felt a lump in my throat. I set the diary on the coffee table and decided I'd wait to ask my father about this. The thought of the Locus Circle made a cold shudder creep down my arms, but I threw it off. I shoved the diary into one of my bags when I heard Adelaide's car horn blaring. It was time to go.

I caught Jasmine and Penn coming in from the front. I embraced both of them with a fierce hug. "Goodbye, I'll miss you."

Jasmine smiled at me. "You know you can visit any time, right? And, I mean *any* time."

I nodded. "Of course."

"For you…" Penn handed me a new passport. Once again, I would have to go by another name.

I thanked them for everything they'd done for me, and I gave them one final reminder to alert SOE that I was headed back, and that an escort should meet me in Portsmouth. It would probably be Richard, since he split his duties between piloting and escorting SOE agents at the behest of the Royal Air Force. After I gathered my belongings, I got into the car and took off with Adelaide.

⁓

Instead of the usual route an SOE agent would have to take in order to make it back to London, I had to take the long way around. Adelaide drove me across the French-Spanish border and toward the port city of Bilbao in Spain. The passport Penn had obtained for me was under the name "Angela Beryl." I looked through the document, noting its basic information, just in case any questions arose, though I doubted I'd be interrogated by anyone since Spain was neutral territory. I thought of Ernest and Lucien, and had a fleeting notion to find out where they were and visit them. However, I dismissed the idea, knowing I should return to London as soon as I could.

We made it to Bilbao just after sunset. I would have to wait until morning to board the ferry that would take me across the English Channel. My pockets were empty, but Adelaide had some Spanish pesetas in her purse and suggested we try the local inn.

As we exited the car, a tall man with salt and pepper hair, who looked quite fit, greeted us.

"Can I help you with anything?" he asked in Spanish.

"We're looking for a room," Adelaide said. "Just a night's stay. How much does it cost?"

"The owner is my friend. Wait here, let me ask for you." He shook our hands. "My name is Sandalio."

I introduced myself as Angela, and Adelaide stuck with her codename. I told him we were sisters. When Sandalio turned back toward the inn's entrance and was out of earshot, Adelaide said to me, "He's handsome!"

I grinned and elbowed her, but then straightened my expression when Sandalio returned with the owner in tow. "This is Antonio."

The not-quite-fit inn owner smiled at us through his yellow mustache. "Sandalio told me you wanted to stay at the inn, but I'm afraid I've just accepted the last customer for the evening. There are no more vacancies."

Adelaide frowned, raking a nervous hand through her soft brown hair. Just seeing her do that made *me* anxious. I wasn't too keen on sleeping in the car, so I asked, "Is there anyone in town with an extra room? We can pay."

Antonio gestured toward his friend. "Sometimes Sandalio rents his spare room when he needs extra money."

Adelaide shook her head. "What about—"

"Don't worry." He laughed and slapped Sandalio on the back. "He's just a fisherman who helps out with maintenance at the inn sometimes. He lives a few blocks away with his wife and three children. I wouldn't send you to a scoundrel's house."

Sandalio spoke up. "If you'd like, I can show you to another inn, or a hotel."

I glanced at Adelaide. She looked a little disappointed to hear Sandalio had a wife. "I think Adelaide and I will go to your home...if you don't mind."

Sandalio smiled. "Not at all. Ofelia and the children are there now, so I'll call her and let her know to expect you. I'll be there shortly. I was just finishing some repairs inside the inn."

We thanked him and followed his directions down to his place. He lived on the top floor of a six-story apartment building which allowed access to a comfortable terrace on the roof. When we arrived, we agreed to leave everything in the car except our toiletries, and I sealed the vehicle shut with a spell to protect the items inside.

Adelaide and I arrived just in time for dinner. After a quick wash in their tiny bathroom, we gladly accepted Ofelia's invitation to sit at their table. After a half hour, Sandalio came in with his toolbox and set it by the door. He greeted us, gave Ofelia a tender kiss, then sat down to enjoy his plate.

"Have you ladies been to Spain before?" Sandalio asked.

"Adelaide has," I said. "I think I would be lost around here without her."

Ofelia smiled. "Well, hopefully your studies at the University of Paris can continue. I think it's nice that you both have each other."

"When I was young, I traveled the world as well." Sandalio grabbed a pitcher of water sitting on the table and filled our cups.

"Then he met me, and it was all over!" Ofelia chuckled.

"How long have you two been married?" Adelaide asked, watching the two young boys and their older sister at the other end of the table.

"Has it been ten years, Ofelia?" he asked.

"Eight...you see, for men it passes by slowly." She smirked and headed over to the children, bribing them with sweets so that they'd eat everything off their plates.

After we finished our modest meal of fried fish and vegetable soup, Adelaide and I offered to do dishes and helped Ofelia put the children to bed. When we saw all the care Ofelia took to save any scraps, to make sure all the children ate well before she even fed herself, and without rest, began mending and sewing the family's clothing, we felt guilty that we couldn't offer more money for our night's stay.

"Ofelia," Sandalio said as he kissed her on her forehead. "You're going to pass out in the living room, dear. Go to bed."

She kissed him back and then rose from her seat. She gazed at us. "Angela, if you or your sister need anything, don't hesitate to ask."

Adelaide smiled at her. "God bless you, and your husband. You have a lovely family."

Ofelia left for her bedroom and the two of us sat on the couch drinking coffee. Sandalio took out his pipe and began stuffing it with tobacco. He bristled when a knock on the door interrupted him. He walked over to the door, and after looking through the peephole, opened it and tilted his gaze downward.

"Good evening, Tomás."

"Good evening, Señor Vega," we heard the squeaky voice of a boy respond. He began rattling off a list of maintenance jobs that needed to be done around the building.

Sandalio turned to face us. "You'll have to excuse me, ladies. I've become the unofficial repairman for many of the tenants here."

Tomás stuck his head in and waved at us. "Hello!"

We waved back. Sandalio bent down and reached for his toolbox. He excused himself once more and headed out with the boy.

Adelaide opened her coin purse and tried to scrounge up some money. "I wish I had a little more to leave them."

"I think they'll be fine," I stretched and yawned. "Let's just hope the war doesn't spill over to this side of the border and destroy what they *do* have."

"Do you want to go see the terrace?"

I really wanted to drag myself to our little guest room and curl up on the bed. "Sure, that sounds nice."

Adelaide ran into the kitchen and got a couple of glasses. She went over to the cabinet where Sandalio kept the wine and poured us some Amontillado. She placed the wine bottle back inside, took off her wrist watch and left it on top of the cabinet as payment.

We went to the rooftop terrace and felt a cool breeze blowing toward us from the nearby estuary. Tomorrow morning I would be over there, boarding a ferry and making my way through Biscay Bay. Then, I'd go through the English Channel and land in Portsmouth.

As I stood on the rooftop watching the stars, I thought about my father and whether or not he had a place to stay tonight. Did he have to run and hide, even in the dead of night? Could he even sleep for an hour, knowing that seven wizards were commissioned to kill him? The Gray Tower wasn't even interested in detaining a Drifter; they would not take him as prisoner.

"I'd like a family one day," Adelaide said, cradling her glass of Amontillado.

I drank my wine. "Got a sweetheart?"

"No, but you know how it is with this line of work."

"I think you did a good job, driving us back to Jasmine's house. We could've been captured, or caught by the Gestapo."

She snorted, though there was a hint of a smile around her lips. "I was a nervous wreck!"

"Believe me, I understand. I actually wanted to retire." I took a seat in one of the lounging chairs. "Now...I'm not sure what I want."

When she saw that I had finished my drink, she gestured for me to give her my empty glass. "Do you want some more wine? I have a pair of earrings I can leave."

I laughed. "No thanks, I'll be fine."

"Well, this war can't last forever. One day, I'll have what I want." She set my glass on the table and took another sip from hers. She stood there, looking up at the sky with a wistful expression.

"What do you plan to do after tomorrow?" I asked.

She brushed a wisp of her shoulder-length hair aside. "I'm going back to France to work with the other SOE agents in Paris. My mother had family there."

"Father Gabriel said he knew your father."

She nodded. "They were schoolmates in Italy, at the Borghese gardens, when a lot of British boys used to go there."

I sped through the names of everyone I've heard of in SOE, and tried to puzzle out her family name. "If you don't mind me asking, would I know your father?"

"I'm not sure, but whenever you're in London, just look up Edwin Grey." She winked at me.

"I'll remember that. If you see Lucien and Ernest again, can you tell them I said thanks?"

"I will."

I thought of Ernest's original mission and prayed that he'd be careful. "I hope they find that assassin who's been bumping off our pilots."

"What assassin?"

"That spy, Galeno."

Her wineglass slipped from her hand and crashed to the floor. She had a startled look on her face, and just as I was about to ask her what frightened her so much, my gaze fell onto her white blouse, now sullied with blood flowing from her right shoulder.

I got up and caught her just as she sank to her knees. Sandalio emerged from the house with his gun in hand, and a silencer attached to it so that no one could hear his shots.

Adelaide reached for her shoulder, probably trying to stem the blood flow. My muscles stiffened, and I felt the ache of fear restrict my movements. I knelt with her and began working on controlling the bleeding and closing the wound.

"Don't try to heal her, or I'll shoot her again."

My throat went dry, and I could barely speak. None of this made sense. "Why did you do this?"

"Because Sandalio Vega always gets his target. When I'm done with you, I'm going back to finish off your friend Ernest Wilson. Don't take it personally, Miss George, it's just business." He gestured for me to step away from Adelaide with his gun.

"You're Galeno...did someone from SOE hire you? Are you working for the traitor?" I tore myself away from Adelaide, my chest tightening and stomach aching as each vital moment passed. She just lay there, quiet and still in a pool of blood.

"No," he said.

"But I bet you're on the same payroll."

"My employer has eyes and ears in many places." He approached and kept the gun trained on me.

"So does Ofelia know about you? How about your kids?"

"They know nothing, and I plan to keep it that way."

I wanted to spit in his face. "That's going to be a little difficult, since you just shot a woman in cold blood."

With his free hand, he pulled a thin gold band from his pocket. The circle was too wide for it to be a bracelet, but it would fit perfectly around one's neck. "I presume you know what this is?"

"I've seen one before." Nearly every country banned possession of imperium collars, except in the case of law enforcement. Like the one used on Veit Heilwig, they were control devices used to either prevent wizards from using their powers, or to control how they used them.

"Then you'll permit me to place this around your neck? I will administer jade powder to Adelaide and heal her. Quickly though, she doesn't have much time."

Holding back tears of anger, I gathered up my hair and tilted my head forward. When he opened and placed the imperium collar around my neck, it clanked shut by itself. I felt like someone had his hands around my throat. I wanted to claw at it and scream; it felt unnatural, and I immediately felt my magical energy fall into submission.

"Now heal her, Galeno...please." My hands fell to my side.

"You will not use any of your powers against me. Do you understand?"

"Yes." The collar tightened, and I knew I had been bound.

He seemed satisfied with my compliance and slipped the gun into his holster. He pulled out a tiny black pouch, reached in, and sprinkled the dark green powder onto Adelaide's wound. When I saw her arm move and heard her soft breaths, I calmed down a little.

"Erase her memory, Isabella."

"What?"

"If she remembers how she ended up like this, I swear I'll shoot to kill next time."

"I'm not a mentalist."

His finger rested on the trigger. "I'm sure you can think of something to alter her mind."

I couldn't stand arrogant people like him who found out how to use a few enchanted items, maybe even associated with wizards, and thought they knew everything about us. I lowered myself to my knees and cradled Adelaide's head between my hands. I concentrated on a form of mind control, where I strongly suggested to her mind that she had suffered an accident, but would be all right. It was the best I could come up with. When I explained to Galeno what I had done, he grinned at me then helped Adelaide to her feet. He overlooked the fact that although my mind control spell would lead her to believe she suffered an accident, it didn't erase or suppress her memory of what just happened.

"Adelaide, my dear. You had a nasty fall, but Angela here helped you. Why don't you go downstairs to the guest room and lie down."

Adelaide's body trembled, and she winced as she reached for her head. "I...fell down?"

"Y-yes," I said, trying to keep a calm expression. "Just rest, Adelaide. You'll be okay in the morning." I eyed Galeno as I said this last part. He obviously wanted me alive—for now, but Adelaide's safety wasn't guaranteed.

"I promise, she will be fine." He gave a cryptic nod.

"Oh...then, goodnight." Adelaide reached for me, wrapping her arms around me. She turned toward Galeno. "Thank you, Sandalio. I'll see you in the morning."

"Goodnight, Adelaide." He accepted her embrace with a smug expression, but then broke away when she yanked his gun from his holster.

Before he could stop her, she fired a shot into his chest. He stumbled backward and fell to his knees, mouth gaping and eyes widening in shock. He hit the ground face first, and Adelaide doubled over, half-crying and half-gasping.

I took the gun from her. "Are you all right?"

She nodded and wiped the tears from her eyes. "Let's get out of here."

Just then, Ofelia came onto the terrace and began screaming. She ran over to Galeno and knelt beside him. She shook him and called his name. She gazed up at us with fear and bewilderment in her eyes. I felt terrible seeing her cry over him, mostly because she hadn't been aware of the other life he led. Part of me wanted to tell her that she had married a fraud, a man who killed for money without conscience, and who, in between jobs, visited brothels. I just shook my head and said nothing.

When neighbors in surrounding houses began turning on their lights and poking their heads out of windows, Adelaide grabbed my hand and pulled me along. We dashed downstairs, not even bothering to grab our things from the guest room, and made it to the lobby level and out to the car. As we hopped inside and drove away, I looked into the rearview mirror. Cars with sirens came zooming down the street. I let out a sigh, relieved that they stopped at Galeno's building and weren't yet on our trail.

"You just saved my life." Adelaide stared straight ahead and sped north up the road.

"I think you just saved mine." I didn't know what Galeno had planned to do with me, but the fact that he had access to my information, and had dangerous items on him, like this imperium collar, truly frightened me.

"We'll go to Santurtzi." Her hand was in her hair again. "We'll sleep in the car if we have to, and then you can catch the ferry from there."

"Thank you, Adelaide." I touched the imperium collar and felt a mixture of fear and disgust. It still bound me. It still prevented me from using most of my powers. I would have to find a wizard skilled at enchantments in order to break free, and I'd have to do it within three days...or else I'd be in a world of trouble.

CHAPTER 19

After I parted ways with Adelaide, I took a ferry up through the English Channel and landed in Portsmouth, where Richard awaited me. When he saw how uneasy I looked, he ushered me into the back seat of the car and quickly took off. I had borrowed a scarf from Adelaide to wrap around my neck so that the imperium collar wouldn't be exposed—it wasn't something you'd necessarily want seen. There's no telling who else would recognize it and would want to take advantage.

Richard cleared his throat. "This must've been a tough one. Only once or twice have I seen you come back this way."

My hand went to the scarf, but I forced it back down. "It turned out to be one of my toughest, but...I'm glad I made it. Is Agent Warren in London?"

"Yes, do you need him for something?"

"Have him meet us at Brown's."

"You want to go to a hotel? Don't you think we ought to get to Baker Street?"

His tone of voice told me that he felt uncomfortable with the idea, which didn't surprise me. Richard liked doing things by the book, and protocol dictated that he take me directly to SOE headquarters.

"Please, it's important. And I'm not exaggerating when I say it's a matter of life and death."

Richard sighed. "If Warren isn't there within an hour, then I'm taking you to Baker Street, and you'll have to try to reach him from there. Understood?"

"Yes. Thank you."

I began nodding off and felt my eyelids droop. Adelaide and I had been so anxious after our escape from Bilbao that we didn't even sleep. My throat felt itchy and dry, and my stomach threatened rebellion if I didn't eat anything soon. However, I was so exhausted that a nap appealed to me more than a meal. I finally gave in and closed my eyes, only vaguely hearing Richard tell me that he was glad that I had safely returned.

~

When we made it to the Mayfair district in the London area, we checked into Brown's, much to Richard's consternation. It didn't even cheer him up to learn that the Prime Minister had arrived earlier and was staying in his usual suite. Richard phoned MI6's London office and asked Neal to come meet with us. They seemed to exchange a few words over the phone, then Richard's face tightened, and he hung up. His dislike for Neal Warren probably stemmed from the time Neal had asked Stella out on a date, even though it was obvious Richard had his heart set on her. When we made it to our suite, he began complaining.

"Who does he think he is, telling us which room and on what floor to stay in? SOE should've never absorbed Section D—those MI6 agents finger more paperwork and doilies than they do weapons."

I helped him with the luggage. "Come on, he's not that bad."

Richard took off his coat and slung it over a chair. He loosened his black tie and headed over to the bar to mix a drink. "Of course not. It's none of my business if the bloke looks like he just stepped out of a rake novel."

"Forget I said anything." I went over and opened the double doors that led to the bedroom. A faint stream of sunlight fell through the window, but receded when the clouds in the sky closed in.

"I brought you a change of clothes." He pointed to the suitcase sitting in the corner.

"Thank you." I went over and took out the clothes, but decided I'd wait until after this monstrous gold collar was off my neck.

"I hope your friend Warren shows up. He's got twenty minutes, then we have to go."

"He's not exactly my friend."

Although Neal and I had trained at the Gray Tower around the same time, and we were on speaking terms, I knew better than to allow him to be a confidant. And, I didn't mind keeping it that way. However, I sought his help because, as a Philosopher who also specialized in enchantments, he had the knowledge and skills necessary to unlock the collar. If I could be confident in one thing about him, it would be the fact that he was always willing to assist a member of the Order without hesitation.

I heard a knock on the door, just as I downed a glass of cool water. Richard went over to answer, but I gestured for him to head for the chair in the corner. The last thing I wanted was for them to aggravate one another.

I opened the door and stood face-to-face with Neal. He wore a black trench coat and carried a small black case with him. He wore his dark hair slicked back and had apparently started growing a beard since I last saw him.

"Good afternoon," he said.

"Hi, Neal. Come in." I grabbed his hand and led him inside.

He spotted Richard in the corner, pretending to read a newspaper. "Lieutenant Carr, good afternoon."

Richard gave a quick nod and glanced back down at the newspaper, but suddenly stood and followed us when he saw us go into the bedroom. I sat on the edge of the bed and began unwrapping the scarf that concealed the imperium collar.

"Can you help me take this off?"

"Well, this is going to be interesting."

"The *collar*, Neal..." I pulled away the last of the scarf and tilted my head back so he could see the gold band.

"Now, how did you get into a situation that would force you to let someone put this ghastly thing on you?" He approached and stood over me, running his finger along the band. Richard stood in the doorway with his arms crossed, probably not sure of what to say because he knew it had something to do with magic.

"A Spanish spy who went by the codename Galeno. It was either this, or let another SOE agent die." I had seen enough people lose their lives, and I just couldn't stand there and watch Adelaide bleed to death.

"Was he a warlock?" Neal opened his black case and took out a small knife whose blade faintly shimmered with colors. I grew uneasy at the sight of an unassembled sniper rifle in there as well.

"No, but he was obviously in league with warlocks. Someone in SOE is a double agent, and if we can find this person, then we can find whoever hired Galeno."

"Why do you think it's important to find Galeno's employer?" He made gentle scrapes along the band with the knife. He uttered a Word. I never understood what Philosophers said when they spoke like that, but I always imagined it as the opposite of the infernal language of the Black Wolves.

"They know who I am, and, because of that, it blew my cover and cost lives. Galeno said his employer had eyes and ears in many places. It's in our best interest to find out exactly where these eyes and ears are—especially if they extend to the Gray Tower, don't you think?" I sucked in a quick breath when the collar heated up on its own in reaction to Neal's counterspell. It burned like hell.

He went around the circumference of the band again with the knife, and I felt energy flow from the blade into the band. "This could be worth looking into."

"Are you all right?" Richard asked, now pacing back and forth.

My eyes watered from the pain. "Yeah. We're almost done."

"There we are..." Neal loosened the collar and then pried it open far enough to slip it off.

"Thank you." I rubbed my neck. He placed the band inside a warded bag and tossed it into the case.

"That's what it means to be part of the Order, Isabella. We help one another."

"Don't start with me..."

He looked at his wristwatch and then took off his coat. He reached for the rifle parts in the case. "Excuse me, can you give me just a moment?"

"For what?" I eyed him in astonishment as he assembled the rifle then went over to the window.

"Three assassins are staying across the way. They were sent by the Nazis to go after the Prime Minister." He opened the window and gazed across the interior courtyard to the other building that also made up part of the hotel.

"You've been tracking assassins this whole time?" Richard went over to get a better view of the courtyard.

"We intercepted a message last month hinting at an attempt on the Prime Minister's life, and we knew to expect them, but no one knew when they'd come or where they'd go. I took into account the little information we had, the likely profiles of the assassins, and calculated all of the possibilities and determined with nearly one hundred percent accuracy that they would be rooming here at Brown's, today, in that room across the courtyard, and, from there, would try to strike."

"Seriously?" Richard asked.

"Seriously."

"What if you're mistaken?" I asked, eyeing the window his rifle was trained on.

"I'm not."

We saw a man in all black, with gloves on and his own rifle in hand. He cracked his window open and took aim at a lower level window on our side, completely unaware that we were watching him from two floors above. Neal fired his shot. The sniper went down. When his partner came into view, he took a bullet as well.

"All right hotshot," I said. "What about the third assassin?"

"If he's as good as I suspect he is, then he's already on his way here."

"What? You mean he's coming to our room?" Richard reached for his gun.

"Excuse me." Neal gestured for Richard to stay in place. He got up, headed toward the door, and then just stood there. He counted a few seconds before opening the door, he caught the assassin by surprise when he tried the knob, and the assassin came stumbling in. Neal grabbed his wrist and twisted it, so that he'd drop his revolver. He spoke another Word, and the man fell unconscious.

Richard ran over and closed the door behind them, picking up the assassin's weapon. Neal dragged him over to the closet and threw him in.

"Is he dead?" Richard asked.

"No, this one I'll take in for questioning. He won't wake up for another eight hours though."

Richard handed him the gun. "Well...good job."

"Thank you."

He went back into the bedroom and grabbed the rifle. He disassembled it and placed everything back into his black case. I went over to the bar and poured another glass of water. I drank it before taking a seat on the couch. Neal came over, placed his case on the coffee table, and eased on the seat next to me.

"Now that I've helped you," he said, "I think you know what I want as a token of gratitude."

"All right..." I bit my lip and thought about what I wanted to share. Richard shook his head and went back over to the bar to finish his drink.

"And it has to be something more profound this time," Neal added.

I took a deep breath. "I almost killed my would-be fiancé. I was so certain he was corrupt or had betrayed me, that when he tried to propose to me, I almost stopped his heart from beating. I was a paranoid mess."

"Bloody hell," Richard said.

"Fascinating." Neal leaned back and gazed at me.

"What, are you a psychologist too?" Richard quipped.

I faced Richard. "When Neal and I first met, he said I had an unusual mind. He swore some kind of enchantment had been placed on me, but no one else could detect it. I think he only said that about me because he couldn't figure me out."

Neal leaned forward, never taking his eyes off me. "And it drives me mad to not figure you out. I can project and anticipate what every person in this hotel will do the rest of the day, but you —you're like a nebulous cloud."

"Thanks," I said. "So, whenever he does me a favor, I repay him by sharing one truth about myself."

"And most of them are shallow truths by the way," Neal said. "You should've had that enchantment lifted years ago, Isabella."

I shook my head. "You're the only one who thinks I have one."

"Now, let's follow this line of reasoning and see where it goes. Who would place such a powerful enchantment on you? One that is apparently innocuous, yet meant to obscure your mind. Daddy, perhaps?"

I cringed on the inside, but kept my composure. "Richard, why don't you go downstairs and have breakfast. I'll join you shortly."

"Breakfast is over."

I glared at him. "Please."

"Fine." He went for the door and threw me a slightly anxious look before leaving.

When I felt certain that Richard had gone down the hall and wasn't listening at the door, I asked, "What do you know about my father?"

"I know enough."

"Do you know who he is?"

"Yes."

"Are you...one of the seven?"

"Seven what?"

"Don't play games with me. Are you one of the seven?"

"No, I'm not."

My gut instinct told me not to believe him. "Who are the seven wizards tracking my father?"

"Obviously Brande Drahomir couldn't hide this from you if you know there are seven. Such a task would have been given in secrecy."

"Can you take your prisoner and get out of here?" I should've known better than to get into a tangle with a Philosopher.

"Don't you want to know who gave Galeno that imperium collar?"

"Okay...I'm listening."

"After I broke the collar, what did you taste in the metal?"

"Mostly gold, a little silver, copper, and even a bit of bauxite."

"That particular combination has been consistently used by a certain buyer on the black market, whereas other buyers overwhelmingly opted for pure gold."

"Who?" I decided not to ask why he snooped around the black market.

"Who's our favorite Russian spy?"

"Praskovya? Does she even have the money for that?"

"If there's one thing I'll credit her for, she loves to work, and she gets paid well for it."

"The last time I saw her, we were in a lab that I blew up. I can't say for certain she's dead." And if she wasn't, then I knew I'd have to take precautions.

"I wonder if Galeno was going to hold onto you for her."

"That would've been a disaster."

"Just try to be careful, Isabella. Believe it or not, it would pain me if you were killed."

"Thank you, Neal. I'll...see you around."

He grabbed his case and headed over to the closet, pulled out the unconscious assassin, and doubled him over his shoulder. He spoke a Word, and disappeared in a flash. By this time, my stomach ached and my limbs felt weak. I knew I needed to have some food. I quickly dressed and then went down to join Richard for a meal, relieved that he didn't ask about my exchange with Neal.

CHAPTER 20

Richard and I exchanged few words about my Paris assignment during the rest of the car ride, as was protocol. Anything I had to divulge about my mission would be shared with Ian. I debated with myself whether or not to tell Richard about Stella's fate, and it seemed every time I was on the verge of saying something, I would choke up or pause. Finally, I told myself that I would only share what I knew about Stella if he asked me. He never did.

As the car slowed and parked in front of the building entrance, I called to mind the names of each person who fought, sacrificed, and laid down their lives for me to reach this place. I meant it when I told Ken I had grown tired of this war, of spying, and especially of losing friends. However, if I stopped fighting, I would feel as if their sacrifices were all in vain.

Once again, it seemed, Ken was right about me. I had too much fight in me, and too much heart to just give up and stand on the sidelines. I'd see this through as long as necessary, and I'd do it as a wizard, and not try to escape into a life I knew I'd probably never have. If I ever met the man of my dreams and got married, then that would be fine—if not, then that would be fine too. As long as I followed Renée's advice and remained true to myself, then I could find peace in that.

"Thank you, Richard." I gave him a grateful nod as he opened the car door and held an umbrella over me. I stepped out of the vehicle and went into the building. Despite the warm July weather, the clouds that had formed earlier now began pouring down rain.

I wore a black dress under a fitted black coat, and my affinity for fedoras led me to ask Richard for his. I placed it on my head and tilted it forward, shielding my eyes from the gawking of others. I didn't feel sociable at all; I wanted no greetings, no "welcome back" statements, and especially no small talk. I did acknowledge some other agents and employees in passing with a quick nod here or there, but they found me reluctant to stop and say anything.

"Welcome back, Agent George." Bernadine smiled kindly from behind the reception desk.

"Good afternoon, Bernadine." I *especially* didn't want to talk to her, but I had learned a long time ago to never provoke the anger or resentment of the one who administered the office, mailed paychecks, and held keys.

I gripped the handle to the briefcase I carried, which contained the formula case. I had also included a file folder where I secured the papers I had stolen from the lab. Before leaving Brown's, I had sent the diary by courier to Jane Lewis, as I've done other packages in the past. I didn't dare bring the diary in with me, because I didn't want anyone to know about it, and besides, it had more to do with Gray Tower affairs than SOE.

I went down the hallway and up the stairwell that would take me to Ian's office. Both of our offices were on the same floor since he headed my department. As I passed my tiny office, whose door had no lettering, I considered asking for a new one...a bigger one. Why not? I had risked just as much as any man would.

Taking a deep, calm breath, I removed the fedora and knocked on his door. I entered at his behest and sat in the chair facing his desk. His usual jovial demeanor had turned somewhat subdued, probably because Joshua Morton from MI6 stood at his side.

"Glad to have you back, Isabella." Ian gestured toward a cart carrying a teapot and cups, cream and sugar, and some pastries.

"Thank you, but no. Let's get this over with." I picked up the briefcase and gently set it on his desk. As I opened it and offered the small case inside to Joshua, I handed the papers to Ian and recounted everything that had happened to me—except the parts I wanted them to know nothing about.

"So you failed to extract Veit Heilwig," Joshua commented at the end, examining individual vials from the case.

"Yes...sir."

"But you destroyed the true stockpile, captured the new formula which they will never be able to duplicate, gathered intelligence from Simon Vester's office, *and* even disposed of some Black Wolves along the way." Ian folded his hands under his chin and shifted his gaze toward Joshua.

"Well," I slightly smirked at Ian. "I had some help."

Ian's expression grew serious. "And we'll find the double agent who betrayed your identity. In any case, I do believe you've done well."

"She's done well enough." Joshua placed the vials back inside the case and shut it. "I'll take these down to our lab and have an update for you by next week."

"Very good, then. Was there anything else you needed from Agent George?"

"She can hand in her written report by the end of the week. This debriefing is over, thank you." With a solemn air, he grabbed his trench coat from the coat rack and headed out the door. I could have burned a hole through the door the way I glared at it.

"Hmph...*well enough*. At least acknowledge all the hell I went through to get this formula here."

"I hope you don't take his indifference to heart, Isabella. You did a brilliant job." He went to his wine cabinet and pulled out a bottle of Sherry. He had probably been waiting all day to bring it out.

"Thanks." I gladly accepted the glass he poured me, taking a long, slow sip and slouching in my seat. "Why don't we go down to Finley's and have a real drink?"

"Because, some of us have loads of paperwork sitting on our desks to get through."

"Fine." I couldn't really strong-arm him into it when I only patronized the local pub once every couple of months. He had gone maybe once or twice before giving up and just keeping Sherry in his office.

"That reminds me, I have the resignation documents ready for you, and all they need is your signature. Are you ready to retire?"

I slowly shook my head. "Not yet, but I would like some leave time."

"If that's what you need, then of course." He looked rather pleased as he sat on the edge of his desk near me and drank his wine.

"Would a few months be asking too much? I want to return after Christmas, but before the New Year."

His grimace told me maybe it was asking too much. "Perhaps...I can go talk with the director. I mean, you have done us a great service, and if I went through half of what you did..."

"And what about a bigger office?"

"Let's work on getting your five month leave, shall we?"

"Did I ever mention how much I admire you? You're like a second brother to me."

He downed the rest of his drink. "And you're the spoiled sister I never had."

"Well are you going to see about it, or what?"

"You know, I think I will. That way, at least I won't have to deal with you for a few months." He winked at me and left for the top floor, where the heads of the organization had their offices.

I decided to head back to my tiny dungeon and fight off any spiders or insects that may have invaded and settled while I was away. I set down my wine glass, not really having the stomach to finish it all, and walked down the hall to office #221B. I fumbled for my key before remembering that I had left it with Bernadine when I last left London. I didn't feel like going back down and coming up again, so by chance, I tried the door to see if it was unlocked.

With a satisfied grin, I went in ready to settle into my chair and check any mail awaiting me, but froze at the sight of what used to be Stella's side of the room. The furniture was still there, but there were other things in place that certainly weren't there before. A notebook and three pens sat on top of the desk, and a single red rose lay across toward the front. A stack of papers were arranged with a degree of neatness that I didn't like, and when I looked at the wall adjacent to the desk, I saw a large poster of Amelia Earhart.

Before I could finish processing what I saw, a bubbly brunette who looked like she was late for her high school sewing class walked into the room and smiled.

"Oh my," she said, pressing her hands to her mouth and beaming at the same time. "I didn't think you'd be here until later this afternoon."

"I'm sorry...who are you?"

"Hello, I'm Bianca. I've heard so much about you, Miss George, and I think it's *swell* that we have so much in common."

Ian came bursting through the doorway. "Ah, there you are. I was going to tell you about your new officemate."

My gaze went from Ian to Bianca, and then back to Ian. I wasn't sure how to respond because I felt like they had thrust this upon me during the worst possible time. When I didn't feel like having a chattering neighbor next to me, especially in the space where Stella used to be. Yes, I knew she would never come back, but I wanted time to mourn for her in my own way, which included leaving her belongings alone until I've reconciled myself to losing her.

I didn't know if I would cry or explode, and so I refused to shake the girl's hand and hastily excused myself. I stalked down the hall, back into Ian's office, and shut the door. He came in after me and grabbed me by the shoulder. I stiffened as he pulled me into a hug.

"I knew you wouldn't like it, but if I knew you'd take it this hard, I wouldn't have done it."

"I told you I wasn't interested in a new officemate." I pulled away.

"I'm sorry."

"Can I get my own office? At this point, I'll take a broom closet."

"Oh stop it, if you talk to her, I'm sure you'll like her."

"What exactly do we have in common, besides dark hair and green eyes?"

"She's American, her father is a military man, and she likes those flowery hats."

"I like fedoras."

"And the best part is, she's a Practitioner. You can be sort of a double mentor to her."

A Practitioner acquired the lowest level of wizardry training at the Gray Tower. Practitioners weren't required to advance to higher levels, though many chose that route. Most people who left the Tower at this level were usually the types who wanted to either live quiet lives with just the basic knowledge of controlling their magic, or to hone their magical abilities in service of advancing other vocations. It could be a midwife who seemed more knowledgeable than the local doctor, and had never lost a mother or child—she was probably adept at body magic. Or, consider a detective with extraordinary skill and impeccable reasoning—probably a Philosopher.

Bianca was young and definitely green. She probably went to

the Gray Tower expecting one thing and completely experienced something different. Now, she had found her way to SOE, perhaps the result of a desire for adventure and her father making a few phone calls on her behalf.

I faced Ian. "I'll go and talk with her. But if I don't like her, will you send her to another office?"

"You have my word."

"Thank you, and what about my leave?"

"I'll have an answer for you in a few days."

"Good."

I walked out and went back to my office. With a stern face, I sat in my chair like I had wanted to earlier. Bianca wasn't at her desk, and for a moment I thought I had scared her off. I recanted the thought when she came back in carrying a cup of coffee. My cheeks burned with embarrassment, and I felt a twinge of remorse when I saw her watery eyes and crestfallen expression. She surprised me when she set the coffee on my desk and asked me if I needed anything else.

"No, thank you. Listen…I'm usually a lot more friendly, it's just that I came back from hell, and the girl that had that chair and desk before you is a pile of ashes in a Nazi death camp. That's quite a bit for me to cope with."

She sat in her chair and wiped her eyes with the back of her hand. "I'm sorry. They didn't tell me where I was going or who I was going to be with until the very last minute. When I found out it was you, I was excited."

"I should be the one apologizing. I hope this doesn't tarnish your image of me, even though I didn't know I had one."

"Of course not."

"Welcome to the Special Operations Executive." I took a sip of coffee. Well, at least she knew how to make good coffee.

"Miss George, I know I'm the new girl, and I have a lot to learn, but it doesn't mean I can't do the job. My father hates the fact that I'm here, and I probably left the Gray Tower for the same reason you did. I don't want to be treated like a child, and I don't want to be judged based on assumptions."

I paused for a long while and considered her words. "Fair enough."

She smiled. "Thank you."

"Have you been on assignment yet?"

"No, but I've been training."

I took another sip of coffee so she wouldn't see me frown. "Well, we all have to start somewhere. What were you doing at the Gray Tower?"

"I tested and they told me I was best at body magic. They also said I could be a Philosopher."

I nodded. "You didn't enjoy it there, though?"

"I did, but then my brother was killed. He was in the Navy, like my father." She turned and reached into her desk drawer, pulling out a small picture and handing it to me. A young man with a piercing gaze stood in a naval uniform. He looked no older than his sister.

"Handsome fellow. What's his name?" I gave her back the photo.

"Eric...Eric Raye. He died fighting for us, and I was sitting in the Gray Tower, oblivious to the world."

"So you felt like you were wasting your time?"

"Did you?"

"I have a complicated relationship with the Order. There are plenty of reasons why I'm not at the Gray Tower."

"I might go back, but right now I want to do *something*. Why can't we all just get together and end this war with our powers?"

God, she had a lot to learn. "Isn't that what Octavian Eckhard wants to do? Create world order under the leadership and rule of wizards? Get his hands on the Akashic Record so mere mortals can quake in his presence and worship him?"

She lowered her gaze. "I guess I didn't think about it in that way."

"Well, I'm sorry about your brother. I understand why you want to fight."

We continued talking for the next two hours, and I made up my mind that I'd like her to remain my officemate. In fact, she reminded me of myself, in some ways, when I had first started at SOE. I didn't know how much of a mentor I could be, since I hoped to be back in the United States as soon as possible. I also hesitated over the idea because I feared she would end up like Stella.

My eyes burned and I felt a lump in my throat at the thought of her, and Renée, and others. As I sat at my desk writing up my report for Morton, I kept repeating to myself that I had to keep fighting, that I wouldn't quit. At the end of the workday, I said goodbye to Bianca and grabbed my coat. I headed out the door—I was ready for a real drink.

CHAPTER 21

Finley's Pub stood right at the end of Baker Street. It had become the haunt of several SOE agents who'd drift in after a hard day of work. On an evening like this one, I was certainly one of them. We'd mingle at Finley's with people from neighboring office buildings, bored twenty-somethings looking for conversation, companionship, and even Air Force officers who were off-duty.

Of course SOE agents knew better than to discuss the nature of their work while patronizing Finley's, even if sincerely trying to blow off steam. I came around for a drink maybe twice every couple of months, and I still used the name "Emelie" while at the pub. I liked going to Finley's because it felt like I still had a semblance of a normal life. Some nights I'd just sit and enjoy the banter and raucous jokes of the Air Force officers, or watch with amusement as one of the uptight businessmen asked one of the cute twenty-something girls to dance. Sometimes I'd sit at the bar with two or three other SOE agents, and we'd just give each other the I-Know-What-You're-Going-Through look without uttering a word. It also helped that the barman always gave me free drinks.

I opened the front door, painted an ugly green, and went inside. I took off my coat and hung it on the coat rack. The lingering smell of cigar smoke wafted from the pub's smoking room, and the lights were dimmed. A few businessmen sat at one of the booths in the far corner, drinking and singing along to *I Don't Want To Set The World on Fire* playing on the radio. The barman, Hal, dusted off the bar counter with a rag with no particular enthusiasm, but his face lit up when he saw me, and he gestured toward one of the stools.

"There's my girl! How are you?"

"I'm well. I'll have a martini."

"It's good to see you, Emelie." He began mixing my drink.

"It's a little slow tonight." I looked over my shoulder and saw the businessmen down the last of their drinks and then head for the door.

"We have our highs and lows. Next week, I'll hardly manage to keep all the orders straight." He garnished my drink with an olive and handed it to me.

"Thanks, Hal." I set my martini in front of me. I grabbed a handful of chips from a half-empty bowl on the bar counter and devoured them.

For a second, I thought about going to Jane Lewis's place to see what she was cooking. I'd have to stop by and see her anyway to pick up Heilwig's diary that was dropped off by courier. I buried my face in the martini glass, nearly quivering at the thought of casting that Locus Circle. If I really wanted to, I could do it, but if I made a crucial mistake or if my mind proved weak, I'd end up insane or dead.

However, if I didn't cast the Circle, then how could I know or understand the rest of the diary? I thought about how it felt to open the first page and begin to read, knowing that I could not turn back once I knew Heilwig's knowledge and secrets—nor would I want to. My whole life had been shrouded in mystery and filled with questions I could never get answers to. Now, I had a way to satisfy my inquiries and understand what had happened with my father these past sixteen years—what his plan was for the Gray Tower, and for me.

And the only thing that stood in between me and that knowledge I yearned for was that damned Locus Circle.

"Ah," Hal sighed, beaming with pride over the drink he had made. "She likes it."

I finished off the martini and saluted him. "You're too kind. You know, E.B. White said the martini is the elixir of solitude."

"Who's that?"

"A poet. I think he writes magazine articles too...I like him."

Hal reached into one of his compartments beneath the bar counter. "That reminds me, I just got another one in."

"Did you?" I watched him pull out a small red book.

"This one's by Elinor Glyn." He shoved it toward me. The title read in fading black letters, *Three Weeks*.

"When I asked for book recommendations," I said, flipping through its pages, "I thought you'd give me something like Austen, or Brontë."

He snorted. "This is what the ladies are reading nowadays. No one wants to go out for a beer and talk about bloody Elizabeth Bennet."

"Hey—that's classic literature, buddy." I held up the red book. "This...this is...smut."

"Suit yourself, your highness."

I flipped through the book again. "I mean, look at the vocabulary in here. How many times does this woman have to use the word 'pleasure'?"

"All right, you've made your point." He reached for the book, but I set it on my lap.

"I didn't say I wasn't going to read it." I made a mental note to go back and read page forty-five.

He chuckled. "Would you like another martini?"

"A hot soup would be nice."

"I'll be right back."

Just as Hal headed into the kitchen, I heard the front door open and shut. I didn't care to take notice of the newcomer until she came and sat right next to me. When I saw who it was, I immediately rubbed my vitriol bracelet to enhance my clarity of mind, all the while resting my right hand on the book, my left hand in my pocket, on my silver knife.

Casandra regarded me with a tentative smile, and though her tight red dress, golden locks, and attractive face would make any man's head turn, seeing her made my stomach turn. She was a Cruenti who claimed to be reformed, but damned if I had ever met one.

"You're Emelie, yes? I'm Casandra." She offered her hand, but I sat there like a statue.

"I know who you are." I'd seen her at the pub before. She would spend her time drinking and socializing until it was time to stumble out the door with her latest flame. Granted, she seemed to only date non-wizards, but there was just something about her I didn't like—aside from the whole being a Cruenti business, *and* in addition to resembling Nikon Praskovya.

"I don't think you do know who I am, love." Instead of widening the gap between us, she seemed to lean in a little closer.

My heart pounded in my chest, and I clenched the knife. "I'm surprised Hal even let you in here."

She sat up straight. "I haven't harmed anyone...and I have rights like any other citizen, don't I? A girl can get a drink, can't she?"

"How long do you think you can go without feeding on a wizard? Assuming you're not lying about abstaining."

"I see that I'm speaking with a Tower Slave." With a smirk, she leaned in again and drew in a deep breath. "An alchemist."

"It's impolite for someone like you to read a wizard like that." I began slowly pulling the silver knife out, but halted when Hal returned with my soup.

"Here you are, Emelie. Good evening, Casandra, what can I get for you?"

"Gin and tonic, Halden. Thank you."

He began making her drink and smiled. "Casandra, I thought you'd bring in Edan."

She waved her hand through the air. "He's old news."

"So it didn't work out, eh?" He gave her the gin and tonic.

"I just didn't find him amusing anymore." She sighed and took a sip.

"You've got to tell me..." Hal leaned over the bar counter. "Did you bite him?"

She joined him in laughing. "No, I didn't!"

I rolled my eyes at their exchange. Hal and others wouldn't find her so fascinating if they possessed magical abilities and had to fend her off. I made another mental note to make sure Edan hadn't shown up in any recent missing persons reports. Just in case.

"I have to go, Hal." I left my soup untouched.

"So soon?" His smile faded. "The Air Force officers are coming in tonight. The tall one, Jack, asked about you last week."

"I have to go," I repeated in a low voice. I held the book with both hands so I wouldn't be tempted to reach for my knife again.

I went over to the coat rack and slipped the book into one of my coat's outer pockets. I pulled on my coat and buttoned it up, throwing one last glance in the direction of the bar. Hal had gone into the kitchen again, and Casandra sat there—staring back at me like she wanted to drain me.

"Maybe I'll see you around again," she said.

"Hmm...yes, let's just hope I don't have a stake or sword in hand." Having gotten in the last word, I opened the ugly green door and headed out.

Since I lived within walking distance of Baker Street, I left the pub without hailing a cab. I headed down the street just in time to catch the beautiful sunset peeking through the clouds that had parted since the afternoon. Darkness seemed to settle almost immediately, and so I quickened my steps. The streets glistened with the slick dampness left by the rain and the air had already started to cool. Even amidst the cold metals of parked cars and lampposts that I tasted, the sweet familiar essence of gold stood out. I headed straight for a red telephone box just past the public gardens and closed myself inside. I dialed the operator and gave her a name. I waited for my call to connect.

"This is Morton."

"Why were you at the debriefing today?"

"Miss George?"

"Yes, why did Ian need you there?"

"You know why."

"So did you find our leak?"

"Not yet. Seems SOE's made a few enemies."

"I've made a few myself."

"I'm shocked."

"It's good to know I have friends, though."

"Friends, eh?"

"You should come see me, so we can discuss it in detail...bring some of your friends too."

"Well...goodnight then."

"Goodnight."

I hung up and went another few blocks until I reached Wesley Street. I made a right turn and headed up the familiar steps of the building I called home. I stopped at Jane Lewis's flat on the first floor, declining an invitation for tea, and grabbing the package that the courier had brought. As I trudged up to the third floor, fatigue finally started to take hold of me, and I breathed a deep sigh when I made it inside.

Everything was as I left it, which wasn't saying much. Newspaper clippings lay scattered on my coffee table, both opened and unopened letters were stacked high on the kitchen counter, and my nose alerted me to a few undone dishes that I resolved to just throw into the trash. I drew a hot bath and got inside, but quickly got out once I felt myself nodding off. Tonight, I would have no terrifying dreams of battles and bloodshed.

I pulled on my robe and grabbed the package, which I kept with me the entire time. I couldn't describe it, but I felt both exhilaration and anxiety at looking at the diary again. I also wondered who the "others" Heilwig spoke of were, and whether or not their names would be listed. These could very well be the people loyal to my father, or who were at least willing to side against the Tower in this matter. Either way, they'd be my closest allies.

I set the unopened package on top of my cluttered newspaper clippings and sat back on my sofa, staring at the package on the coffee table and contemplating a thousand more questions. My fingers tingled as I reached for the package, so I could finally open it. I immediately halted when I felt a strong hand on my left shoulder and the cold blade of a golden knife—*my* golden knife, resting against my throat.

"You didn't think this was over, did you?" Praskovya asked.

"How did you find me?" I asked, feigning shock.

"I kept your knife, from the university. A precious possession should never be left in the hands of an enemy. I tracked down a wizard just so he could cast the spell I needed."

"And the imperium collar?"

"I gave it to Galeno to use on you, just in case you made it out of France. If you really think about it, I am showing you mercy. Octavian would have your head because of Marcellus's death." She pressed the blade into my skin and made me hiss. A warm trickle of blood streamed down.

"And what about you, Praskovya?"

"What about me?"

"You're standing on a Putrefaction symbol. You'll decay and corrode if you cut me again. I promise you."

She paused in her breathing and made a low laugh. "I should have known. Is there anything else I should know about?"

"Yeah, you fell for the bait. This time, I won."

She got the hint and ran toward the window, but armed MI6 agents came crashing through and shouted orders as they surrounded her in a semi-circle. Four more armed agents came in through the front door, as well as Joshua Morton and a redheaded woman.

"You're late, Morton." I took the handkerchief he handed me. I blotted the stream of blood from the superficial wound on my neck. When I had called him and told him to "bring his friends," he must've been shocked that I had used the code phrase he once gave Jane if she ever needed his help. Luckily, he had decided to take a chance and show up for me.

The redheaded woman approached Praskovya after the agents deprived her of my golden knife. The woman pulled out cuffs and bound Praskovya's hands in front of her. Two of the men, one on each side of Praskovya, held her still as a third agent clamped leg irons around her ankles.

"Nikon Praskovya," the redheaded woman said to her, "you are hereby under arrest and will be taken into the British government's custody."

I turned to Joshua and whispered, "Who's the Irish woman?"

He bent to my ear. "I thought you would know. You-know-who sent her a few weeks ago to partner on a few missions dealing with the Black Wolves. She's also been trying to monitor your most recent assignment."

"And she asked you to be at my debriefing today."

"Correct."

My chest tightened and I grew angry. Apparently the Gray Tower had been watching me more than I thought. I wondered if

SOE wanted me to extract Heilwig from France, only to hand him over to her.

"Give me the head cover." The Irish woman gestured toward the agent who secured Praskovya's legs. He handed her a black hood with a glowing symbol on it.

"What's that?" Praskovya made a futile attempt to back away.

"Don't worry, Nikon. It's just to ensure that you don't run away from us."

"No! The Russian government will pay my ransom. I will not be your prisoner."

The woman straightened out the hood and opened it. "Unfortunately for you, I already informed them that you had turned on them and voluntarily remained with the Nazis. Thus, you are worth nothing to the Russians."

Praskovya squinted her eyes, gritted her teeth, and in an instant the two agents next to her went sliding in opposite directions across the room. Before anyone could react, Praskovya shrieked and fell to her knees when what looked like a lightning bolt struck her. Praskovya flashed an angry gaze at the woman. She commanded the golden knife to fly straight toward the woman's face. However, the knife disintegrated into powder, and when the golden powder passed her, it reassembled back into a solid knife and hit the wall. The cuffs and leg irons restraining Praskovya glowed red hot, and she fell to the ground, screeching in pain.

"There we go..." The woman slipped the black hood onto Praskovya as two more agents came forward and grabbed her. This time, Praskovya said nothing and fell limp as she slipped into unconsciousness.

Joshua faced me. "How did you know Praskovya would track you here?"

"In some ways, she and I really *do* think alike. It's what I would do. Besides, once I detected my golden knife, I knew she had it and was following me. She wouldn't have come here though if I gave any sign that I was aware of her presence."

"Well done, Miss George," he said.

"Thank you."

"Let's go," Morton said to the MI6 agents. He placed a hand on my shoulder in a parting gesture before heading out the door. The agents followed, carrying Praskovya with them.

I rose from my seat and retrieved my knife still lodged in the wall. I faced the woman and began taking in the breadth of her power. I grew a little anxious. "That was impressive."

"You could have helped." She picked up my package, still lying on the table. "You have over sixty symbols hidden in this flat."

"It didn't look like you needed any help. Besides, let's just say I'm not heartbroken when a Gray Tower wizard kicks the bucket." I approached her and opened my hand; she handed me the package.

"Spare me your vindictive attitude, Miss George. You are part of the Order as much as I am, and whatever happens to one of us should concern all."

"You're an alchemist." I cradled the package tightly in my arms, ignoring her statement.

"I'm the *Master* Alchemist, to be exact. I've been away, working for the Order, but I'll be returning to the Tower soon."

"Cathana Erin. I know about you. Did you know Veit Heilwig?"

"I did, and your father was also a friend of mine. He's an absolutely phenomenal wizard."

"Spare me your flattery."

"My dear, it wasn't meant to be mere flattery. It's the truth."

I set the knife on the table and thought about how she had made it disintegrate and reconstruct without creating a symbol. I had seen Heilwig, an Elite Alchemist, create blazing symbols with his fingertips. Cathana went beyond that—she had mastered alchemy, and could do every alchemical spell by constructing the symbols with the power of her mind. She could direct her spells without any physical gesture.

"If Heilwig really was your friend, then I'm sorry."

"Thank you," she said.

"All my time at the Gray Tower, I had never heard of him. Why?"

"Sometimes...when one of us falls into disgrace, his name may be struck from our records, and those who know him are forbidden to speak of him."

"Sounds typical. I suppose you guys like to throw people away."

She stiffened. "Veit stole something from us, and he decided that helping your father was more important than the Gray Tower."

"Well, Veit's dead now. Is that what you wanted?"

"No," she lowered her gaze, "it's not what I would have wanted."

I didn't know why, but her response deflated my antagonism. "Well...it was interesting meeting you in person, Master Erin. By the way, can you tell Leto Priya to stay the hell away from me?"

"I'll deliver the message." She turned and headed toward the door, but then paused to face me once more. "You know, if you'd come to the Tower for more training, you could probably match Veit's level within months."

"Thank you for the suggestion." *Could you please go now?*

"I don't take Apprentices, but for you...I'd make an exception."

"Thank you, Master Erin."

I closed and locked the door behind her, then I went over and sat down in my chair, wondering if the prison they planned to lock Praskovya in would hold her for long. For a moment, I thought Master Erin had detected the diary and would try to take it. I carefully unwrapped the package and flipped the diary open, gripping it as if reassuring myself that it was here and all mine. I began re-reading the page that instructed me to cast the Locus

Circle. Although I tried telling myself that there must've been a good reason for the spell, and everything depended on me following Veit's instructions, I still hesitated over doing it.

Perhaps I would stick with my original plan to just ask my father when I saw him again. He'd probably know what to do about this. The image of him in the park that day flashed in my mind, and I thought about the enchantment he placed me under. He said he intended it for my memory, but he didn't explain why.

Fear gripped me when I thought of Neal and how he kept claiming that an enchantment obscured my mind. What if he was right? I had been so overwhelmed with emotion the day I saw my father that I didn't even question what he did. My heart grew resentful as I realized that my father hadn't bothered to explain the enchantment because he was responsible for altering and locking my memories. When we were together in the park that day, he had wanted to fortify earlier enchantments from years past. He must've woven the memory spells with such intricacy, that the Locus Circle would be the only way to break through them.

Why would my father and Veit do this?

I glanced toward the bottom of the page, reading through the list of materials I needed in order to cast the Locus Circle. Most of them I already kept in my flat, and I went scouring through my kitchen, closet, and nightstand drawers for them. I knew I didn't have the last set of materials on my list, but Jane Lewis did.

I ran down the stairwell to her front door. I knocked a few times and she answered with a sleepy face and a slightly surprised look in her eyes. I felt guilty for waking her up, but if I didn't do this now, I would lose any resolve I had.

"Isabella...is everything all right?"

"Yes." I nodded and quickly ran my fingers through my hair, trying to appear somewhat presentable—well, as presentable as one could be as she stood outside her friend's flat in a bathrobe.

"Come in." She pulled the door open further and gasped. "Is that a cut on your neck? What happened?"

"Hey, you know those pebbles you brought back from Dover Beach?" I turned to face her and didn't bother taking a seat on the sofa.

"Y-yes...let me take a look at that." She approached and swept my hair to the side. "Why didn't you heal yourself?"

"It's just a little cut..."

She ran over to her first-aid kit in the kitchen and pulled out a band-aid. "I feel silly giving this to you, but..."

"Thanks." I let her place the band-aid over the tiny wound. "Praskovya paid me a little visit."

"What? Where is she?"

"Don't worry, Joshua arrested her. It looks like your brother finally did something useful."

"*Half* brother," she said with a smirk. She went over to her bookshelf and grabbed a silver and turquoise jewelry box. She flipped the lid open and counted ten large pebbles.

"Great, I'll need just nine of them." I took the box from her and gave her a peck on the cheek. She still looked confused and worried.

"Are you in trouble? Do you need help?"

I started to shake my head and tell her "no," but it occurred to me that it would benefit me to have her be there. I would need Jane to pull me out of the Locus Circle if I couldn't do it myself. "Actually, yes. Come with me."

For a moment she seemed to have regretted her offer. "Oh...well...all right."

∽

After assuring Jane that I planned to fix my broken window as soon as possible, she finally started helping me set up the Locus Circle. She carefully placed seven of the pebbles in a large circle around me as I sat on the floor with my legs crossed. She followed up with a line of amber dust tracing the outside of the Circle.

"This had better be worth it," I muttered, as she crushed petals from a single gilded rose and followed the same outline of the amber dust. I had bought the rose from Penn a few months back and wanted to save it for the right spell. Amber repelled fear, and gilded roses fortified one's mystical energy, acting as a good luck charm.

"When do you want me to start it?" She held the last two stones in each hand and faced me. She would have to place the eighth stone in front of me to complete the Locus Circle and send me into the recesses of my mind. The ninth stone would bring me back.

"At my word. Just pull me out if you see me in distress. It won't affect you."

Her eyes widened. "What should I look for?"

"Screaming, vomiting, passing out..."

"Are you sure you need to do this?"

"Yes." But it didn't mean that I had to like it.

"Be careful."

I felt a knot in my stomach. "Okay, do it now."

As soon as she completed the circle with the eighth stone, a bright light illuminated the inner circle, and everything else around me faded. When the light slowly dimmed to gray, I knew I had entered the dreamlike state of the memory palace.

A door that looked wrought of iron stood in front of me. I took a deep breath and opened it, and to my surprise, I walked into my childhood bedroom. I stood there and watched my ten year-old-self climbing my tall bookcase, with no shoes or socks on, my eyes focused on a large white box at the very top. Several stuffed animals littered the floor to cushion any possible fall.

When young Isabella slipped, I rushed forward and shouted a warning, but she neither heard nor saw me. Luckily, she didn't fall, but kept climbing up the sturdy bookcase until she reached the white box. Hanging on with one hand, she used the other to grab a hairpin from the base of her ponytail and shoved it into the keyhole on the white box. Just then, my father opened the door and came in. Young Isabella faltered and fell down into the protective cushion of her toys. She immediately jumped to her feet and held my father's gaze.

"Daddy, hi."

"Isabella," his voice sounded stern, but his eyes showed kindness. "You're supposed to be writing standards like your mother told you."

"I did!" She ran over to her desk and grabbed a few sheets of paper. She handed them to my father. "I wrote it five hundred times, like she asked. And I wrote an extra two hundred just in case I did something else bad later on."

My father smiled. "Very good, then. But that doesn't mean you should try to get your dolls out of the box until your mother says you can."

She pulled a face. "I said I was sorry."

My father approached and cupped her chin in his hand. "You do know that what you did wasn't...normal?"

"It wasn't?"

"I'm quite sure big brothers don't instantaneously suffer from purple blisters on their faces."

"I told Johnnie to stop teasing me."

"Well," he grabbed her hand, "I'm going to teach you how to control it. First, you'll have to be tested, like I was when I was a boy."

My mother's voice carried from the end of the hall. "Carson...Carson!"

When my father and young Isabella stepped out into the hallway, the room pulsated like an underwater vibration, and I followed behind. They both stood there and eyed my mother who, despite her beautiful face, could look rather scary when angry. She wiped her hands on her apron and stepped toward us.

"Carson, what are *they* doing out there?"

"I told you, I have to take her for testing."

My mother's lip quivered. "But I asked you to give her some time."

"It's been two years. That's more than enough."

She looked over her shoulder as if expecting whoever "they" were, to come barging in and grab me. "But...she's just a girl."

"It's just testing, Mary. I went through it as well when I was her age."

She rushed toward us, almost knocking over the blue vase sitting on a stand in the hallway. She grabbed young Isabella's free hand. "I already have to sit here worrying about whether or not you're going to make it home to us. Now you want to get our daughter involved with the Order?"

My father's expression looked apologetic, but he never let go of young Isabella's hand. "We'll be back in a few hours."

She pressed one hand against my father's chest to stay him, and kept her grip on young Isabella with her other. "Johnnie came out normal," she said in a half-whisper, "why can't she?"

That question stung me, and the look on my face as a little girl proved that it must've hurt me then. Father Gabriel called his powers a "gift from God," but seeing this memory unfold showed me why my mother always treated my abilities like a curse. She had never opposed my decision to enter the Order, but I could always tell that she didn't approve.

My father regarded her with a tender look. "We have to go. I promise we'll return soon."

"Wait!" my mother shrieked when my father started down the hall again. She grabbed young Isabella's wrist and tried to pull the girl toward her. My father simply uttered a Word, and my mother let her slide out of her grasp.

"I'm sorry, Isabella," he said when he saw tears running down her tiny cheeks. He scooped her into his arms and headed toward the living room.

"Bring her back!"

My father dodged sideways and avoided the vase my mother threw at his head. He pivoted with an amazing degree of swiftness, caught the vase, and placed it on another stand in the living room.

"Calm down, Mary. You could've hit Isabella."

She shadowed us into the living room. "If you take her to them, then don't come back. Do you understand? I can't do this anymore."

The entire house pulsated this time, but only I noticed or felt it. My father and young Isabella headed toward the door, and she raised her hand in a half-wave at Johnnie, who sat on the sofa pretending to read a book. I couldn't tell if my brother's tears were those of anger or sadness.

My father instructed young Isabella to get inside the car that waited at the curb. An invisible force drew me behind her like a magnet. Wherever she went, I would have to follow. She wiped the tears from her eyes and walked through the front yard. She approached and opened the wooden gate. I stood next to her as she threw one last look in the direction of the house, where my mother stood in the doorway with my father, in a loving embrace.

When young Isabella saw it, the tension around her mouth eased. However, from my vantage point, it looked like he had placed my mother under an enchantment. I didn't like that. Let her scream and cry and throw vases at his head all she wanted, but who was he to manipulate her like that?

I turned and followed young Isabella to the car, and the back door opened for her. She crawled inside and sat down next to Veit Heilwig. He smiled down at her and said nothing, but the driver did turn around to speak with her.

"Good evening, Isabella. My name is Serafino Pedraic."

A third person sat in the passenger seat, but neither she nor I could see who he was. My father slid in next to her and closed the door. She looked up at him with complete trust, a trust that would now be plagued with suspicion and doubt.

He framed her face with his hands and said, "Don't be afraid."

Her eyes rolled to the back of her head. She let out a soft gasp as she fainted. This was probably the first of several memory enchantments. As the car took off and I stood at the curb, I wondered why my father had buried this memory—besides the fact that it made him look like a nicer version of Leto Priya. The atmosphere around me pulsated, then my vision blurred, and suddenly everything turned gray. I felt like I was falling.

When I opened my eyes, I was back at the house, except this time I stood in the backyard. Young Isabella carried a long red ribbon and ran in a large circle as a Labrador puppy chased her. My father and Veit, with beer bottles in hand and barbecue aprons on, watched us from the porch.

My mother emerged from the house with a petite woman at her side. "We're going to pick up Johnnie's cake from the bakery," she said.

The petite woman bent over Veit and planted a kiss on his lips. "Do you need anything while we're out, dear?"

Veit stroked her light brown hair and smiled. "I'm fine."

Johnnie came out. "Mom! Are you ready?"

"Yes, let's go." She put on her gloves.

"Happy birthday, Jonathan." Veit handed him a beer.

"Veit," my mother shook her head and snatched the beer out of Johnnie's grasp, "we don't drink at sixteen over here."

"When will you be back?" My father grabbed the beer from my mother.

"We shouldn't be more than an hour. Come on, Rosa. I want to show you this beautiful dress I saw yesterday down at the shop." She gave my father a parting kiss and steered Johnnie toward the house. Rosa followed.

"Do you want to get started with the barbecue?" Veit asked.

"Be my guest."

Veit drew a fire symbol in the air, and the pit lit up. Young Isabella paused to watch, the Labrador seized the ribbon in between its teeth and took off with it.

"Did you do that with your powers?" she asked.

Veit nodded. "You can do the same, too."

The puppy came back around and nipped at her heels. She squealed and started up the chase again. I moved in her direction to follow, but, oddly, something forced me toward my father and Veit. They were in the middle of a conversation.

"...and we've secured everything, Carson. You don't have to worry."

"Thank you."

"Are you...going to tell them goodbye?"

He shook his head. "Robert's going to phone me tonight, make it seem like I have an assignment with the Army."

Veit nodded. "You won't be able to see your family again. The Masters will dog your every step, and you'll have no rest."

"It has to be this way."

Veit smiled and watched young Isabella. "There has to be a reason for this, don't you think? And, no one made us infallible. Neither the Masters nor the Three can answer that question—what if they are wrong?"

My father drew in a deep breath. "I apologize for getting you involved."

"I knew the risks. We all did. Serafino and Jerome may have their reasons, but I'm doing this because you're my friend."

"What if *we're* wrong?" My father gazed at him and awaited an answer.

"Stop weighing yourself down with so many 'what-ifs.' Besides, don't you think it's a sign from God? Imagine, after a hundred years, the fourth Drifter arrives, the only female one."

No. This was wrong. What was this?

Young Isabella broke out into a long scream that resonated

throughout the backyard. The puppy yowled and ran in the direction of the tool shed, and my father and Veit followed.

My father swung the door open, and with a stunned expression, he saw her crouched in the middle of the tool shed, blazing like a torch. When he saw that the flames didn't consume her, he called to her and held out his hand.

Something inside me made me want to extend my hand as well, though I knew no one could see or feel me. Just as all three of our hands were poised to meet, a black hole surfaced in the upper right corner of the shed. It grew larger and began to swirl like a mist, until I saw a familiar pair of eerie red eyes peek out from the center.

I jumped back when the corpse-like Black Wolf weaseled its way through the black hole and came slithering toward me like a snake. "Jane! Pull me out, now!"

I called out for Jane again, and suddenly a strong hand on my shoulder guided me out of my nightmare. I went flying through gray space again. The bright light of the Locus Circle blinded me, and then an immense pressure hit my chest. I took a deep breath, and when my vision returned, I saw that I was back in my flat. I lay halfway outside the broken Circle, and Jane sat on the floor with her arms wrapped around me.

"I've got you," she said in a steady voice, though her entire body trembled. "Please, don't ever do that again!"

"Jane..."

"What is it?"

"You can't tell anyone about this. Not Joshua, not Ian...no one."

"What happened?"

I stared into her frightened eyes. She may not have completely understood what I just did, but I couldn't risk even a small part of it being communicated to anyone else.

My mouth felt dry. "Was I on fire?"

"For a moment, but it went away. There's not a mark on you. It's a miracle." She helped me to my feet and steered me toward my reclining chair. "Poor dear, you're shaking. Let me fix you some tea."

I watched her go into the kitchen, and I wanted to groan. When I thought about what Jane just said, I felt the way my mother did. This *gift*, this *miracle*, caused turmoil within my family. It made my father leave us and lead the Gray Tower to believe that he was the one they wanted. Veit, my father, and Serafino Pedraic and whoever Jerome was...they must've found a way to mask my true powers with those of an alchemist. However, it had been sixteen years, and each day the façade slowly crumbled. My arms felt numb, and I would've been screaming and kicking things if Jane weren't here with me.

"Here's your tea." Jane set the cup down in front of me and ran over to grab my broom. She started sweeping up broken pieces of glass.

"Thank you." I took a sip and nearly dropped the teacup.

"You can stay with me tonight."

"Jane, I—"

"You're not getting out of this one. You're coming with me." She grabbed the dustpan and swept the glass inside. When she threw the broken glass into the trash, she came over to me.

I mustered a smile for her. "Let me grab some things, and I'll meet you downstairs."

She nodded and headed for the door. When she closed it behind her, I stood and went into my bedroom. I took a few articles of clothing and a book to read. I went back into the living room for my knife and sheathed it before placing it into my robe's front pocket.

I shuddered at a cold breeze coming in from the broken window. I watched my cream-colored curtain sway in the wind. I went over to the window and carved Earth and Air symbols into the windowsill. The breeze went away, and my invisible barricade sealed off the window.

As I headed out with my things, including the diary, I

wondered if I would lose my powers as an alchemist, and what I would do with the powers of a Drifter. However, first things first—I needed to find a mentalist I could trust who'd be willing to put a seal on my mind. If Leto Priya went prying in there again, he'd discover my unlocked memories and kill me on the spot.

I'd be lying if I said I wasn't afraid, or that I stood ready to face this challenge. My father, despite his flaws, bore the burden for me all these years so I wouldn't have to endure what he did, or worse. Now I had to show that same strength and learn how to keep fooling the Gray Tower while staying out of the clutches of Octavian and his Black Wolves. I withered at the grim thought that I couldn't afford to make a single mistake, but I had no choice.

If I didn't protect myself and stay a step ahead of my enemies, I was as good as dead.

ABOUT THE AUTHOR

Alesha Escobar writes fantasy to support her chocolate habit. She enjoys reading everything from Tolkien and the Dresden Files, to the Hellblazer comics. She lives in California with her husband and six children.

If you've enjoyed this ebook, please consider leaving a review at your favorite online retailer. It helps other fantasy readers like you to find this book. Thank you!

Want free and discounted ebooks? Join my readers lounge today!

Join Fantasy Mashups and Mayhem Readers Lounge

www.aleshaescobar.com
alesha@thecreativealchemy.com

facebook.com/AuthorAleshaEscobar
instagram.com/fantastli

ALSO BY ALESHA L. ESCOBAR

The Magic & Mayhem Series
The Wayward Wizard (Magic & Mayhem #1)
Hexes and Bones (Magic & Mayhem #2 - Coming Soon)

The Aria Knight Chronicles
Sin Eater (The Aria Knight Chronicles #1)
Revelations (The Aria Knight Chronicles #2)
Legacy (The Aria Knight Chronicles #3)

The Immortal Brotherhood Series
The Immortals (The Immortal Brotherhood #1)
A Discovery of Faeries (The Immortal Brotherhood #2)
The Man Who Broke Time (The Immortal Brotherhood #3)

The Diviners Series
House of Diviners (The Diviners #1)
Order of the Black Sun (The Diviners #2)

Made in the USA
Columbia, SC
14 October 2024